Second Chance

By
Ed LeCrone

© 2014 Ed LeCrone
All Rights Reserved.

No part of this publication may be reproduced, stored in a retrieval system, or transmitted, in any form or by any means, electronic, mechanical, photocopying, recording, or otherwise, without the written permission of the author.

First published by Dog Ear Publishing
4010 W. 86th Street, Ste H
Indianapolis, IN 46268
www.dogearpublishing.net

dog ear
PUBLISHING

ISBN: 978-1-4575-2643-5

This book is printed on acid-free paper.

This book is a work of fiction. Places, events, and situations in this book are purely fictional and any resemblance to actual persons, living or dead, is coincidental.

Printed in the United States of America

Acknowledgements

I wish to acknowledge and thank my lovely and understanding wife, Darlene, for her assistance in this, my fourth book. Other accolades should be given to my granddaughter, Larin Carlson, and my youngest daughter, Mimi Book. This work flat out could not have been completed without the direction and suggestions provided by these three members of my family.

Summary

A fictitious novel set in the period immediately following the end of the Civil War and encompassing the international intrigue during the occupation of Texas.

To the casual reader, the American Civil War ended with Lee's surrender of the Confederate forces at Appomattox Courthouse, Virginia, on April 12, 1865. In reality the conflict continued for an additional forty-four days at which time the Trans Mississippi command capitulated. The occupation of the subdued southern states was maintained under the administrations of three presidents. Rutherford B. Hayes signed its termination during his presidency.

Texas did not come easily back into the folds of unification due to several issues. The Lone Star state had stubbornly held out in its remoteness even continuing to hold Union prisoners in a concentration site at Camp Ford in Tyler, a full sixty five days following Lee's signing the peace accord. Additionally, the Texas state government had all but disappeared and the enforcement of the law had halted due to the famed Texas Rangers having been conscripted en masse into the Confederate cavalry arm. The bulk of the former law officers were sent out of state to fight against the Union forces leaving a void in the laws which the officials wished to see up held. Those surviving Rangers who plodded home in 1865, were unacceptable to the Union occupiers in there former capacity and were forced to take lesser civic positions until they could regain their lost reputation.

Texas, as lawless as it had become, was a tranquil fairyland compared to what was transpiring within the borders of its southern neighbor, Mexico.

Encumbered by debt payable to the European powers, the Mexican government defaulted on its obligations triggering an invasion by France, Spain, and Great Britain.

Faced with the ire of the United States, the latter two powers withdrew their naval blockade and land forces.

France, in the regime of Napoleon III, continued to access land with its armies and eventually forced the rightful government out of the capitol, Mexico City.

Emperor Napoleon sought to establish a puppet government in order to collect debts owned his nation and offered his newly instituted position of monarch to his brother in law, Ferdinand Maximilian of the Austrian-Hungarian royal lineage. The young Austrian naval officer was at first reluctant to accept the post but Napolean convinced him that he could reconstruct the backward and indolent Mexico into a country in the likeness of a progressive European power.

Chaos resulted with the Austrian's installation. He was supported by thousands of French and mercenary forces as well as Mexicans known as Imperialists who had longed for the deposition of President Benito Juarez with his popularity among the peons. So the conflict spiraled with Emporer Maximilion counting on Austrian volunteers, French army forces, Hungarians and Confederate ex-patriots clandestinely crossing the Rio Grande. The Juaristas, a people's army, sought to depose the Austrian interloper with the assistance of a country with whom they had fought a war less than fifteen years before; the United States.

Standing alone and willing to fight anyone in power for their independence, were the Mayas living in the Yucatan. Seeing an opportunity to break away from the beleaguered Republican government in Mexico City, the indigenous people rallied around the cause of complete secession from the restraints under which they had suffered.

President Juarez allied himself with several generals who had been previously active in the war with the United States that ended in a humbling defeat for Mexico in 1846. Fighting against the Imperialists, the former president sought to regain his elected position in Mexico City and continue his republican form of government.

On the northern side of the Rio, President Johnson and Secretary of War Stanton filed protest after protest with Emperor Napolean regarding his thinly veiled attempt at colonizing Mexico. Gaining nothing but rebuffs from the French, it was decided that arms and equipment would be sent to the Juarez forces and an American army would make a demonstration of force to convince the invaders that the United States meant business regarding the Monroe Doctrine.

United States General Philip Sheridan, was not permitted to take part in the Grand Review of the victorious Federal army in Washington, D.C. on May 23 and 24, 1865, but instead was ordered to Brownsville, Texas by the most expedient manner possible.

Men in the Union service deployed at the time in Mississippi and Louisiana were shifted from transport destined to carry them back to their home states for decommissioning and marched instead to Hempstead,

Texas. Traveling in early summer heat in woolen uniforms, General George Custer, the force's commander, drew the undying wrath of his troops. Foot sore, home sick, and agitated at being passed over for mustering from the service, the Union army of occupation seethed and sulked on the north bank of the Rio Grande.

General Sheridan, aware of, but unaffected by the morosity spreading through the ranks of the assembled men, busied himself with secret meetings with Juarista generals and the selection of tough, devil may care body guards for their protection. Sheridan, at one time, reported that he had seen to the shipping of thirty thousand muskets to the Mexican people's army from the arsenal at Baton Rouge.

Gaining wind of the possibility of an armed conflict with a European power so soon after peace had been restored in the United States, gangs of reporters flooded into Brownsville and the surrounding area. They reported to the northern presses that they were witnessing Mexican soldiers parading about in new blue uniforms on the southern bank of the Rio looking more Union than the American soldiers observing them.

'Second Chance' is intended as a sequel to the earlier; 'Fire on the Prairie, A Civil War Novel' published in 2010. The previous work featured the characters; Chance Neunan, an infantry private from Moultrie County, Illinois, and Andrea Edwards, a beautiful, well educated, former slave, who is employed by the Freedmen's Bureau located in Brownsville, Texas. Both are vainly trying to reconnect with each other after passing through the fires of the American Civil War.

Regarding the characters in this novel

The majority of the characters in the manuscript are fictitious with the exception of historical personages such as George Custer, Philip Sheridan, Benito Juarez and others.

Major Robert Tyler, of the 4th Wisconsin Cavalry is based loosely on a larger than life officer, Major Henry H. Young, the right hand man for General Sheridan. Major Young was tragically killed with several of his bodyguards on the American side of the Rio Grande in an ambush set by ex-Confederates and Mexican renegades. Major Tyler's philandering ways and efforts at self aggrandizement are in no way a reflection of the life of Major Young. Young's death during the winter of 1866, is inserted in the manuscript to illustrate the dangers of occupying south-eastern Texas immediately following the close of hostilities.

The farrier, Homer Nichols, was also a living player in the difficulties between the United States and the French forces in Mexico. Nichols, my wife's great grandfather, enlisted in the Fourth Illinois Cavalry and hailed from Chillicothe in that state. This small town was located on the Illinois River mid-way between Rock Island and Peoria. Nichol's received his training at Camp Dickey, situated in Ottawa, upstream from his home. On February 7, 1862, while engaged in pursuing retreating Confederates who had evacuated Fort Henry in Tennessee, the young trooper's horse slipped on an icy hillside, rolled over his body, and severely injured him. Nichols' chest was crushed and the broken ribs and breast bone partially disabled him for the remainder of his life. The Illinois cavalryman spent a period of convalescence in Natchez, Mississippi, recovered somewhat, and then was assigned to be a hospital steward in that facility. He was able to return to his regiment late in the war and was with his unit when it was consolidated with the Twelfth Illinois Cavalry on June 4, 1865, in Louisiana.

Homer Nichols retained his rank of farrier throughout his enlistment and marched overland from Alexandria, Louisiana, to Hempstead, Texas, as a member of the Union occupying force.

On or about September 20, 1865, Private Nichols went 'Absent Without Leave' or in the military vernacular of the time, 'took French leave'.

Nichols was caught and sent back with a few other mal-contents to face desertion charges. He was returned to his command with a dressing down but little else. When at last, he was mustered (discharged) from the service on May 29, 1866; he was assessed seventy five cents from his pay for having lost his haversack.

Ex-trooper Private Nichols returned to Chillicothe, married his sweetheart, Charity Caldwell, and started a blacksmith business. As he aged, his wartime injuries afflicted him more and more until he was forced to apply for a government pension. He died on September 16, 1927, with the attending physician signifying that his demise was brought on by injuries he had received in the service of his country.

MAY 22, 1865, ALEXANDRIA, VIRGINIA

Neunan was the only transfer, though an illegal one, within the group of green recruits gathered in by the 12th Illinois' captain who'd established his office in the vacant store front.

Captain Ivan Crowder, a wounded convalescent, pale and thin from his injury, had only moderate success with his efforts to find replacements for his unit on the Western frontier.

Barriers to the officer's attempts came about due to the demobilization of the military forces at the cessation of hostilities some six weeks earlier. During the next two days of May 23rd and 24th, a great and final review of the Armies of the Potomac and of the West would take place in Washington City. After that a virtual flood of men heading to points north for mustering out and decommissioning would over tax all modes of transportation. Only those elements of the military positioned in the field within the conquered southern states were allowed to stagnate where they were. They would await further direction from the Washington officials.

A seasoned veteran, you say, Neunan. We aren't getting many of your kind right now. All the boys want to go home and I can't see as how I blame them.

Captain Crowder removed a printed form from a field desk set up on a table in the window of an empty building on E street in Alexandria.

Just take these papers here over to that empty desk over yonder and fill 'em out. You'll find pen and ink there and when yer finished I'll swear you in. Of course, we'll have to reference your past records with yer infantry unit and that could take months. Don't you worry none, we'll get things straight so's you won't be considered a deserter or any such thing. You'll travel with some other fellows and we'll try to catch up with the 12th in Louisiana. Any questions, Neunan?

* * *

Chance ached from his abbreviated sleep on the hard ground in the Sibley tent in Hempstead, Texas. His compliment was met at the rail station by a crusty sergeant and marched to the cavalry camp on the town's outskirts. Neunan could hardly keep his eyes open or make his legs work as the group trudged to an abandoned warehouse and stood in the light of a cadmium arch lamp. There, the replacements were shown items of equipment 'sans' the horse which would make them mounted troopers in the service of the United States.

The end of the week long trek came with the bone weary acceptance of a gray wool blanket and a spot on the dirt inside a tent. Chance had no idea how many men were in occupancy. All he recalled was tripping over a number of bodies in the pitch blackness.

Chance straightened his kepi as he fell in for morning roll call. The sun was doing it's best to dry the dew from the previous night but its intensity was still weak. By noontime, without interference from cloud cover, Sol's rays would be sharp enough to raise blisters on unprotected flesh.

Troopers, in a hodgepodge of uniforms, were walking up to the assembly point to be counted. Once their presence was confirmed within their company, they were checked off and marched off to the mess tents. Those with ailments answered sick call and were dismissed to be examined at the hospital facilities.

Chance looked around and spied several familiar faces belonging to men who had enlisted at the Virginia recruiting station with him. The mop headed, swollen faced youngsters were his train companions as their journey brought them to the Rio Grande to swell the ranks of the occupation forces.

"Now you boys with the last name ending in the letters A-L are to report to the stables and corrals to be assigned your mounts. These animals will become your best friends during your duty in the army of the United States. You will feed and care for this animal above your own health. You will curry it, shelter it and you will never become separated from your charge unless you or it are killed or become incapacitated." The sergeant paused, savoring his use of the last word he'd spoken. "Do you have any question?"

The three striper, whom Chance was to learn later that morning, was named Fredrick Aldridge. Neunan feared that all the better horses would be assigned before he was given the opportunity to make his selection. He took a place at the rear of the line ambling for the mess tent and accepted a tin plate, cup and spoon from a mess orderly.

* * *

"That one there in the corner is about as fine a horse that you'd ever find in this last herd moved over from Mississippi. His name is Zeus and he is a three year old gelding."

"If he's such a prize why is he one of the last animals in the corral?" Chance asked.

Neunan turned his attention from the handsome equine to a sandy haired farrier wearing a leather apron. The man leaned on a post which was part of the fencing.

"Oh, he's got a fickle streak, that one does. He can sense the uneasiness of a rider by the tension he feels in the man's body. He got swept up in a horse roundup durin' the war and none of the Reb citizenry, at least as far as I know, has put in a recovery claim for him. I'd expect that he was some young girl's pet. You ever ride a horse, mister?"

"Yes, I sure have. Back in Illinois 'fore I joined the infantry. I was raised on a farm in Moultrie County."

"You aint a total green horn like the most of these recruits, then?"

"I'm new to the cavalry but I've been across half of this nation in this damned war on foot."

Chance extended his hand to the slender, blonde young man.

"Name's Neunan. Chance Neunan."

The farrier returned the handshake with a strong grip.

"Homer Nichols of Chillicothe. I came into this giant skirmish in '62 with the 4th Illinois and have been all over hell just like you." The horse shoer spit into the fine dust at the base of the corral post. "Never get used to the dust nor the smell of horse shit in my occupation but I enjoy my work. Now, as I've told you, Ol' Zeus there, would be a fine mount for you. You've got experiences with the horses and you'll know how to handle him. You just go over to the sergeant and tell him your name and give him the number, 314. That's his government identification used at this post."

"I'll take your advice, Nichols. You're a real friend to do this."

"I liked your looks when you walked up and I liked you even more when I heard you speak. I says to myself; this fellow is a down stater just like me."

* * *

In the weeks after the replacements reached Hempstead, Chance received all the equipment that the recruits were shown on their first night at the cavalry camp. He was learning the use of the saber mounted and the carbine while dismounted. Neunan was discovering too, that the work involved with caring for a horse was double the load of that of a foot soldier.

The excitement of being in a different branch of the service was however, beginning to wear off. The green recruits were outsiders and were given the worst details to perform. They were forced to be content to stand on the periphery of veterans and listen to their adventures. Making friends from within the diverse group of men was difficult but Chance and Homer Nichols got along famously.

On Monday morning of the last week in September, Sgt. Aldrich intercepted Chance in the mess line and took him aside out of earshot of the rest of the men.

"Neunan, you're to report to a Lieutenant Wilson over at headquarters. If you don't know where that is, it's located in the old Texas Ranger station near the main entrance to camp."

"Is there something wrong, Sarg? Is there a problem with my papers? You know that I transferred into the regiment not exactly on the square."

Concern creased the young cavalryman's face.

"Beats me, Neunan. Me and General Sheridan ain't been talkin' very frequently as of late. You just eat your grub quick, hit the sinks if you have to and get on up to headquarters."

* * *

Wilson was a young man perhaps two or three years older than Chance. He had career soldier written all over him with his neat attire of a cavalry short jacket with its polished buttons. The officer rose from behind the table where he was sitting and returned Neunan's salute.

"Have a seat, Private. I've been going over your records which arrived last week. You've had some interesting war time exploits in your days as an infantryman."

"I had my share of excitement."

"Yes, you certainly did. No back water deployments for you."

"I didn't plan it that way, Sir."

"But it's the way that you handled yourself in those situations that stands out. You are shy about this but you are cut out of different cloth than most men."

"I just took care of myself."

"And so you did."

The lieutenant laid the papers he referred to on the desk in front of him and stared intently at Chance.

The cavalry private never averted his eyes from the officer's face.

Wilson cleared his throat breaking the silence.

"From what I've discovered in your files, I wish to broach a proposition to you."

"What can I do for you, Sir?"

"If you have been truthful in the factual material you provided the recruiter in Alexandria, Virginia, and I believe that you have been, then you could be a very valuable man in an upcoming operation."

"Go on, Sir." Neunan looked down at his folded hands.

"You do speak Spanish?"

"Yes, my dad fought in the 1846, war with Mexico. He brought the lingo back with him and taught a little to me. I'd not want you to think that I can horse trade with you using the 'Mex' though."

"And French as well?"

"My mother went to a girl's finishing school in Kentucky. Yes, I know a bit of the language. I can read it better than I can speak it."

"Excellent. Now tell me why you chose to transfer to the cavalry and come to Texas. You could have gone to your state capitol, been mustered out, and gone home like ninety nine percent of the men did. Why did you come to Texas, Private?"

"I pretty much figured to chase Indians and keep the French from invading our country."

"I don't believe you one bit, Neunan." Wilson looked away and through the window indicating that he was disgusted with the answer. He remained reticent for a few more seconds before turning back to face the Illinois private.

"I'm going to offer you a position in a top secret information gathering unit. Once I've revealed what it encompasses, you will be sworn to secrecy under penalty of death if for any reason you disclose even the smallest of details."

Neunan scooted his chair backward and held up his hands in mock surrender. "Wait! It's getting damned dangerous to talk to you any further. As I've said; I came down here to chase hostiles, protect our border, and I guess to help the blacks who are newly freed. I've developed some real compassion for the sable race and all they've gone through."

Wilson had been studying Chance in an effort to evaluate his sincerity.

"We have people and organizations to handle these problems, Private Neunan. You could be much more valuable to our efforts here in Texas if you'd consider volunteering for this mission."

Chance leaned forward having noted the depth of his importance in the officer's plan. Neunan wanted answers to questions that he'd had on his mind since his last letter from Andrea. Chance was in a position to squeeze information out of the lieutenant if he played his cards right.

"What of the freed slaves? What's being done for this group?"

"I'm informed that the Freedmen's Bureau will be establishing a regional center in Brownville within the coming days. The Twelfth Cavalry which is, as you know, stationed there and will be in a position to assist this group as called on. You have heard of the Freedmen's Bureau haven't you?"

"Oh yes. Oh yes I have, Sir."

* * *

Private Neunan was securing Zeus' reins to the picket rope erected a half mile out on the prairie from the Hempstead cavalry camp. The exercise was being tried for the first time involving the newly assigned mounts and although the animals had received some previous training, this was a new routine for them as well.

Chance turned as a horseman trotted up and halted behind him.

Sergeant Aldridge dismounted and tethered his house in a space next to Zeus.

"Dang it Neunan, I thought you'd be out here and, by golly this is where I found you. That Lt. Wilson wants to see you back at headquarters and he sent me out to find you and about a dozen others. He gave me an order that will get you and the other fellers dismissed to meet with him. You don't know any boys named Larson or Avery do you?"

"What's that jasper, Wilson, up to now?" Chance leaned forward and dusted off the thighs of his uniform pants before standing erect and grinning broadly. "No, wait a minute, I shouldn't ask such a question of you, should I. General Sheridan hasn't notified you of his plans for the day has he?"

Both men laughed.

"Well, all I can say is that Wilson sent me out here to round up a number of men for some reason. They're all pretty top specimens of horse soldiers and I'm hopin' that he ain't plannin' to transfer them out of this company. It he does, this outfit is bein' handed the short end of the stick."

Aldridge paused and wiped a string of white lather on the side of his hand onto the skirt of his saddle blanket.

"So what gives here, Neunan?"

Chance smiled a mischievous, smaller smile and shook his head in the negative indicating that he was not going to divulge anything to the NCO.

"Sarg, I don't know either of the two men you've mentioned that you're looking for. They could be in this unit. I don't know since I haven't become acquainted with everybody in the outfit."

"Well Shit!" Aldridge kicked at a clod positioned at the base of a thin pole cut from a sapling which supported the line. Both horses shied and tried to turn around but their reins were tied fast.

"Bollix!" The sergeant spoke with a normal voice. "I'd best be a little calmer around these spooky sons-a-bitches."

"As I've said I don't know of these men and if Wilson is looking for them, I don't care to know why. I just know that Lt. Wilson wants me for something and that's all I care about."

"Yeah, but now I've got to ride all over creation to find these fellers. I figured if I found you that you could give me some information that'd make it easier for me,"

Aldridge turned to his horse, placed his boot in the stirrup and grasped the saddle bow before turning back and saying; "Sure is some mighty queer things goin' on around here."

* * *

Lieutenant Wilson, nattily attired as always was standing watching out the headquarters window as the sun slipped below the distant horizon.

Private Neunan's knock on the room's door brought the officer out of his reverie.

"Enter."

Both men saluted and stood opposite each other, Neunan in his unbuttoned cavalry jacket with dirt on his face and the officer in all his finery. The silence between them was awkward.

"You sent for me, Sir."

"Yes, trooper, I'm notifying all those involved in the mission that we are leaving by train for Fort Brown on the Rio tomorrow morning."

"So soon, Sir?"

"Yes, it's imperative that we get our observers in the field as quickly as possible. We've got to get our eyes and ears across the border so that we can determine which way the French are going to jump."

"I see, Sir, but why didn't you assemble all of us together tonight after mess call? There must be a fairly large group of us since Sgt. Aldridge said he was pulling a dozen or more men together for you."

"I'm proceeding in this manner for security reasons. There will be more men aboard the train than will be involved in the operation. Some of these troopers will be decoys and masking our initiative. You see, you won't know who the second person is in your two man spy cell until you get together with him to cross the river. Keeping the operation broken into cells will mean that if one unit is captured or worse, the others can continue with impunity."

Chance looked down at his dusty boots and wondered silently about the decision he'd made.

"Private Neunan, here are your orders. We will transport you and your mount on the military train tomorrow morning to Brownsville and the cantonment at Fort Brown. I'll provide two men to assist you with your equipment locker and see that it's aboard the cars. We will depart from the station here at exactly six A.M. to commence our journey. I'm emphasizing the time; six A.M., trooper. I will not tolerate any tardiness, Private Neunan."

"Yes Sir. Do we have any idea of just how long this jaunt will be?"

"It will be strenuous for both man and beast. The distance is three hundred sixty miles give or take a few. We should expect, with refueling and exercising the animals, a journey of nine to eleven hours in duration. My intent is to remain on the move with as little interruption as possible."

* * *

The slender farrier stood rinsing his eyes with water from an iron strapped, wooden bucket sitting on a bench. He'd made the mistake of watching his helpers unload a rack full of hay into the stable mow. Nichols had positioned himself at a safe distance from the activity in the structure's gangway.

A gust of wind took up a fork full of the fodder and showered him with chaff and filled his blue eyes with hundreds of dust particles.

It was his fault for not practicing more caution in observing the work of the three troopers who were sent him by the upper command. They were an incorrigible trio and sullen in their temperament. The men were serving as a work detail at the stables for some minor discipline. Homer would have just as soon done without them.

Nichols dried his face on a dish towel he'd obtained from the mess tent and reasoned whether the errant fork full of hay had been an accident or not. He concluded that it was more than likely not.

These boys are making my life pretty damned miserable, he thought, *perhaps four hours on the gargantuan manure pile beyond the corral would teach them humility.*

Homer looked forward to his departure from the Hempstead location on the train tomorrow morning and his relocation in a new posting. He hoped that the personnel at Fort Brown would be more professional and willing to put their all into their duty of protecting their country.

As for himself, his spirits were flagging. The period of enlistment and unit consolidation was nearing five years. Because of his value as a farrier, he had not received a furlough as most others had in March of '64. He was suffering from severe pangs of home sickness and the correspondence from

Charity Caldwell was contributing to his malaise. The monotony of military life and the daily drudgery without rest was wearing him down to the point that he was questioning his own devotion to duty. Only his newly acquired friend, Trooper Chance Neunan, prevented him from doing the unthinkable; deserting or placing a revolver against his temple.

No, he could stave off his melancholy by entraining south to the cantonment at Brownsville. A change of venue could be the elixir that would save him.

* * *

The engine and its cargo rattled and shuddered as it passed over a long neglected roadbed heading south. The occupants closed the cars' windows to prevent the smoke and burning embers being poured out by the enormous, funnel shaped stack from entering the carriages' interior.

Chance's saddle valise was wedged against the smeared carriage glass as he leaned on it vainly trying to sleep. A half cup of over- brewed coffee and a hard cracker constituted his breakfast and now the *mélange* was rebelling inside his stomach. Sleep, at present, was eluding him thanks mainly to the joisting and jolting of the conveyance.

He felt a nudge on this left shoulder which caused him to open one eye.

Homer Nichols, both hands on the seat back above Chance's head, stood beaming.

"Ain't no way you're gonna get any sleep, Pard. Track's too rough."

"Homer? What in tarnation are you doing here?"

The farrier friend continued to smile. "Got a rather forlorn letter from my girl, Charity, and it made me pretty blue. You know the stuff she wrote: When are you coming home, all the boys are returning daily and where are you? That kinda stuff."

Chance nodded that he understood his friend's heartache.

"You got a sweetheart, Chance? I don't believe that the topic ever came up in our conversations?"

"Yes, I do, but I haven't had word from her for nearly a year. I'd hope that she still had feelings for me."

Neunan adjusted his sitting position and waved to Nichols to take the seat opposite him.

"Let's change the subject, Homer. The love letter thing you've brought up is pretty painful to me as well."

"Sure thing, pard."

The train rattled and shook as the two friends sat looking at one another without speaking.

"Did you accept a position at Fort Brown for any particular reason?" Chance asked taking his make shift pillow from its location beneath his right ear.

"An illness amongst the stable staff at Fort Brown. It had to be filled and I figured a change of scenery would sooth the hurt that I was feelin'."

Chance studied Nichols and recalled Lt. Wilson's mentioning mission decoys ensconced aboard the train. These men would, while active as a part of the operation, more than likely had no knowledge of the role that they were playing in it.

Could Nichols be one of those men or was he a full fledged spy just as Chance was?

* * *

A WEEK LATER......ACROSS THE RIVER

The leather straps supporting the corn shuck filled mattress squeaked as Neunan readjusted his aching body. The air in the room was hot, fetid and reeking from the smells entering through the lone, shuttered window.

Some noise had roused Chance. Fatigued and half conscious, he couldn't determine from which direction the sound had originated. His sleep was fitful, drifting. His rest was far from having been deep. He'd tossed about on the unsteady bed with his perspiration trickling down his back and puddling in the divot beneath his Adam's apple.

Two pesos had been tossed on the bar with no questions asked. Neunan was glad of that for his Spanish was the weakest link in his false façade and except for a few words inquiring of the location of his accommodations, both men remained stoic. The proprietor of the cantina didn't look more than a few seconds at the black haired, black eyed, and sun burned hombre. In his work, it was indiscrete as well as dangerous to one's health to gaze too long at a customer.

Chance was unsure if the owner saw through his disguise. A serape, sandals, cotton clothing and a sombrero, did not make him a Mexican. Even if the old man had recognized him as being a 'gringo', he was smart enough not to use English in the transaction. The cantina's bar served as the hotel desk and the owner had shooed away a formation of flies and wiped a clear place on the wood surface with a tattered sleeve. He produced a dog eared ledger from beneath the bar and withdrew a stubby pencil from the book's spine. An arthritic digit sporting a yellowed finger nail was the only gesture the man made. Neunan obliged with a hastily scribbled signature; Juan Marcos.

"Gracias, Senor". The stubble bearded older man swiped up the coins and pocketed them. He raised a section of the bar and tottered past Chance and motioned to him to follow. They passed a half dozen empty tables and entered a dimly lighted corridor. Stopping before the first door on the right, *sans* any kind of lock, the proprietor swung the massive door open. The portal, suspended on leather hinges, dragged at its bottom but gave way after a nudge from the sole of the elderly man's sandal.

"Tenga una buena noche," he grunted and shuffled back toward the empty cantina's main room.

Chance appraised the room and drew back the coarse blanket on the shuck mattress.

No insect skittered away and certainly no cock roaches which was the scourge of the entire country.

A lumpy pillow with a sweat stained ticking cover augmented the set of bed clothes. Beside the bed stood a flimsy night stand constructed from the roughest wood Chance had ever seen. The furnishing supported three burnt candles of various heights shoved into wax drizzled bottles. On the stone floor next to the stand, sat a crockery basin and a large, pottery jug decorated in a gaudy white, blue, and a pale green motif. It appeared that the night stand would become a dry sink when the sun rose on the morrow.

Neunan didn't like the room's layout; a lock- less door opening onto a hallway leading to the bar and a shuttered window opening out to the dusty street.

Not a secure place by any means but it would have to do. He picked up his blanket role and tossed it atop the thread bare blanket on the bed. Chance untied both ends of the bedding and refolded the sky blue uniform pants that the canvas covering protected.

Somewhere out in the approaching twilight two men were on his trail. Paid assassins doing their dirty work in the name of General Marquez and his Imperialist army allied to Maximilian. How close they were Chance could only guess but the sixty odd miles remaining for him to reach the spy camp were unattainable without rest. His body told him that this was a fact. The observations and the counts of men and material he'd made would be of unfathomable importance to Major Tyler and eventually to General Sheridan.

Chance eased onto the shuck mattress and removed his right sandal. His eyes perused the stitching in the shoe's sole where the thread had been broken and resewn. The envelope he'd made by doing this created a thin storage area to hold all the information he'd acquired over the past two weeks.

The shaft of sun light streaming through the crack between the shutters became paler as twilight approached. From the bar at the end of the corridor, laughter and music commenced.

Chance fought back the urge to roll onto his side and sleep but tension and the oven like heat of the room prevented that.

No, he'd have to be prepared for the two trackers when they came to kill him. Chance knew that this would quite possibly be the last opportunity that they would have to do him in before he reached the safety of the spy camp.

The forty-four Remington revolver was removed from where it rested in the waist band of his cotton trousers. He wiped the moisture from the glistening blue of the firearm and rotated the cylinder to see if all the percussion caps were in place. All five of the nipples on the chambers held the igniting caps in their correct position. The sixth chamber was unloaded with the hammer resting on a bare cone as a safety for the pistol.

"I'll be ready for you my 'muchahos'", Chance uttered under his breath.

In the hallway, the clinking of glasses mingled with hysterical laughter issuing from one of the bar girls.

Satisfied with his main source of defense, Neunan scooted the bed against the unlockable door. One thing in Chance's favor was that the room's lone portal opened inward. By positioning the furnishing in such a way, Chance would be awakened by anyone wishing to gain entry.

A drink from a bottle with a screw topped lid refreshed the young trooper and softened the sharp edge of his nerves. He was surprised to see how easily slumber crept in and commenced to erode his senses. Even the din wafting down the corridor had little effect on his desire to sleep. His peasant clothes were damp with perspiration but the wetness soothed his tired muscles.

Shortly, his breathing deepened and became more rhythmic.

* * *

Neunan had no knowledge of when the mariachi band packed there instruments away and left the bar or when the last cactus whisky besotted customer was escorted out the door. He didn't hear the proprietor secure the cantina's front door. Extreme fatigue had overtaken Chance and he slept a sleep that was three breaths away from death.

SECOND CHANCE

A dog began barking in the street outside his room's lone window. This noise and the stench of cheap tobacco wafting under his door roused the sleeping spy. Chance rolled from his side to his back and rubbed his eyes trying to identify where he was or how he managed to get into such a place. Every inch of his body ached and the action of moving his hands up to his swollen eyes sent a sour smell of body odor wisping into his nostrils. He clarified his vision permitting his eyes to follow a gecko's passage across the ceiling above his head.

A scraping sound of metal against wood brought the young trooper's gaze from the lizard to the window directly above his head. In the flickering light of one of his room's candles, Chance observed the long blade of a machete sliding up and down in an attempt to lift the horizontal clasp at the window from its fastening.

Just as Neunan's mind registered what was transpiring, a body slammed hard against the bedroom door knocking him sideways on the rickety bed. In an instant, the Remington revolver was in the young man's hand and exploding in an orange flash sending sparks and smoke into the room. The weapon bounced a second time before it was swung upward. In the flash of the load's ignition, Neunan saw the body of a dark form being flung backward from a sitting position on the window sill.

The residue from the three pistol shots fell on the thread bare blanket of the bed. The worn material caught fire immediately and with such voracity that Neunan was skittering sideways to escape the flames.

Leaping to his feet, he grabbed up his sombrero and bedroll and made for the door. He hefted his shoulder against the half open portal, moving a prostrated body away from his escape route. As he passed the prone form his sandal slipped in something wet and sticky which was spreading across the tile floor. The trooper ran into the bar area past a jumble of tables and chairs and made for the door to the street. As he moved hastily through a gauntlet of furnishings, Chance spied a door, behind what passed for a bar ,beginning to open. Silhouetted in the dim light cast by the fledgling fire, he made out the proprietor shouldering a double barreled shotgun.

"Imperialist or Juarista!" He shouted as he leveled his pistol at the half dressed figure.

"Juarista, Juarista!" came the frightened reply. The shotgun clattered to the floor as the door was slammed shut.

Chance made the street and began shouting; "*Fuego! Fuego!*" as he ran. The fire would create the perfect diversion for his escape.

Turning the corner at the outer edge of the building, Neunan's passage took him next to the cantina's wall and near his bedroom window which was belching smoke and flames.

"Madre! Madre!" A withering man clutching his mid-section was attempting to crawl away from the façade of the blazing cantina.

People were flinging open entrances to the street and pouring out in an excited frenzy.

Chance avoided the growing mob by cutting down a side alley. He ran in the shadows, his right hand clutching the nearly empty revolver as his body scraped past scrub thorn back yard fencing. His running feet carried him to the edge of town and to an adobe hovel where he'd paid to board his horse.

Neunan vaulted the top rail of the corral frightening his animal and two others which were incarcerated within. Quickly the young cavalryman checked to see if his saddle was still on his mount and took valuable seconds to pull the cinch tighter around the horse's belly.

Mounting, he checked the other two steeds and saw that both; a bald faced roan and a pinto had recently been boarded. White lather foamed on their withers and streamed down their forelegs indicating to him that they had been ridden hard in order to gain entrance into the town.

By God, he thought, *these two cayuses belong to the two hombres that had just tried to kill him.*

He untied their reins and led them to the gate, leaned down and opened the enclosure. Then, as the rider and mounts were bathed in the orange glow of the burning cafe, the rider and group of animals bounded away into the darkness of the arid landscape.

* * *

Chance lay in the scant shade of a mesquite shrub, his lips cracked and his tongue swollen. He'd ridden too long and too far in the blazing sun that blistered every inch of his exposed flesh. The skin on the backs of his hands was beet red and swollen from the affect of the biting rays. Only his wide brimmed sombrero offered protection for his face but did little to shade the front of his neckline. His animal and the extra horses he'd released from the corral were suffering from the inferno heat as well.

White swatches of sweat beaded on their chests and whithers as they continually chewed at their iron bits. The dehydrated equines seemed to believe that their yellowed teeth could somehow squeeze moisture from the metal to allay their thirst. Neither of the three were of the stuff that Chance's cavalry horse was made of.

Neunan had been forced to give up the beautiful animal with the US branded on its left shoulder because its appearance in the midst of the group of infiltrators which he was a member of could have jeopardized their mission. Having such a mount in the spy group's presence could have caused too many questions. Had Chance been more confident of his command of Spanish he might have attempted to pass off his ownership by claiming that Zeus was an animal he'd stolen or one that he'd taken in battle. As it was, it was difficult enough to pass himself off as a Mexican, let alone discuss the merits of good horse flesh in a foreign tongue.

The oppressive heat and the searing sunlight weakened his strength as Chance's head began to spin. His vision faded in and out of focus and he felt that his ability to control his consciousness was waning. A translucent void crept over his eyesight and a ringing like the call of a thousand cicadas filled his ears. The stricken soldier fought to separate hallucination from reality

"Some parade, aye, Chance? Has to be the biggest doins' I've ever been in. How about you?"

Pete O'Donnel stood outside a pup tent that he shared with Neunan. O'Donnell's image was a shimmering silver gray in Chance's fevered mind. Chance was cognizant of being a part of a peaceful dream at another time and in another place.

"Yep. Lots bigger than Phianis Rosewells' Traveling Medicine and Freak Show". Chance laughed as he unbuckled his accoutrements and allowed them to fall on the ground. "Ever see such a crowd in your whole life? I got a good look at General Grant in the reviewing stand and he looked the part of one determined man, he did."

"Yeah, I got a good look at him when we did eyes right." O'Donnel unbuttoned his four button sack. His shirt was plastered to his back. "Did you see Sheridan? I don't believe that he was there with all the rest of the big wigs."

"General Sheridan wasn't on the reviewing stand. Haven't you seen a newspaper in the last couple of days?"

"No I h'ain't. What's in 'em concernin' General Sheridan?"

"It appears that there's a movement afoot to send an army down to Texas to run all the foreigners outta Mexico."

A fly landed on Chance's forehead and moved upward to his hair line. The insect roused him from his overheated lethargy. The water from his pint bottle was long gone. If he didn't fine better protection from the sun he could expire within the hour. Neunan closed his puffy eyes and tried to suck saliva from the lining of his cheek but nothing formed on his tongue.

"Hey Chance, *you'd better get a move on. We're formin' up down to the depot. We're catchin' a train ride back to Springfield. No more marchin' for us.*"

"Don't plan on doing any of that for a while."

Pete shot a disdainful look at Chance and urged him to get up and move. "*Get up offin' yer ass and put your gear on. We're goin' home, Boy.*"

The wavering image of Chance and his best friend, Pete O'Donnell, faded away as Neunan's thoughts returned to the present and the ungodly heat that clutched at his body. Another vignette shaped itself in the private's mind as he turned from the writing desk where he was sitting in the cheap boarding house in Georgetown on the outer edge of Washington, D.C. The capitol was bustling with regiments marching to points of demarcation in order to return to their home states. In sites of demarcation all across the nation the men were transported generally to their state capitols where they were mustered out of active service. Arms were surrendered and equipment turned in at the arsenals. A written discharge and in some cases a bounty payout was given to the departing warriors to finalize the severance of their duty to the United States of America.

In an image so real and lifelike that Neunan swore that he heard the burning sand crunch under O'Donnell's shoes.

"I want to give you something, Pete. Actually, I'd like to give you two things."

The young man from Moultrie County reached inside his sweat stained cotton shirt and withdrew an object wrapped in an oily rag.

"What's this, Chance?" O'Donnell looked mystified.

"It's my Colt Root revolver. It's the one I carried at the riot in Charleston back in March of '64'."

"But, why are you doing this? There are still some bad people back home and you'll have need of the gun. There'll be lots of people carryin' grudges."

"Take it, it's yours."

Chance's friend turned one corner of the rag aside to see if the bundle really contained a pistol.

"This is for you as well." Chance produced a tri-folded paper and placed it in Pete's free hand.

"The letter is addressed to Mr. Winford Dixon back home in Moultrie County on the Kaskaskia. He's been in charge of the home place since I've been gone. I've kept up a correspondence and he's seen to renting out the ground."

"I don't understand, Chance?" O' Donnell looked at the paper with puzzlement creasing his features.

"I'm directing Winford to allow you to live in the house, use the outbuildings, plant and harvest the crop on half shares with me. Would you like to do that?"

"I sure would, but ain't you goin' home? You're young and you've got your entire life ahead of you."

"I'm not going back to Illinois, at least not at this time."

"Why? There's got to be a reason."

"You see that big box over there against the wall?"

"Yeah."

"Inside that box is the nicest, most beautiful pair of cavalry boots you'll ever see."

"You've stumped me, pard." *The private stood dumb founded.*

"I'm not going to the regimental formation and go home on the train. I'm not going except to whatever place I choose."

"You'll not get your mustering out pay."

"I know but I've had Mr. Dixon bank my last year's crop revenue in Sullivan. I'll be alright."

"I think that what you're doing is deserting." Private O'Donnell shook his head in disbelief at what his friend was contemplating.

"Not really, You see, I've joined the Twelfth Illinois Cavalry and rumor has it the ..uh; what's the new president's name?"

"Andrew Johnson."

"Yes, Johnson. Anyhow, it's said that he's sending a force down to the border with Mexico. It's likely that the United States will have a go with the French there real damned soon."

"What in tarnation do you want to go and join up with the cavalry? You ain't no horseman and besides, I'd think that you've had enough of flag wavin'."

"I have my reasons."

Pete O'Donnell slid the rag covered pistol into his front pant's pocket and refolded the document that Chance had given him. This he placed in the inside pocket of his sweat stained tunic. When he was satisfied that all was in order, he turned to Neunan and said; "It's the mulatto woman ain't it."

* * *

FREEDMEN'S BUREAU
THE FORMER BAXTER PLANTATION
BROWNSVILLE, TEXAS

Andreaine Edwards rolled onto her side in her oversized bed which faced the upstairs window, her night gown clinging to her moist body. She was aware of the rooster's crowing in the chicken yard and the bumping of hardtack boxes being stacked on the porch of the house's lower level. She sat up and rubbed her eyes.

A gentle breeze not yet tainted by the heat from the sun ruffled the gingham curtains on the floor to ceiling window. The young woman shucked her sleeping garment before bending to pull the china chamber pot from beneath the bed.

She relieved herself and shoved the receptacle into its hiding place. Later that morning a maid would retrieve and empty the vessel as part of her daily duties.

Andrea took stock of her visage in the freckled mirror that had frost around its edges.

Her dark hair was tangled in an alluring way and her lips were puffy from her nights rest.

Taking a bone handled brush from a set on the night stand; she brushed her tresses into a more presentable style. She selected a cotton dress from the room's closet before returning clothed, to the window.

Before her stretched several acres of lawn and shade trees that once had belonged to Carlton Baxter. At present, the magnificent, though poorly maintained plantation with its slave quarters and out buildings, was the leased property of the United States. Colonel Baxter was making his way back to the Brownsville area following his release from a federal prison in Ohio. His political and military involvement stood in contrast with the Union cause. In his absence, his wife was given a demonstration of how desperate things could become for those who failed to co-operate with the Federal occupiers. Mrs. Anna Bell Baxter agreed to an eight year lease with an annual compensation from the Union authorities.

In spite of unfavorable comments from the residents of Brownsville, the property was turned over to the Freedmen's Bureau to be used in any way they saw fit.

Andrealine Edwards came on the scene soon afterwards and set about establishing a mixed-race committee dedicated to the education and betterment of the former slaves. Edwards anticipated more racism and opposition in her endeavor than she received. It seemed that the local populace held more contempt and rancor for the Hispanics than for the newly freed blacks. This most recent addition to Texas society was met with ambivalence and a silent expectation that when the Yankees departed things would revert back to the old ways.

A movement caught Andrea's gaze in an area to the right of the window. A line of black people were qued before a stable turned warehouse. Even in the early hour, throngs of people silently moved toward stacks of food stuffs which were being distributed to the hungry. Government rations, and locally raised fruits and vegetables were being placed in blankets and baskets belonging to the recipients. Teams of soldiers and a Bureau official marked off the names of the shuffling destitutes. The supply of such necessities came at a critical time in the heat of the summer. The slaves had foolishly left their plantation cabins to be nearer the military force that had stricken the shackles from their legs. Leaving the only shelter that they had ever known, the black folks were reliant on the Union forces and the Bureau which its own army protected. Vacating the gardens and field crops, they allowed the produce to wither away. This had not been the best decision that the ex-slaves had made. But the year of 'Jubelo' had arrived and in the weeks following the close of hostilities, the black people were in dire straits.

Andrea pulled a chair closer to the window and took up a pair of army issue brogans. The heavy shoes served her well in the field for her duties called on her to oversee a series of activities where dainty dress was not expected. She would go now to her administrative office and wrestle with what ever crisis that had arisen.

A hot cup of chicory coffee drawn from a silver samovar would constitute her breakfast in the dining room on the mansion's lower level. She marveled at the beauty of the steam vessel and wondered at how such a treasure had escaped the conquering occupation troops. Its massive size possible had saved it. At the cook house she'd coax one of the cooks into frying up a 'johnny cake' or two for her. Such meager fare would start her day.

The executive walked down the spiral staircase and into the parlor. Two butlers dressed in the appropriate livery stood facing each other on each side of the ornately carved double doors as Andrea approached. She passed between the men and noticed a deep bow from each of them.

"Stop that! I'm not your mistress! You don't bow to anyone! Now, straighten up and act like free men because that's what you are!" She paused and realized that she'd spoken too harshly to the pair. "I expect politeness and courtesy from you but there will be no more bowing and sniveling in my presence."

An aide, a pretty, but slightly plump girl whom Andrea was considering for a full time position, opened the doors leading out onto the front veranda.

"Mornin', Missy Edwards. They's five, white, cavalry soldiers come onto da grounds wantin' to serve as volunteers."

"Bring them up to the porch. I'll question them to see if they really will be of value to us."

Andrea chose to remain on the upper step of the stairs as her young charge went to the shade of the trees where the five men were waiting. Andrea had learned a few things about psychology and by placing herself on a higher level than the young soldiers, her dominate position would be the first step in gaining a modicum of respect over the interviewees.

The cavalrymen, dressed in a variety of uniform parts, lined up at two feet intervals and straightened their shoulders. Their gaze was steady and fixed on her face.

"Well, well, we've finally received some help from the army."

A dark complexioned fellow wearing a pork pie hat adorned with a yellow cord raised his hand as though he were a schoolboy seeking permission to speak.

"Beg your parden.Ma'am, but we're all cavalrymen."

"Oh, yes. I'm sorry for the mistake."

"Apology accepted, Ma'am."

"May I continue?"

The men answered in unison in the affirmative.

"You are the first help we've had offered here. What made you decide to come to the Bureau to assist us?'

"Name's Howie Livingston, Company B, First Iowa. I volunteered so's I could avoid stable duty."

"That all? Sure you didn't wander down here to spark one of my little darkie girls?"

Livingston's face reddened.

"No Ma'am. Just wanna help out the Bureau."

Andrea nodded to a man standing next to Livingston.

"What's your reasons?"

"Name's Sam Blackwell of the same regiment as Howie. He says to me, "Lets go over to this place and see what it's all about and bein' kinda bored, I tagged along with my pard. If we can get away from camp life it seemed the right thing to do."

"And you, Sir?"

The cavalryman with his pants stuffed in his boot tops appeared taken aback at being addressed as sir.

"Henry Conklin, Ma'am. Me and my brother, Frank, here, decided that camp was getting danged slow so we put our names on the list to volunteer here at the Bureau that the Captain put out. We want to help you 'uns."

"You two from the First Iowa as well?"

"Yes, Ma'am."

The men's' eyes followed Andrea's as her's coursed down the assembled line.

"What's your name, there?"

She pointed a finger at a fair haired, blue eyed, slender man at the end of the formation.

"I'm Homer Nichols, Miss Edwards."

"And how do you know my name, my good man?"

"I took note of whose name was listed to report to written on the top of the sign up sheet. I just put two and two together."

"Yes."

"I always like to get ahead of the game."

"Good point. Are you an Iowian too?"

"No, Ma'am, I'm from Illinois. I'm a farrier in the Twelfth Illinois Cavalry."

Andrea Edwards' eyes brightened as she recalled her time in the 'Prairie State'.

"Where exactly do you come from in Abe Lincoln's home state, young Mr. Nichols?"

"Chillicothe up in the north-central part on the Illinois River."

"Oh." Her hopes were deflated but she covered her disappointment and continued with an additional inquiry. "A farrier, you say. That's a horse shoer isn't it?"

"Yes Ma'am. I got tired of the flies, the horse sweat, and the horse shit, er, the horse manure. I had to treat a lot of sick animals as well. You see, the cavalry is awful hard on horse flesh."

"Well, I hate to paint you a picture of some other duty but if you come here we'll use you in the stables. We've got the most wretched teams of horses and mules you have ever seen, most of which we got skinned on when we purchased them."

"I didn't expect to be in that ol' line of work but I suppose I can continue it. I think that I can help you folks with your stocks' health and replacement."

Nichols kicked the toe of his boot into a tuft of grass growing in front of him.

"Besides the scenery is a heap better here than back in camp. Ain't that right, boys?"

The young men chuckled.

Andrea paid little heed to the compliment she'd been given. She sought to change the subject.

"How are you gentlemen holding up in this Texas climate?"

Frank Conklin looked up and said; "T'ain't too bad 'cept 'bout dark. You see, our camp ain't very far from the Rio and the danged skeeters and flies like to eat us up at that time."

"You'll like it a lot better, here. We're nice and open and there is usually a pleasant breeze blowing." Andrea placed her hands on her hips and continued; "We'll send a Bureau wagon to the camp to pick you up at seven in the morning. You'll have eaten your breakfast and we will give you dinner on the grounds. It will be better than the fare that you get from the government. At least tastier. At the end of the work day…er, what time do you men have supper?"

"Five, parade is at six-thirty." Private Blackwell had stepped forward and offered the information.

"Thank you, Private. We'll get you back to camp no later than four-thirty in the wagon that has transported you here."

Blackwell moved forward again and offered; "Ma'am?"

"Yes private, what is it?"

"The big-shot officers call our camp a cantonment."

Andrea laughed lightly as the men guffawed.

"I stand corrected. In the presence of your big-shots, I shall refer to your camp as a cantonment."

Andrea smiled and continued; "You soldier boys have provided a bit of levity missing from this place and I appreciate your coming and your desire to give us a hand. Go with Angie Sue, there, and she will take you to the warehouse next to the stable. There you will be given your assignments. I will send a courier to your cantonment, er, camp, informing your commander that we will put you men to work straight away. We, here at the Bureau, thank you for your service.

The group of males turned and looked about in order to locate their guide named, Angie Sue.

"And, oh, Private Nichols, I'll come to the stable in the afternoon to hear a report from you regarding the status of our transportation herd. Can you have some figures compiled for me that quickly?"

"I'll do my best, Ma'am."

* * *

UNION ARMY ENCAMPMENT
FORT BROWN
BROWNSVILLE, TEXAS

A banjo and a harmonica were being played somewhere in the rows of white Sibley tents. The Fourth Wisconsin exchanged their easily carried 'dog' tents for the larger, bell shaped shelters. Eight to ten troopers could reside in one tent and enjoy the luxury of being more sheltered against the weather that with the punier issue. Regiments assembling on the banks of the Rio Grande knew from the time that they unloaded the sturdier shelters that their stay in Texas was going to be a long one. Another sign that the military force would be stationed indefinitely at the location adjacent to Fort Brown was the building of corrals and the removal of the rope picket lines for the horses.

Wisps of white wood smoke drifted down the company streets as the cook fires died down to embers. Inspection had ended and the men had returned to the canvas abodes to repair equipment, play instruments or cards or write letters to loved ones.

Outside, guards were posted and commenced their monotonous pacing.

"Lieutenant Wilson, I'd like a report on the detachment who've volunteered for duty at the Freedmen's Bureau plantation." Major Robert Tyler closed his writing desk and latched the clasp that secured its lid. The senior officer was handsome in the extreme with a well groomed, rust colored beard and flowing, shoulder length hair. As he spoke, Tyler turned sideways in his folding chair to see the tent flap part and the junior officer enter.

"Oh, at ease, Wilson."

"Thank you, Sir."

"You may begin with your report, Lieutenant. I'd like to determine if this experiment of Captain Adams and yours will be of benefit in raising the moral of the men. It would seem, on the surface, the plan has some merit. If handled properly it would ease the boredom of the troops. I must admit that the repetitiveness of our work here is very tiresome."

Lt. Wilson opened a ledger book and studied it.

"Cigar, Lieutenant?"

"No thank you, Sir. With your permission, Sir?" The younger officer thumbed the top button of his short cavalry jacket.

"Yes, yes, make yourself comfortable, Wilson. Then let's get on with your report. I don't relish lighting a candle in my tin lantern in this heat."

"Certainly, Sir" Wilson cleared his throat. "We've had five men sign on for a week of duty at the Baxter place. Excuse me, Sir, the Freedmen's Bureau. The plantation was originally known as Glen Haven by the residents."

"Yes, yes. You may skirt that portion of your report. We senior officers have been briefed on this local. Please continue."

"Our men, from our command, have signed on for a week of duty providing assistance distributing food and clothing. Two are building a communal privy and the farrier, Nichols, is signed on to bring the Bureau's stable animals up to snuff."

"Up to snuff?"

"Sorry, Sir. To treat the live stock for their health and see that they are well shod."

"We can spare this man; what was his name, again?"

"Nichols, Sir."

"Yes, we can spare him. He has two apprentices trained. He's come to me twice previously to ask for a furlough to go home. He's very, very homesick and done with war. I thought it would be good for him to spend some time away from his duties here."

"And what does this man do? He agrees to do the same type of work for the Bureau as he does here." Tyler shook his head sideways in puzzlement.

Wilson unbuttoned his jacket's second button.

"May I sit, Sir?"

"Yes, yes. How ungentlemanly of me. We are in conference and should make ourselves comfortable. However, we officers must conduct ourselves according to our rank in the presence of our troops."

"Of course, Major."

"Please continue." Major Tyler took a long draw on a cheroot which he'd lighted.

"This is not in my report, Sir, but the chief administrator of the Bureau operations is a woman of ravishing beauty. She's black but not at all like the field hands whom we're accustomed to. From the description that the volunteers bantered about the camp, she's of mixed blood with a white lady's features. Our volunteers returned from their first day, crowing about her and asking if they could sign up for the following week. I'd suspect that she's charmed the men and Nichols especially so."

"That's most unusual, don't you think?"

"That the woman is sure a beauty?"

"No, that the government would appoint a woman to head such an important establishment in the heart of rebel country." Major Tyler tapped the ash from his smoke into an empty oyster can sitting atop his writing case.

"On the face of things, it is a puzzlement. But she comes with sterling credentials from the national office and, in particular, an endorsement from its director, General O.O. Howard."

"You've checked all this out?"

"Yes, Sir."

"This is all very interesting, Wilson."

"The five men selected for this first week of work have returned and have the regiment from whence they've come in an uproar. We have more volunteers than we know what to do with and all, I dare say, because of this woman's loveliness."

"Very good, then, Wilson. You, in essence, are saying that this volunteer practice could lead to a lifting of the moral within out immediate command?"

"Yes, Sir. Will that be all, Sir?"

"That will do for this evening, Lieutenant." The major took another draw on his dwindling cigar. "Oh yes, Wilson. How could I have been so forgetful regarding such an important matter?"

"Yes, Major?"

"Headquarters wants to know if we've received word from the spies we've dispatched into Mexico for information gathering. Those soldiers are from our brigade are they not?"

"Yes, Sir. Three are from the Third Iowa and two from the Twelfth Illinois. I'll get together what I have but it won't be much. It's as though they've all been swallowed up in some void once they crossed the river. I'll look into the matter tomorrow morning at first light. You'd like a report on that operation, Sir?"

"Yes. Put something together that sounds credible but leave out any references to 'up to snuff'. Good night Lieutenant."

As the sound of the junior officer's footsteps grew fainter on the gravel company street, Tyler scooted his camp chair back from his desk. Taking a match safe from his vest pocket he struck a Lucifer on its seriated top. The flame rose from the wick of the wax candle in the folding lamp and bathed the tent's interior in an amber glow. Tyler hung the lamp on a nail driven into the center post of his shelter and adjusted the mirror on the rear pole of the support structure.

Standing before it, he studied his image, turning first left and then to the right.

Not too bad of a specimen, he thought considering the wars he'd come through and the scrapes he'd survived. A nasty little war in Nicaragua with a lunatic American named Walker. The crazy conqueror starting his own country he wanted known as Walkeragra, marching with Garibaldi to Rome in the Italian Unification War, and the recently concluded unplesantries between the North and South. As the images of bygone adventures flickered through his mind, he curled the fingers of his right hand and pulled them through his red hair. His hair color was exotic to the South American and Mexican senoritas, an aphrodisiac to them which opened many a bedroom door to him.

Tyler's conquests had been more numerous than he could recall. New Orleanian ladies of the night, courtesans in Alabama, and lonely officers' wives and widows in Washington. He threw caution to the wind in his love making, accepting anything and everything from the opposite sex. A sobering visit to a venereal disease ward in a military hospital in Pittsburg pulled him back from a catastrophic end. Viewing the poor wretches, blistered over their emaciated bodies and steadily going blind brought a degree of understanding he'd never had before. The saying; 'One night with Venus and a lifetime with Mercury' brought an acknowledgement that the 'French disease' could not be cured. Tyler had escaped the ravages of the insidious affliction and now he would be more discreet, more careful than he'd ever been before.

No, he would woo his next amorous interest in a socially accepted manner. But before that occurred he would attempt one last frivolity. He would initiate a dalliance with the mulatto woman at the Freedmen's Bureau. From what he'd discerned, she was proud, indescribably beautiful, and a worthy adversary for his lecherous intent. Her spirit and intelligence would be challenged to the hilt by his powers of persuasion.

Yes, tomorrow, in the company of Lieutenant Wilson, he would ride over to Glen Haven under the subterfuge of inspecting the facility. He would commence to spin his web of seduction at that time.

* * *

IN UNKNOWN TERRITORY
THE MEXICAH DESERT

Chance Neunan passed out for a second time and slipped further into delirium. He was no longer conscious but drifting between light and darkness. His overheated brain flipped through one image after another until it settled on one scene.

Eight men were huddled around a map laid atop a door taken from an abandoned building. The flat surface was supported above the tent floor by a pair of saw horses. The two supporting devices had legs no thicker than darning needles and there was no possible way that they could be supporting the massive door. The make shift table appeared to rise and fall with the beat of Neunan's heart. Those men examining the topographic chart were faceless and unknown to Chance.

All their features were as though they had been painted in watercolor and then the rain had washed them away. Yet, one of the figures looked familiar. As Chance fought to clear his mind to complete the identification, the realization came to him that the man he was struggling to remember was actually him.

At the head of the table an officer was pointing with two fingers, or was it three, at a spot on the map. The man with the smudged face had blazing hair and a blue coat with extremely bright and extremely large buttons in four rows up the front. As Neunan stared, the buttons began to undulate and spin round and round. the brass of the fasteners glimmering and enlarging before retreating to a smaller size, The insanely brilliant buttons kept shifting up and down as the speaker's mouth moved but no sound was emitted from his lips A younger, junior officer with an even shinier coat kept nodding his head and moving his lips Gesturing and waving the officers were quite animated as the six smaller soldiers stood stoically as if they were uniformed mannequins.

Words, at first unidentifiable, grew clearer as Chance's hearing intensified. Zones, spying, disguises, and deception. Code words, and counter signs, were mentioned as well but the meaning of the words tailed away and Chance could not lock them into his brain. When he was handed a small, tissue paper map, he examined it only to discover that the paper was blank. The befuddled soldier's head was spinning as he fought to make sense of and clarify the goings on within the gathering.

"God go with you" were the parting words of the lieutenant wearing the ridiculously shiny coat.

Neunan attempted to force his swollen eyes open but they were sealed shut with some sort of mucus that oozed from his tear ducts.

A rock being turned over and the shuffling of feet in the sweltering gravel outside the circle of meager shade which Chance occupied, roused the dying trooper. Moisture from a soaked cloth was dripped in the corners of each of his eyes and a third swipe was given to his cracked lips.

"Who's there? Who's beside me?" Chance whispered.

"We'll he ain't dead, yet." An unfamiliar voice spoke to an accomplice. "Suck on this rag fer a while and don't try to talk. Don't move around, Pard."

"Cal, I got some saddle dressin' in a can in my goods. Let's wipe a bit on his face and backs of his hands. Maybe that'll soothe them parts. Don't let him drink much neither. That could kill him."

The original speaker continued to drop water from a gourd jug on the moistening cloth. "Cal, you get on over there and take care of that horse. Don't waste no water on her, she's done for."

One of the equines which Chance had liberated from the corral in the town he'd recently terrorized was down on its side in the blazing sun.

"I can't shoot her. The sound of the pistol shot will travel for miles."

"Cut her throat. She'll kick around a bit but we won't chance givin' our position away to anybody that's trailin' us."

"I hate doin' that."

"It's got to be done. Now go do it."

Chance's tormented hearing registered a horse's scream followed by gurgling sounds and then silence. In a few minutes returning footsteps sounded and a man said disgustedly, "There it's done."

The unseen speaker hocked and spit.

"Don't ever ask me to do such a thing again. I hate seein' horses hurt. I've had a belly full of seein' them hobblin' around with a leg shot off trippin' on their guts after they been in a skirmish."

* * *

The temperature beneath the rock shelf was at least twenty degrees cooler that in the blistering sun. Chance's two rescuers dampened his sombrero and tied a wet bandana over his eyes before moving him to a more hospitable location. From the elevation that the men had chosen, they could survey the singed landscape spread out beneath them. The site offered them the advantage of observing the advance of any contingent of men approaching from any direction.

"Did the right thing, didn't we, Cal? Movin' up here allows us to see what kinda outfit General Marquez has put on our trail. He's more than likely got a couple of Yaqui Indians signed on as trackers. In the meantime, I'd like to ask this sorry traveler we picked up, a thing or two."

"Would you look at that flock of vultures flyin' over that dead horse we left? That Mexican general won't need no Indian help, at all. He can just foller the scavengers to where we was."

Chance was in a sitting position; his back resting against a massive rock. The two men turned from the jumble of rocks where they'd been watching and walked to Neunan. Chance managed to force his swollen eye lids open to mere slits and although he had difficulty seeing, he was conscious and able to communicate. The corners of his mouth were deeply cracked and his lips blistered. The man called Cal stepped closer and kicked the sole of Chance's sandal.

"Abe's." He uttered the word forcefully and studied Neunan's face for any type of response. Chance rolled the word around in his mind trying to make a connection to why the ragged man had said it. Then it came to him! It was as if someone had lighted a candle in a dark room.

"Beard." He replied weakly. Yes, 'Abe's Beard'. That's the password."

Cal smiled broadly and said, " So you're the bad man who half burned down Los Rios and killed two 'Peralists', stole two horses plus scarin'a good part of the province half to death."

"Yeah, that was me." Chance smiled a quick smile which hurt his mouth. "Who are…?" The young cavalryman paused.

"Yes we're the two spies comin' crossed Tamaulipas province makin' for the spy assembly point. We were doin' jest fine, makin' good time 'til we run inta a hornet's nest at Los Rios. There was Imperialists patrols all over the place. You are one lucky pilgrim to have been travelin' the same route as us. But then, you and us was carryin' the same assembly map."

"I hadn't any time to take a look at my map. I was just trying to get out of the scrape that I was in."

"Any way, stranger, it's fortunate that we met up like we did. A couple more hours out here and you'd have been fried bacon."

"Name's Chance Neunan." The Illinois horseman offered his hand.

"I'm Calvin Hawbacker and my ugly lookin' pard there is Lewis Carter. We're the Third Iowa's contribution to this here mission. Don't remember meeting you at the conference we had before we left Fort Brown. Guess we didn't go through any introductions, did we? All part of the secrecy of 'snoopin' the 'Frenchies'."

"Or the Mexicans or whoever else the high command thought that we might be going to war with." Chance finished Hawbacker's sentence for him.

Lewis Carter smiled a smug, little smile and added; "We took the liberty of goin' through yer clothes and stuff when we found you. We located yer map and part of your uniform. You shoulda took better care not to have had them things so easily found."

Chance drew in his cheeks to discover that he had saliva in this mouth. He spit into the chipped rock underneath his sandals. It was a gesture that he added for emphasis.

"I think I've shown that I can take care of myself if I get into a scrape." Calvin Hawbacker laughed and added, "Yes, I suppose you have, that's for danged sure, Mister Chance Neunan."

Private Carter unbuttoned the blousy striped shirt that he was wearing and continued where his accusation had left off. "Yes, but you showed yerself and that could've bollixed up the whole mission. Because you showed yer hand, the operation could've gone to hell."

"Not necessarily. I'd gathered all the information that I felt was needed. I assume that you fellows have done the same. Those sons-a-bitches which I did in were intent on either capturing or bringing me in dead. I acted to save my skin. Now that I have some traveling partners all we have to do is get back across the border. Once on the good side of the Rio, the higher ups can tabulate our figures."

"Oh, is that all? You think that the trip is gonna be easy?" Carter continued to bait Chance.

"I expect that we'll get back, maybe not at the appointed time that the Major set for us, but we'll get back."

Hawbacker returned to the pile of rock and gazed acrossed the sun baked vastness. Pausing, he raised both hands to his eyes and cupped them against the slice of the sun's rays. The heat simmered in undulating waves on the distant horizon.

'Wish I had a telescope or a pair of them fancy French made binoculars."

"Why's that, Calvin?"

"Take a look at that dust cloud risin' in the direction we've just passed through. It's 'bout up to where Neunan's horse is layin'. Betcha a dollar to a donut that it's a Mexican squadron loyal to Maximilian tryin' to ride us down."

"Can you sit a horse, Neunan?" Private Carter was standing over the resting young man.

"You're damned right, I can. If my hide is at stake, I can ride."

Hawbacker came running back to the pair and pulled Chance to his feet.

"Mount up then and we'll make for that patch of pines at the base of that little rise. Don't ride your horse full out. He's stressed and he'll have to get you in among those craggy rocks. We get in amongst the trees and boulders, we got a chance."

* * *

FREEDMEN'S BUREAU
BAXTER PLANTATION

The sun bore down relentlessly as it neared its noon time zenith. Andrea Edwards felt as if any further exertion would cause her to faint but she knew that her position dictated that she carry on. She would have to set an example demonstrating toughness for her workers at this furthest station of the Freedmen's' Bureau.

Angie Sue Parker passed along the line of hungry, newly freed slaves and approached her employer.

She thrust out a white, cotton cloth which had been dipped in camphor to Andrea and said, "Dis will help you draw in breaths easier in dis hot, humid air. Jest sniff on de rag once in a while but don't get it near your eyes or your mouth. It'll burn like sixty if you do."

Angie touched the back of Andrea's neck and added, "You should get yourself over dere in de shade. The folks in line has to stand out in de sun but you don't."

"Thank you, Angie." Andrea took the cloth and touched the outer edges of her nostril with it. She watched her aide walk away and noted a massive ring of perspiration forming on the dress fabric under each of her arms. "Angie," she called, "I'll be going to the front of the line to taste the stew. It's intolerably hot to be serving such fare but it's all we've got that will produce the best use for our vegetables and government beef."

"Yessum, Missy Andrea."

The executive turned and followed Angie Sue before hailing her and handing her the relieving saturated cloth.

Andrea shooed away a fly and placed her hand on the young girl's arm. "Incidentally, have you had an opportunity to observe the five men who've been given release to assist us here?"

"Yessum. Two of 'em is workin' at de front of de line and sweatin' like I h'ain't never seed Yankee men sweat before. Why dey's soaked in sweat clean through."

"And the others?"

"The other two is paired off and sawin' and hammerin' on the big privy. I axed dem if they wanted help from some of de men in de food line but they allowed not. Said the fewer, the better. This way dey can stay longer. Sides they are thankful dat dey can work in de shade most of the day."

"The farrier. Have you done any errands down near the stable?"

Angie looked puzzled.

"The blacksmith. He's called a farrier."

"Oh, I h'aint seed him 'cause I got no call to go over in dat direction."

"Very good, Angie Sue. Check on the mothers in line that are nursing. Give them one of these red cards which will permit them to get back into line when their time comes. Have them take their babies and rest in the shade of the Live Oaks."

"Yessum, will dat be all?"

"No, I haven't gotten to the kettles in the stew line. From there, I'll be off to the stables and I'll be looking up this Homer Nichols, fellow."

"Yessum, Missy Edwards."

* * *

THE STABLES
FREEDMEN'S BUREAU

Homer Nichols drove a dozen animals into a small enclosure built onto the side of the stable building. His aim was to examine the conditions of their mouths, hooves, and assess their overall health. The heat forced the private to remove his linsey-woolsey shirt down to his long johns. Over his under wear, he tied his heavy smithy's apron and pulled on a pair of blacksmith gloves. One at a time he separated a single animal from the milling herd and forced it into a narrow examining fence that pinned the horse or mule solidly against the side of the building.

Within a quarter of an hour, Nichols was wet to the skin with perspiration. The young man from Chillicothe, Illinois, set a ratio of a half dozen animals per hour for his medical perusal. Once his requirement was met, Nichols' commenced to remove shoes and fashion replacements at his forge. Finished animals had a splash of white wash dabbed on their right rear flank. Time spent with the livestock gave the farrier clues to the disposition of the animals and forewarned him of problem stock. Thus, he was acquainted with their little quirks and how to deal with them. Nichols was oblivious to the goings on nearer to the manor and the pounding emanating from the area where the new privy construction was taking place.

"How are they looking, Private Nichols?" asked a voice from behind the bent over soldier. Nichols turned, shielding his eyes from the sun and made out a slender figure of a woman sitting atop a corral rail. Homer allowed the mule which he'd just finished to drop its hind leg. He stepped away from the animal and brought his hand up in order to shield his eyes from the sun.

"Who wants to know?"

"Andrealine Edwards, the administrator of this site."

"Oh, sorry, Ma'am. I couldn't see you very well with the sun at your back. Some of the lil'darky,...." Nichols caught him committing a massive faux pas.

"Go on, Private. What were you saying?"

"Beg pardon, Ma'am. I meant no disrespect. It's just that things are so different now."

"You were mentioning some of the girls who come daily for their rations."

"Yessum. They come around the corral either to admire the horses or watch me. I guess that I really don't mind. Some of them even climb on the fence and laugh and snicker."

"You weren't expecting me?"

"Well yes, I knew that you'd put in an appearance some time. It's just that I'm not used to seeing ladies sittin' on the board fence."

"I'm not an ordinary lady, Private."

"Yes, I'm finding that out." Nichols pushed the rumps of two horses aside so that he could stand parallel with Andrea and out of the sun.

"Getting back to your opening question, Ma'am, They're in better shape as a whole than I expected." Nichols exhaled a big breath and continued. "A couple of 'em are wind broke and not of much use, another three are lame but with rest and care, I think I can bring them back to bein' half way decent. Two jennies are going to foal in three months but other than that, you've got a pretty good bunch of transportation animals."

"Good, thank you for your evaluation."

A cool wisp of a breeze drifted around the edge of the stable and ruffled Andrea's hair and soothed Nichols' perspiring face.

"Pretty hot aren't you, Private. Is this your canteen hanging on the post?"

"Yes."

"Here catch."

The cavalry trooper caught the wool covered container, uncorked it, and took a gulp of the warm contents

"Could you help me down from here, Mister Nichols? I would jump but I'd probably destroy your image of me with my dress yanking up above my knees."

"Of course, Miss Edwards."

The two made their way past the animals and into the cooler stable interior.

"So you've made your way to Texas all the way from Illinois. That's a pretty good distance, is it not?"

"Yes Ma'am, You don't have to remind me of that."

"Where did you tell me you were from when I interviewed you two days ago?"

"Why, Illinois, you just mentioned that a minute ago."

"Where specifically within the state, then?"

"Chillicothe, up on the Illinois River north of Peoria."

Andrea shook her head indicating that she wasn't certain of the location of the cities or the river that Nichols had mentioned.

"You learned your craft from whom?"

"My Dad. He had a shop so I had a good background in the trade. That's why I enlisted in the Fourth Illinois Cavalry as a farrier or smithy. They're one and the same in my book."

"But you're serving in the Twelfth now."

"It's a long story, Ma'am. It's too long and too boring."

"I have time. I can make time to listen to you. You're easy to talk to."

"You're sure?"

"Yes, I'm sure. You take a seat over there on that pressed hay bale and I'll sit opposite you on this one."

"All right, I'll keep the story of my simple life as brief as I can."

"No, don't. Talk as long as you'd like and I'll see that you don't miss your noon-time rations."

"Well, all right. What do you want to know?'

"Did the Fourth Illinois see much action?"

"Sure did. I got bad hurt at Ft. Henry. Well, it was in an area where the Rebs was evacuating one fort and escapin' cross country to get to Fort Donelson. That was in Tennessee in February. We had 'em on the run and we were about to gobble them but the weather turn real bad. It was snowing, sleeting, and colder than ol' Ned. All the roads were about impassible and the hillsides were nothing but a sheet of ice."

Nichols paused, removed his kepi and set it next to his leg on the hay bale.

"We were gaining on them in every minute and they were leaving behind everything that they had extra of. You see, they were afoot and we were mounted. Me, and the boys were sliding down one slope and up the next when ol'Lute, that was my horse's name, slipped sideways, lost his footing and fell backwards right over me. Everythin' that ol' horse had on his back came smashing down atop of me and pretty well put a finish to me. I mean everything. Saddle, carbine, sword, saddle bags and a thousand pounds of horse."

"Oh my!" Andrea's hand went to her mouth.

Nichols waited a few seconds to allow Andrea to process the seriousness of the accident.

"The boys all thought that I was a goner 'til I got up spitin' blood. From that time until eight months later I couldn't take a full breath that would expand my chest. The military sent me to a hospital in Natchez, Mississippi to recover. I got better and after a while the doctors made me a hospital steward which was simply helping nurse the boys who were sicker than I was. Finally in the next summer after my spill I was fit enough to rejoin my regiment."

"The Fourth?"

"Yes. I caught up with the boys outside the battlements at Vicksburg."

"My Private, that is quite a story."

"There's more."

"All right, I have yet to figure out your involvement with the Twelfth."

"This here is the highlight of my young life. Seems Company A of the Fourth was the headquarters guard for General Grant in that momentous battle. The company was to furnish a farrier to serve with the contingent but their man was ill and couldn't perform his duties. I was called on to replace him and, by golly, I got to see all the big officers and curry and maintain Grant's horse. It was quite an experience and one that I'll tell my kids about 'til the day I die."

"That is an experience that most people could only dream of. Now, fess up and give me the tie in with the regiment you're attached to."

Nichols took out a red bandana and wiped his face and patted his throat.

"You see, the war was going strong and the Fourth had lost a passel of men and the regiment was so small that it wasn't effective. The secretary of war or some big shot in Washington decided to merge my old regiment with the Twelfth Illinois. I was set to go home, get mustered out, draw my pay and traipse back to Chillicothe. Then the President decides to send an army down here to chase the Frenchies out of Mexico. We are in Louisiana and halfway to Texas so we're the likeliest to make the move. I tell you, Miss Edwards, I got no grudge against these French fellows and to be honest, I think that goin' home is a damned good idea. Pardon my language but I can't see that we are making much of a difference here."

Andrea straightened from the position she'd assumed when the story telling commenced.

"I don't think that you will have much chance of being released to go home until President Johnson makes a decision on how to handle this dilemma."

"No, I suppose you're right."

"It's all going to be decided when the French issue is settled. May I change the subject, Private?"

"All right. I'm getting tired of the one we're on."

"Do you have a love interest back in Illinois? I should think that a handsome young man like you would have amorous interests. I don't mean to be forward, but it's just a natural thing."

"Yes, Ma'am, I do. Her name is Charity Caldwell, and a right pretty one she is. Lives across a forty acre field from our farm. We attended school together."

Andrea looked away and spoke as if she was remembering a long lost dream. "I had a love interest once. He was in the Union infantry and was from Illinois like you. I visited him at his home once. That was in Moultrie County. Have you ever heard of that county?"

"No, I'm sorry I haven't."

"That's why I questioned you a bit more than the others when I interviewed you all earlier in the week."

"What's become of him? Are you corresponding with him?"

"No. I realize that I made a dreadful mistake with not continuing to fan the flame which I had for him. I thought that we could never be successful as a married couple because of our racial differences. Instead I rebuffed him and threw all my interest and time into the Freedmen's Bureau."

"Well, Andrea, may I call you by your first name?"

"You may do so in private but not publicly. I must maintain a standard of decorum here at this location. Do you understand?"

"Yes. Andrea. Your story is sure a sad one. At least I have hopes of returning and finding Charity waiting for me. It's a long time since you've heard from this man?"

"It's been months. The last missive from his hand was forwarded to me through the Bureau's Washington address. He was in North Carolina."

"And after that, no further word?"

"No." A tear broke from Andrea's right eye and coursed down her tawny cheek. "I fear that he has met with harm."

"Maybe not, Andrea. What is this lucky fella's name?"

"Chance Neunan." Andrea added dreamily, "I truly loved that man."

There was silence from Nichols.

"Excuse me Private Nichols, why do you look so amazed?"

Homer Nichols drew in a breath as though he was about to say something, but he stopped and looked down. The farrier's continence had changed and his complexion had paled.

* * *

SEEKING TO ESCAPE MEXICAN DESERT

The three scouts saved the strength of their mounts as they rode, trotting for short distances and then walking for half the length they'd covered, then kicking the animals back into a trot. Loping along behind the riders was the remaining horse that Chance had taken from the corral in Los Rios.

"Damned animal, he'll tag along behind us and lead them hombres right up to where we're hidin'." Carter spat out. "Ain't no sense in makin' it easy fer the bastards."

With that, the cavalryman clad in mufti turned his horse back to face the jaded equine following.

BANG! Carter's revolver barked and the riderless horse flopped down and began kicking. The horses that the three were astride flared their nostrils and poofed their green stained lips as they picked up the scent of fresh blood.

"Didn't want to do that but them fellers are closin' fast and that ol' horse would've let them know where we'd gone in them pines."

Carter clucked to his mount and urged slightly more speed from the exhausted animal.

In a few more minutes, with the judicious maintenance of their pace, the three men entered the forested base of the small mountain that they sought. It would be here that the trio would make their stand.

The rolling cloud of tannish hued brown dust grew closer as the cavalrymen dismounted and drew their guns. Forms began to be discernable and red pendants attached to the tops of lances became more distinguishable.

"Hawbacker, you and young Mr. Neunan tie your horses up to that patch of chaparral on the backside of this rock. Stay low and don't expose yourself. I'm climbin' up higher and I'll give them spear boys more grief than they're expectin'." Carter spoke out of the side of his mouth as he unrolled a Spencer, seven shot carbine from a blanket tied behind his saddle. "Wasn't supposed to bring any government issued nor anything when we crossed the river. Now, I'm glad I disobeyed orders."

Lew Carter jacked a round into the gun's chamber.

Chance had gone to one knee and was concentrating on reloading his revolver which was partially empty from its usage two nights before. He fumbled with the paper cartridges, breaking apart two of them before he calmed himself and rammed fresh loads into the empty chambers. The excitement of the coming fight frustrated him and he kept telling himself to stay calm as he applied percussion caps to the gun's cylinder.

"Calvin?" Carter shouted from his elevated position.

"Yeah."

"Can you see that leanin' cactus out yonder?"

"The big devil?"

"Yeah."

"That's about thirty rods h'aint it?"

"I'd say so. Why?"

"When them fancy lancers hit that mark I'm gonna start shootin' with the Spencer. You and Neunan hold off firin' and fight how many ever gets past me."

"Lew, can you tell if the group is splittin' up inta two parts?"

"Looks like they could be makin' to try to flank us."

"Yeah and if they succeed the militia and the Yaquis will snake in among the rocks and wait us out 'til our water's gone."

Chance heard Hawbacker curse.

From across the arid plain, through which they'd just passed, a peal of thunder rolled. A massive, angry cloud as black as a witch's hat advanced toward the two groups of antagonists. Streaks of lightning splintered from the formation and pile drove into the thirst quenched desert.

"Well, would you look at that?" Carter shouted above the explosions of nature's pyrotechnics.

"Looks like we're gonna get ourselves caught in a real toad strangler. Maybe this will even the odds a little bit."

Chance took hope that an avenue of escape was forming for them.

Chance shouted to either of his two rescuers, "Is there any hope that we can sneak outta here when that storm hits?"

"Maybe. Right now I'm takin' in the spectacle of them lancers. They sure are purty.'Bout as purty a Pickett's boys was at Gettysburg."

"You'll not think them so grand when they're stabbin' at yer guts with them skinny spears." Calvin yelled from behind his protective boulder.

"They're formin' up for a charge by God!" Lewis Carter was on one knee sighting over this carbine's barrel.

An ear splitting crash of thunder and a lightening strike which pulverized a jumble of rocks sent shard of granite pinking against the leviathan on which Carter crouched.

"Here the sons-a-bitches come! Hold your fire down there and don't waste any ammunition!" Carter was calling out directions.

The Spencer began to speak and saddles on the galloping horses began to empty. Plumed shakos and pennant bedecked lances marked the path of the rushing line.

"Give 'em hell boys. I gotta reload!" The uppermost defenders shouted encouragement to Hawbaker and Neunan.

The pounding horsemen surged past the defensive position of the two cavalrymen thrusting their deadly spears at their crouching bodies. Neunan shot two of the gaudily dressed troopers from their mounts just as a gush of rain fell on the debacle.

Carter, with a reloaded weapon fired on the charging line as the mass raced pell-mell into the base of the formation on which he stood. The lancers' steeds crushed themselves into the immovable obstacle and recoiled screaming and kicking in a jumble of riders and equipment. Those few riders who avoided the mass panic reined to the right and left and spurred their animals viciously in an attempt to escape.

"Catch a horse for me! Get yourselves a fresh mount!" Carter was shooting at the recoiling Hussars as they disappeared into the driving rain.

Neunan holstered his Remington, stepped into a group of horses and caught two by their dangling reins as Hawbaker managed to snag another.

"Mount up boys and ride like hell into the storm!" Hawbaker shouted. "Them Yaquis are likely to start shootin' at us as soon as things begin to clear." Hawbaker held out the reins to Carter as the latter slid down the wet face of his stone perch and gained his footing.

"Let's ride boys. We're bound for ol' Rio now."

In the maelstrom the men spurred through they were aware of the zip of musket balls sent their way from the Yaqis and irregulars who'd climbed part way up the rock incline.

* * *

"Whoa! Dammit I said, whoa!"

"Hey, these dumb sons- a- bitchin' horses don't understand English!" Lew Carter sawed left and right on his animal's reins, cruelly burying the bit into the horse's tongue.

"Whoa!" Hawbaker yanked backward on the harness of the mount he was astride.

"Arret!" Chance eased back in his saddle as the confiscated steed he was riding went into a lope before stopping.

"What the hell did you yell at your horse?"

"*Arret*, means stop in French. I didn't know the halt command in Spanish so I tried what little French I know on him." The steeds of Hawbaker and Carter slowed and halted, their nostrils pumping steam in the humidity created by the rainfall.

"I'll be switched if I have to learn a new language jest to ride a dumb ol' horse." Lew shook his head. The older man sighed before turning in his saddle to dismount.

"I'm gonna take a minute to give my butt a rest. I must say those spear fellows sure ride some fine animals and the saddles are miles better'n those broken down Mexican rigs we've been sittin' on."

Carter walked around his steed emitting small groans as he examined the quality of the highly oiled riding harness.

"Let's see here. A breast strap and a double saddle cinch and a crupper. When in the hell did you last see a crupper? There's also a carbine socket which even held steady as we rode over rough ground, a fancy blanket roll with some brass shit clamped onto each end…and saddle bags!"

Lewis Carter unbuckled the storage compartments, reached in one and withdrew a binocular case.

"Well, well, ask and ye shall receive." Carter turned the field glasses over and over in his hands before snapping them quickly to his eyes. "Say, these are just all right. Can't see nothin' for the haze risen up off the sand and scrub, but these will come in handy on our way home. Betcha' I'll be able to trade 'em to one of the boys or get a good price from an officer."

Neunan leaned forward and wrapped his reins in a ring attached to his saddle. "I'd suggest Lew that you stay low key on them things. You go flashin' those around and some pop-n- jay officer'll confiscate em' from you. He'll claim them as spoils of war. Of course, he'll say he's more entitled to having the property of the enemy than you."

Lew shoved the glasses into their protective case."Didn't we say we ain't at war with Mexico or France or whoever is runnin' this show?"

"Well you'll lose, bud. You'll not out argue an officer."

"Aw shit!"

Chance dismounted and patted his heaving horse's neck. "Did you hook your Blakeslee box onto your rig when we made the big skedaddle?"

"Yep. I wasn't about to forget that. Still got two tubes in it plus what's in the gun. That's twenty shots or so."

"I'm hoping that we won't have cause to use any of them on our route to the spy camp."

"Well would you look at that following along behind us?" Chance nodded in the direction they'd just ridden through. "There's two of the crow baits we rode before the skirmish following us."

"They must love us." Lew laughed. "Don't see your cayuse though, Calvin. He must've not liked you or the Yaqis has caught him and 'et' him."

"Cal you tired? You hain't said a word since we reined up." Hawbaker, whose wet sombrero was hanging on one shoulder, shuddered and keeled forward on the neck of his mount.

"What the hell Calvin, are you hurt?" Carter went to the confiscated horse on which his trooper friend sat. Private Carter caught Hawbaker around the waist as the man began to swoon. "Sweet Jesus born of Mary!" Lewis Carter exclaimed as he eased the heavier man down to the wet sand.

"What's the matter?" Chance took two steps and grasped Hawbaker's steed by its halter.

Hawbaker coughed as he adjusted himself on his back and Carter stepped away. Neunan spied the red smear under Calvin's right arm and the stream that ran down the length of the sleeve of the striped peasant shirt he wore. "Thought the big bastard missed me. He didn't but I settled his hash, I did." Hawbaker's voice trailed off as if the exertion of speaking pained him. Neunan took the blood soaked material between the thumb and index fingers of each hand. Carefully, Chance pulled the sun bleached material apart from Calvin's shoulder to his wrist. A deep red gash ran jaggedly upward from his hand through his arm pit. A throbbing artery, blue in color, was visible amongst the clotted hair.

"Jesus, Cal them fellers really got you good!"

"Shut up, Carter." Neunan growled.

"That big guy on the other end of the lance had it aimed right at my gizzard but I parried it....or I thought I did."

"Don't talk." Chance ordered "We're gonna sit you up and bind that arm against your body. We aren't going to dress it just yet. Do you understand?"

"Yes I understand."

"Can you ride?"

"Yes, I think so but my whole right side is about numb."

"We've got to get to some higher ground so we can see what's following." Neunan took a pocket knife and tossed it to Carter." Lew, get the reins off our Mexican horses. They won't need them 'cause they'll follow along with us. That's a good thing 'cause I got a 'housewife' in my saddle gear. It'll be handy in case we hav'ta do some sewing on Calvin."

Once Calvin Hawbaker was cinched to the saddle of his French horse, Neunan and Carter pulled themselves onto their mounts. The animals seemed reluctant to move but a few kicks in the ribs sent them into a trot.

"We'll make for that timbered ridge leading up to the top of that mesa. We can hunker down, treat Cal and keep an eye out for pursuers. You know some of them fellers got away. We didn't get 'em all." The bigger man from the Iowa cavalry troop continued to ruminate aloud.

"Damned Yaquis, they can track a fly over twenty acres of manure, find him and kill him." Carter rode easily beside Hawbacker, his hand resting on his friend's hip. "Things is getting' kinda complicated now that Cal's hurt. We may have to make some adjustments to our return route."

"You're not thinking of leaving him, are you?" Chance looked at the older man intently.

"Me? No. We'll let Cal decide what he wants to do."

"Forget that. He's in no condition to make that kind of a decision."

"What would you suggest we do?"

Chance looked at the wounded man, pale and shivering. "I don't know but the whole mission is in danger of failing."

* * *

THE STABLES
FREEDMEN'S BUREAU

"Do you know Chance? I saw a flash of recognition cross your face when I spoke his name. You can't deny it, you have knowledge of Chance."

The farrier recoiled and shied away from Andrea as she sprang to his side and confronted him.

"Er, Ah," Nichols stammered.

"You know him or have known him! Admit it! Why would you want to hide the facts from me?"

Homer raised his eyes and looked intently into the depths of Andrea's cinnamon colored irises.

"I would get into trouble if I say anything about him."

"Why! What has he done? Tell me?"

Andrea was growing frantic. She grabbed the young man by the shoulder and squeezed feeling the firmness of his arm as she did.

Nichols shrunk back from her grasp knowing full well that the years in his craft could enable him to ward off her aggression.

"I'll tell you about Chance, though Lord I know I should not. If you had word of my Charity that I wanted to know of, I feel you'd tell me. I will give you information but what I'm going to tell you, if it gets out, it'll get us in a world of trouble."

"Tell me, then." The executor sank down beside the farrier on the bale of hay.

"Promise me, Andrea, that this will remain a secret between us. As I've said, any leak and I could go before a firing squad."

"I'll not tell a soul. I've got to know of Chance and if he's safe. I can't believe that he could be in camp not two miles from Glen Haven."

Nichols laid his meaty hand on Andrea's. "He's not exactly in our camp, at least, not at the present." Nichols refused to look the woman in the eye but lowered his head to avoid her gaze,

"Where is he then if he's not with his regiment?"

"I've told you all that I can tell you." The farrier moved away leaving a space between the two of them. The warmth of the beautiful woman's body made him uneasy.

"You have more knowledge that you are giving up. Won't you tell me?" Andrea's voice was pleading.

Nichols exhaled as a sign of surrender to Miss Edwards' request.

"I've known Chance since he came into our outfit. He volunteered in the latter part of May but didn't make connections with us until mid-June, in Alexandria, Louisiana. We moved over land by marching and shipped our heavy stuff by way of the rail cars. We assembled at Hempstead, Texas, after thirty-three days of hell. From that location we moved south east to reach this God forsaken place. That damned vain glorious George Custer just about finished us with the way he drove us to reach Hempstead. Anyway, Chance and me became pretty thick and that was because we had so much in common. We got to talking about things back home and we found we pretty much liked the same things. You see, Chance was considered as being a new recruit and wasn't accepted very well by the veterans in the outfit. Also, a lot of the fellas were from the northern part of the state and kinda uppity with their airs."

"Is that all, Private?"

"Neunan came to the remount station and asked me for help in selecting a suitable horse for duty. Chance wasn't acquainted much with the types of horses used by the cavalry although he said he had ridden quite a bit as a civilian."

"Homer Nichols, I'm getting tired of your round about method of telling a story. I've a good mind to lay my fist against your jaw."

"I could stop right now, you know."

"No, don't. Just get to the point faster."

"Well, Andrea, about two weeks ago, Chance shows up at the corral and turns in his fine horse for the poorest example of a Mexican oat burner you ever did see. He returned every bit of government issued equipment and had me check it off. He was dressed in Hispanic clothes right down to a big ol' sombrero. Said he and four others were gonna slip across the Rio and do some spying.

"A secret mission?"

"I'd expect that it was. I don't know for certain but I do know that we Americans aren't supposed to go traipsing on the other side of the river."

"Did he come back? Had he returned before you signed on to come help us at the stable?"

"Not to my knowledge, Missy, er..,Andrea. None of the five have." Nichols flicked a hand at a buzzing fly before continuing.

"General Sheridan can't send a force into Mexico to determine what's become of them. We have no way of telling if the Imperial Mexicans, the Frenchies or the Yaqui Indians have them. Our men are just gone."

Andrea's eyes welled with tears and her shoulders commenced to shake as the salty secretion flowed down to her lips.

Private Nichols moved closer and wrapped her in his strong arms and held her tightly.

* * *

UNION ENCAMPENT
FORT BROWN, TEXAS

"Lieutenant Wilson, have our scouts made their way into our cantonment from across the river?"

"No Sir, nary a one. I don't expect to see any of them before the scheduled time. Only if they've gotten into trouble would they dare attempt to enter our lines before they're to do so."

"It would be nice to have an update in my report to the Colonel. When were the five to return? I would hope that you've notified the officers in charge of security that we have these men outside our lines to the south. It would be most embarrassing to shoot brave men by mistake."

"They are to come back to us four nights from now. Actually, they are to make their crossing at two o'clock in the morning just down from the ferry and loading dock. Yes, Major Tyler the officers have been made aware of the mission and the sentinels will be doubled and placed on the highest alert."

"Ahem," Tyler cleared his throat. "We've got to guard against the probability that some of our spies may have been caught and that the Mexicans could try to infiltrate our lines in their place. This would be a smear on our security abilities and an embarrassment to General Sheridan."

Tyler never looked at the junior officer but continued to talk and scratch out a note at his field desk. "Four nights from this evening, you say? When will that be?"

"Thursday, July first, Sir."

"I thought as much but was checking to see if you're on your toes."

"I am, Sir. Sir, you expressed a desire to make an inspection of the Freedmen's Bureau grounds and operations?"

"Yes, Wilson. It will be merely a courtesy call and an opportunity to communicate with the staff more fully. Let's set that up in mid-morning, around ten o'clock. Get together a small squad, spit and polish and the horses well groomed. I'd like to make an impression, you know. A show of the colors to let the freed folks see that we're doing a worth while job."

"Yes, Sir. Will there be anything else, Sir?"

"You'll accompany me and have Lil' Ben bring along the guidon."

The major set aside his pen and turned to face Wilson.

"One more thing Lieutenant. My black servant, Sam, is ill and has not been in attendance for my directions today. Would you kindly take my dress boots sitting next to the tent entrance and see that they are shined?"

"Yes, Sir. Of course, Sir."

Robert Tyler waited for a moment or two following Wilson's departure before arising from his chair. The evening dew was creeping under the perimeter of his canvas tent and dampening the trampled grass that comprised the floor of his dwelling.

On the morrow, following the visit to Glen Haven, he'd assign Wilson to find some competent former carpenters within the regiment and have them lay a raised, wooden floor. This would take care of his pesky moisture problem.

Tyler's finger tips went to his face to examine the two day growth of beard sprouting on his throat beneath his beard. *Wilson will be busy tomorrow*; he thought, *especially if 'Black Sam' didn't show up for work at his tent. The lieutenant would have to send the private known for his tonsorial skills to the second in command's tent in order to have him look presentable.* Tyler was well aware of the importance of his initial meeting with the female executor.

* * *

LICKING THEIR WOUNDS
MEXICAN DESERT

"By God, this temperature is cold!" Lewis Carter pulled his shabby serape higher about his neck. "No, it ain't just cold, it's damned cold. It's colder than a witch's tit."

Carter's teeth were chattering as he stamped his booted feet.

Chance leaned over the smoldering fire of dried agave fronds and green mesquite twigs. The flames were puny and provided little heat. He'd constructed a lean-to heat reflector comprised of spindly branches but the fire was so weak that such a make shift devise would be of little use.

"Can't believe that the day would be hotter than hammered hell and the night cold enough to freeze the balls off a brass monkey." Carter complained.

Chance rose from his task and listened to Hawbaker's labored breathing.

"Cal ain't feelin' too good. The poor son-of-a-bitch is burin' up with the fever inside him."

Lewis Carter gathered up a handful of twigs and threw them on the suffering fire.

Neunan continued to study the injured man. Then he tugged Carter away from the prostrated form and whispered," If his fever don't break, he's bound to die."

Carter spit into the cold sand and added, "Sure was a fine job of sewin' that you did on Cal. I'd never seen a hair from a horse's mane used for thread. Where'd you learn how to do that?"

"Learned it from a farrier that I took up with in the Twelfth Illinois Cav. He'd take strands of hair and boil 'em in water before he used them. I don't think that any of the horses that he doctored in that manner ever got an infection. I could never figure out why they didn't."

"We'll that's one fer the books. Like I say, I ain't never seen the likes."

"Fella was from south of Peoria and said his dad, who was a smithy and a vet, used boiled horse hair all the time for sutures."

Chance followed Carter back to the fire and both stood on one foot and held their footwear over the pitiful little fire.

"Sure would like to have a little 'tobaccy'. It would help warm a body on a night like this."

Chance excused himself and knelt beside the wounded trooper to listen to his breathing. As he rose, he heard the Iowan's complaint. Hawbacker was becoming restless and commencing to groan.

"There's a little brandy left in the Frenchman's flask we picked up. I was saving it in case we had to wash out Cal's wound again."

"I'd have a nip of that." Carter quickly stated.

"No, we'll wait. It may do Cal more good than us. I do have a couple of smokes. I found 'em in the same set of saddle bags as the flask. What do you say to that proposition?"

"That'll be just pretty damned fine."

Outside of the flickering light of the fire, a coyote howled in the darkness.

* * *

GOOD NEWS
FREEDMEN'S BUREAU

Andrea sank down on her bed in the master bedroom of the former Baxter plantation. The temperature had risen all day long and as she made her return to the Bureau headquarters from the stables, she was aware of the perspiration gathering on her forehead and nape of her neck. The removal of her thick brogans was a chore but she was finally able to wrench the sweat soaked shoes from her feet. They rested now under the ornately carved dry sink next to the window. She drew her naked feet up tightly against her buttock and unbuttoned the top two buttons of her bodice. Her mind was in a whirl brought on by the affects of the intense heat and the information about Chance that she'd gleaned from Homer Nichols.

*Chance was alive! Or he had been or...God forbid....*Andrea clinched her eyes shut tightly in an attempt to drive the thought from her tormented brain.

It was she who had been the timid, yet all knowing member of the love affair. She had been the one who'd seen the insurmountable barriers that would be erected in their romantic path.

Andrea rolled to her side away from the large window overlooking the sun drenched lawn and commenced to sob. Her tears soaked the lace on her pillow and moistened the open collar of her dress. She had misled Chance at the time of their parting, telling him that she was answering the call to lift up her people, when in reality she was walking away from the man she loved. But time and distance hadn't severed the bonds that the two had made.

Chance Neunan could not be diverted from his quest to find her once more and she knew it.

She was aware that in spite of challenges and bigotry, that the two were destined to be one. Andrea could only hope and pray that Chance would return to her at the conclusion of his hazardous mission.

The sobbing was subsiding as she turned onto her back and wiped at her tears with the heels of her hands. Looking up at the tall ceiling, her eyes took in the floral design painted on the coral background. The motif was executed in calming colors whose presence allowed her to transpose the bitterness of the couples division into happier thoughts.

The last correspondence from the young trooper along with a carte de vista was bound with other missives by a pink ribbon and ferreted away in a velvet clutch in the back of her top dresser drawer. In the quiet at the end of a long day, she'd remove the cherished words and his image and read and reread the intimate correspondences. More than once, Andrea had brought the letters to her cheek and caressed her skin with the paper as she tried to draw tenderness from them. Chance had touched the missives, pondered over just the right selection of words as he wrote, and made promises in them directed to her that he was striving to keep.

Andrea was about to rise from her bed and retrieve her cache from the dresser drawer when she was interrupted by a weak knock on her bedroom door.

"Missy, are you asleep? I don't want to wake you if you is sleepin'."

Andrea heard Angie Sue giggle from the hall where she stood. The girl apparently found her inquiry funny.

"Yes. I'm awake. You may come in, Angie Sue."

"Thank you, Ma'am. I has a 'portant note here from de army camp."

The teenaged aide opened the massive pocket doors just wide enough for her to squeeze her body through.

"I don't know what it says. I h'ain't learned to read yet."

"We're working on that, aren't we, Angie?"

"Oh yes, Ma'am. I intends to be the best reader in my class."

The administrator took the note and broke a red, waxed seal holding the fold shut.

"You been cryin', Missy? I see your eyes is all red."

"It's nothing, Angie. Just some good and bad news all received at the same time."

"If'n it's some folks actin' up and talkin' bad to you, Missy, I'll sic Big Joe and Alvie on 'em. We won't tolerate nobody treatin' Miss Edwards bad."

"No, no, this is no concern of yours. Now don't interrupt so that I can see what the military wants."

Andrea read silently to herself, and then turned the paper over to see whose signature was on the back.

"My word!" Andrea's hand shot to her mouth.

"What is it, Missy?"

"A Major Tyler is coming here to Glen Haven tomorrow morning at nine. He wants to see our operation and to offer more volunteers from the cavalry to assist us."

"Everthing is as right as rain, Missy, thanks to de way you run things. There's no reason to worry at all."

* * *

PARTING WAYS
MEXICAN DESERT

The weak, little fire was trying its best to broaden itself but the wretched wood it was being fed doomed it to mediocrity. Chance walked away from Carter with his cigar as the man sat next to the smoldering entanglement. Private Hawbacker's face, forehead and neck were on fire when Chance touched them. The Iowa trooper's eyes were closed and his cracked lips moved as if he were talking to someone. Neunan knelt next to the wounded man and tried to make an evaluation of his condition. The injured man's rasping, erratic breathing alarmed him. Taking off his damp serape, Neunan covered Hawbacker; then returned to sit beside Carter.

Carter didn't acknowledge Chance's return but sat stoically blowing smoke rings. It was a few minutes before the older man spoke.

"He's not gonna make it is he?"

"No, I'm afraid not."

"Damn!"

"We've done all we could do for him but who can tell. He could rally and be full of spit and vinegar by the morning." The excitement of the chase and fight with the lancers had drawn away Chance's strength. He leaned back against a cold rock and closed his eyes. Several deep breaths followed and soon he felt his consciousness fleeting as he dropped into slumber.

Andrea Edwards, was that really her? The image wavering before him was some type of devious trick. Yet, the smile and the flowing hair looked so much like the woman he was seeking. His tired eyes could only make out her lithe body from her head to her knees. The pale, blue vapor wafted in and out of the rocks and eventually drifted toward him. Misty and hazy only a bit lighter than the nocturnal landscape she hovered beyond his reach in all the naked beauty of a woman. Chance reached out for her but he found that his arms were not long enough to touch her. His finger tips, longing to caress her delectable body, were denied the pleasure by her distance from him. He strained to spread his fingers in order to stroke her throat and hair. Andrea stood before him, smiling and offering herself but she was beyond his reach.

"We could rig a travois and bring him out with us." Carter stood over Chance chewing on the butt of his cigar.

"We'd leave a drag trail that a blind man could follow. The Yaqui would thank us for that."

Carter returned to the fire and kicked a few embers into life.

"Dammit!" The Iowan cursed.

"Won't do any good to cuss, Lew. It won't help any."

"All right, what's your suggestion, Chance?"

"I don't have any."

"Look here, partner, me and Calvin have been together for four years. I'm not about to leave him now."

"Go on."

"Here's what I say we do. Me and Cal'll give you our information and you take it and head for the border. We'll come along after he gets better. That way you'll get back at the appointed time."

"Uh...I don't know..."

"It's the only way." Lew Carter cut Chance off. "Me and Cal won't have it any other way."

"But...." Chance tried to protest.

"That'll do, Neunan. Let me climb up high and take a look around. When I come down, I'll get you our figures."

* * *

"Don't see any lights out there, no where. Guess that I didn't expect any." Carter's statement awakened Chance from the reverie which he'd returned to.

Neunan groaned as he straightened himself into a sitting position. He was embarrassed by his dream and remained silent about it in Carter's presence.

"You sleepin', Neunan? You oughtta been checkin' on Cal." Carter's voice was gruff with his disapproval of the Illinois trooper's conduct.

"I checked on him. I did. He was sleepin' but also tossing at intervals. He's delirious at this point."

"What do you want to do about partin' company?" Lew stood his carbine against a waist high chunk of shale next to his right leg.

"If that's what you want?"

"It ain't but it's the only sensible way to accomplish our mission. Do you wanna start tonight?"

"Now?"

"Yes, now. It's no tellin' what daylight will bring. Them fellers could have us surrounded by then."

"But how am I to navigate across this wasteland in the darkness?"

"I'll loan you my compass. You got Lucifer's don't you? I'll get the compass back from you when Cal and me come across the river."

"Sure, I have matches."

"Then you're set, then. You got a half gourd of water we siphoned from the Indian drinkin' holes we found on yonder ledge."

"Yes, I'll leave more than half of it for you two."

"Ain't necessary. I 'spect that I can find more tomorrow." Carter was unbuckling his waist belt that he suspended his revolver from. "I'll get our figures fer you."

"Where do you have them hidden?"

"No, where do you have yours hid? Me and Cal didn't find numbers or nothin' in yer clothes or belongin' when we come across you yesterday mornin'."

"They're in the sole of my sandal."

"Pretty clever place, Neunan, but not as clever as ours." Lew drew his revolver and placed it on a flat section above the muzzle of his carbine. He located a nearby mesquite bush and broke off a length of stick. He finished removing the belt and tipped the holster upside down and commenced to wiggle the stick up inside the accoutrement. "I have them in the tip of the holster packed down as tight as a shotgun wad."

Neunan reached down and picked up the innocuous circular piece of paper as it dropped in the dismal firelight and examined it.

"We'd better make a duplicate copy of the figures for you and Cal in case I don't get through."

Chance eased down on the damp sand and removed his sandal. Taking out his pocket knife, he slit the stitching on his sole and opened the compartment.

"Once we get things copied, this is where the figures will be returned to," Chance said.

* * *

THE STABLES
FREEDMEN'S BUREAU

Private Nichols was beside himself regarding the information he'd divulged to Andrea Edwards. The factual material he'd imparted to the administrator was of the highest secrecy, so much so that its exposure could lead to an international incident.

Had not he, and Chance Neunan plus two other men from the Twelfth Illinois and two more from the Third Iowa been drawn from the brigade ranks? He had accompanied the travelers without knowing of the choice that they had made to infiltrate dangerous territory in Mexico.

The journey aboard a rickety train from Hempstead had been tiring in the extreme. The track was bumpy and ill maintained all evidence of it's over use during the recent hostilities. Their men's mounts journeyed with them as well and the group arrived at Fort Brown in Brownsville in the occupying vanguard. If the French installers of the Austrian potentate, Maximilian, possessed any intelligence service even of the most minimal kind, they would have sniffed out the clandestine development propigated by General Sheridan. Any spies of either of the forces opposing each other in Mexico, the Juareztas or the Imperialists would have suspected the six, one of whom was a farrier.

Nichols was uncertain of how discrete Andrea would be with the joyful news she'd received. The thought of her gossiping to the house staff or even worse, inquiring within military circles of her lover, gave Nichols chills. The longer he permitted his mind to dwell on the meeting with Miss Edwards, the more nervous he became.

The intensity of Nichols' angst lessened when a behemoth of a man stepped through the partially opened stable doorway.

"What is it Big Joe?" The farrier didn't know the brawny man's last name or even if he had one. Quite likely, he had none and if he did, he'd taken the sir name of the plantation owner who'd recently owned him as property.

"Yes, Sir, bossman. Dey's gonna be a big visitor comin' here to the Bureau tomorrow mornin'. Missy Edwards says to dress the place up for de big brass."

"Is that so, Big Joe? Then let's get some more help and light into that big pile of manure out front and get the stalls cleaned as well."

"Yes, Boss. I'll get Alvie. He's good help when it comes to sweat work."

* * *

RIDING ALONE
MEXICAN DESERT

Chance stood checking the tension on his saddle's girth when Carter approached him in the moon light.

An early moon had risen, blue and pale. It shown down on the jumble of rocks bathing all in a transparent shimmer.

"Best wait 'til the moon sets before you head north." The speaker uttered in a low tone. "However, if you'll wait a few minutes, 'peers like a cloud formation's movin' in and it'll cover the moon sooner. If I was you, I'd light out then."

"I'd like to get started as soon as I can, Lew."

Neunan had switched back to his boney Mexican mount. He hated to give up his French dressage but it would be too dangerous for him to ride about on such a fine animal with such excellent equipment. *No, he thought, the horse called Poco would be the wisest choice to ride on his dash for the Rio.*

"How's Calvin?" Chance tied his damp serape on the back of his saddle.

" 'Bout the same. Out of his head and mumblin'."

Neunan spit into the darkness underneath Poco's belly. It was hell to see a perfectly healthy man give his live away to stay with a dying friend. Calvin Hawbacker was dying and there was no mistaking the fact. Carter knew it too, but he was tethered to his friend with the strongest of bonds; friendship.

"You'll be along soon?"

"As soon as he gets better and can ride. You got everything?"

"Yes." Neunan forced his tongue under his top lip to prevent himself from sobbing. "I took a look at my map and it says to get to big Bear Rock before turning west."

"Foller the map. You're as blind as me and Cal since none of us have ever traveled this way before."

There was silence as Chance placed his foot in the stirrup in preparation to mounting.

On a distant ridge a coyote yapped several notes of its lonesome song.

"Chance?"

"Yes."

I'm givin' you the Spencer. It'll get you out of just about any predicament that you get yourself into."

"You'll need it more than me, Lew. You'll have your hands full tryin' to get Cal to the spy base."

"I'll manage; don't you worry." The Iowa trooper spoke with determination. Lew Carter was the type of no nonsense human being that any man would be proud to have as a friend.

Neunan watched as Carter walked to Poco and slid the carbine into a French scabbard that Chance had secured to his saddle.

"Take care of this little darlin'. I'm expectin' to get her back along with my compass when we get inta the lines."

"I'm much obliged, Lew."

"The Blaksley box is tied to your bedroll."

"Thanks. I'll not forget you fellas."

"We'll be along."

Chance swung up into the saddle and looked down into the shadowy face of Carter. He felt the standing man place his hand on his lower leg and give it a pat.

"You take care of yourself, you hear."

* * *

SETTING THE STAGE FOR SEDUCTION
FREEDMEN'S BUREAU

Major Tyler placed his left foot in the hooded stirrup and pulled himself easily into the seat of the McClellan saddle. Art Fields, his aide, handed the reins to his commanding officer and stepped back. Tyler nodded his thanks.

"Are we assembled, Lieutenant Wilson?"

"Yes Sir. All able men, good and true, riding in double file. You will ride in the center, me on the left and little Ben Sullivan on the right with the guidon. Does that meet with your approval, Sir?"

"Yes, Wilson. You've done a good job. Let us be off, then."

The junior officer waved his right hand in a forward motion and the entourage trotted away. They rode down the company street passing new, unstained Sibley tents and smoldering cook fires. Those troops who looked up from their menial duties sprang to attention as the group moved by them.

Approaching the front entrance to the cantonment, Major Tyler threw his hand up signaling that he wished to halt. Lt. Wilson followed suit and shouted the command, "Troop halt!"

The sound of jingling equipment and the thump of hooves died away almost immediately.

"Lieutenant, what is that large stockade erected there? I knew such a structure was in the works but I have not passed this way very often, always using the sally port, to make my exits and I was not aware of such progress.

"Sir, it's a temporary prison divided into three parts. One section is reserved for the Mexican bandits we catch, the middle section is where we incarcerate our mal-contents who try to desert and the last section is reserved for the rebels whom we capture trying to offer their services to Maximilian."

"Oh, do we have many former Confederates locked inside?"

"Yes, Sir. We have upwards of a hundred such rogues housed in their partition."

"I've heard a rumor that General Joe Shelby has offered his entire command to fight as mercenaries for the Austrian who calls himself the emperor of Mexico." Tyler flicked a particle of straw from his shoulder as though he could care less of the incident.

"Shelby has crossed the border with his motley crew, but I haven't heard if the Imperialists have accepted their service." Lieutenant Wilson offered additional information.

"I'm aware of that occurrence and it's a blight on the record of this army, it is. Shelby should have been intercepted and arrested or at least turned back. This exploit by these brigands leaves an indelible mark on our service record here."

"Perhaps the spy ring we have operational will allow us to prevent such happenings in the future."

Tyler gave Wilson a hard look and lowering his voice, admonished the junior officer for talking openly about the mission.

* * *

"Lordy, lordy, Missy Edwards, da soldier boys are passin' through da front gate and stoppin' in the shade of the biggest ol' Live Oak we got." Angie Sue turned from the lace curtains at the front windows of Glen Haven.

"Thank you for alerting me as to their arrival, Angie. Can we get control of our elation and conduct ourselves as ladies?"

"Yessum. I'm so excited." The young aide gushed.

"I could tell by how you were flitting about."

"Oh, look. Two soldier boys is takin' de reins of the dismounted riders and leadin' off the horses to de corner of the yard. There comes Massa's

Downs and Leonard out to shake hands with the red haired man with de braid on his suit."

"Then I must go and meet our guests. It was not my intention but I see that I will be socially tardy."

Andrea roughed up her hair which had been washed that morning but not coiffured into the drawn back, Victorian style of the day.

"How do I look, Angie?"

"Just beautiful! Lands sake, just plain beautiful!" The assistant stepped to Andrea and pulled up the hem of the executive's dress and looked down. "Good, I didn't want to see any of dem ol' army shoes on yer dainty feet."

"No, Angie. I'm wearing the brocaded slippers I had you fetch me from the chest in the closet. My, you're getting to be like an old mother to me."

"We can't have de fine lady of de house trompin' around de army gentlemens in dem ol' clod hoppers."

The Parker girl followed Andrea out onto the veranda and down the wide, white painted steps. After a few strides, the administrator paused and turned to her assistant.

"Oh my, I've forgotten to have the cavalry volunteers working here at the Bureau on hand to give reports to this Major Tyler. Could you please, look up 'Big Joe' and have him summon the five to this gathering on the lawn?"

"Yessum, Missy. I'll have Joe bring 'em to you right away."

The two officers had parted from their small squad and were approaching the house. They were being accompanied by Downs and Leonard.

Andrea retreated to the step, climbed up to the top level, folded her hands before her and waited for their arrival. She recalled that it was all about positioning in this initial meeting. Standing elevated and relaxed, would send a subliminal message to the major that she was more than a beautiful female, she was his equal. She held an office and managed it efficiently in a difficult time. She was more than an empty headed appointee drawing a government check. Andrea Edwards was a woman with aspirations years before her time.

The junior officer in the group stopped at the base of the steps.

"Good morning, madam. I'm Lieutenant Bryce Wilson of the Fourth Wisconsin Cavalry and you are Andrealine Edwards, Director of the Freedmen's Bureau at Glen Haven."

"That is correct Lt. Wilson."

"Then permit me to introduce my superior, Major Robert Tyler."

"How do you do, Major. We are honored by your visit and I personally wish to thank you for your generosity in allowing us to use your men in our operation. You gentlemen have introduced yourself but allow me to add additional information on Mr. Downs and Mr. Leonard. Mr. Downs is our procurement manager and Mr. Leonard is our minister and Sunday school leader."

"It is a sincere pleasure to make your acquaintance, Miss Edwards. It is seldom in this day and age to encounter a woman entrusted with such responsibilities."

Andrea allowed the condescending remark to pass without commenting. "I believe with your visit you will see the fruits of our efforts. The newly emancipated people are like children having been given freedoms that they have never known. If you or I had been awarded the overwhelming independence as the black Americans have here in the South, I'm certain that we would be as befuddled as they are."

Andrea allowed a few seconds for her declaration to take affect before offering a verbal olive branch.

"Won't you and your lieutenant join the bureau's party for refreshments in the rear garden? I've had the five troopers from your command summoned to join us under the rose bower.

"Splendid." Major Tyler was pulling off his doeskin gloves

"Your men in the yard, should I send them out a bit of food and drink?"

"Of course, if you'd like."

"Then that will be done. Won't you follow me through the house to the garden? In this manner you will observe first hand as to how the interior has been restored by members of the Freedmen. You will be enamored with our gardens as well. Our newly instituted horticulture program is paying dividends. It's amazing what a dose of education will do for people. It gives them hope that they will one day escape from the drudgery of 'choppin' cotton."

The compliment of males followed Miss Edwards through the high ceilinged rooms passing across ventilating wings with gargantuan windows which cooled the mansion's interior. Tyler took note of the ornately carved furnishings and the cast iron ornamentations that stood before each fire place.

"Here we are, gentlemen. Won't you take a seat in the wicker chairs I've had brought out?"

A mocking bird hopped in and about in the damp tangle of a trumpet vine forming the cover for the arched pergola. The gray songster eyed the assembled humans curiously. A squeaking side gate announced the arrival of the five volunteers.

"Ah, gentlemen, the volunteers have joined us along with Big Joe, one of our ablest employees. Have you met these men, Major?'

"Uh, no, I haven't. I placed Lieutenant Wilson in charge of the procurement of assistance for the Freedmen's Bureau."

"Yes, I quite understand. Why would you be bothered with such a mundane matter?"

"Precisely." Tyler was forming an opinion that Andrea was not exactly enchanted with him.

"Would you like a report from these men, Lt. Wilson? Major Tyler and I will retire to a side table and have our small repast. Mr. Downs and Mr. Leonard have their duties to oversee once they've eaten. You may speak to our guest assistants, in private and at your leisure."

Tyler had placed his hat on his head to shade it momentarily from the sun which freckled through the leaves of the bower. He drew a chair from beneath the table they'd chosen, seated Andrea, and removed his head gear and placed in on one of the extra chairs. Wilson took a few dainties and motioned for the five soldiers who'd just arrived to do the same. The group, once their hands were full proceeded to a secluded spot at the furthest boundary of the garden. Downs and Leonard picked through the rapidly vanishing delicacies and then passed out the side gate of the enclosure.

"May I pour tea for you, Major?" Andrea smiled sweetly.

"Why certainly, Miss Edwards." The rust headed officer paused before asking, "May I call you Andrealine?"

"No, you may not, sir. Andrealine is too long and too formal. I believe that if we are to be friends, then we should address each others by our first names. I prefer, Andrea."

"Yes, you are right. You may call me, Robert. Your entreaty to have us speak to each other in this first name basis will put us on the proper footing."

The color which had drained from Tyler's face at the original rebuff had returned. "My full name is Robert Benjamin Tyler. How may I be of service to you?"

The caramel colored woman studied the face of the handsome soldier. Tyler was at least ten years older that she.

"Are you offering assistance to me or to the bureau?'

"Tyler moved the little finger of his right hand until it rested against the executive's hand.

"Aren't you and the bureau one and the same?"

Andrea allowed their hands to continue to touch.

"I'm in a position to help you advance from where you are here to a higher echelon. A very complimentary report and a syrupy evaluation in a quarterly manner could lift you to a position that you could only have dreamed of."

"And what would be expected of me in return for your glowing appraisals?"

The red headed officer's hand slid over the top of Andres's hand.

"My dear, you are marvelously beautiful. Your presence among any group of men causes them to stammer or become tongue tied completely."

Andrea was ready to move to the next stage of her plan. She placed her free hand over Tyler's freckled one

"If I were to reciprocate to your offered favors, would it be possible for me to learn of a certain man who's serving in your command here in Brownsville?"

"Certainly, my dear, that could be arranged and you could be made privy to what ever information you so desire. After all we must survive in this God forsaken place. From this time on our motto shall be: 'Carpi Diem'".

"Let's not be so hasty with what you expect of me, Robert Tyler. Your duties at this location will terminate much more quickly than will mine. The war has, as you well know, completely turned southern society and its bias and bigotry upside down. It will take the Freedmen's Bureau to smooth the quagmire that the conquered people are writhing in. The Bureau will remain here in Texas and the other states in the South until we are no longer needed and true freedom is achieved by those we serve."

Andrea drew her hand away from the majors. She leaned back in her chair and gave Tyler a stern look.

"Frankly, Robert, you have been too liberal with your assumptions about me. I will admit that our mutual friendship can be advantageous to the both of us but your salacious innuendos have dimmed my view of you."

"I,I.." The major stammered.

"You cannot justify your overbearing behavior toward me, can you?"

"I extend my deepest apologies, madam. I have spoken in a boorish manner to a fine lady. My opinion of you was most contorted."

"Hmm;" Andrea rose from her seat at the table and turned her back to the embarrassed officer. When she turned back to face Tyler, her eyes had softened and her features calmed.

"Sir, I accept your apology on one condition."

"And what would that be, Andrea?"

"That you treat me as a lady and not the black whore that you felt that you could speak to condescendingly and control."

"I promise to do that Ma'am."

"Additionally, tomorrow evening you will host a dinner gathering at which time we shall confer again. The meal shall be in your tent in the cantonment at which time you will reveal your knowledge of the missing soldier that I seek."

Robert Tyler paused before answering, contemplating what Andrealine really was getting at or, in short, what reason she had for requesting a conference on his home field.

Major Tyler mused a full minute before replying. He flicked an ort of a trumpet vine bloom from his shoulder before speaking.

The woman is a heady one. She has dashed me to the ground with her accusation, placed a foot on my throat, but reconsidered and allowed me to stand up again. She is leaving me a narrow ray of hope that our relationship could grow.

"Of course, Andrea. I'll comply with your request in searching for the soldier. I'll have Lt. Wilson look over the regimental rosters and locate the man. It shouldn't be a daunting task. Upon my return to the camp, I shall direct my personal cook to prepare an exquisite menu for our pleasure. Would you have any food that you prefer?"

The officer seeing Lt. Wilson dismiss his charges stood and straightened the front of his uniform. He retrieved his hat, brushed its ostrich plume affixed to its crown and held the head gear against his chest in deference to the presence of a lady.

"No, Robert, I shall leave the choice of fare to you."

"Would six o'clock be too early for you? I fear any earlier the sun will yet be warm and much later, we'll have to contend with the insects."

The female administrator went to Tyler, removed a slip of paper from a pocket on the front of her dress and placed the notation in his free hand.

"Here is the name of the man that I'm looking for, Robert. Six o'clock to sup with you will be fine." She brought up her left hand to enclose Tyler's which retained Andrea's right, holding the information. "May I bring or have sent over anything to make our meeting more memorable?" Andrea eyes locked with the officers.

"Andrea Edwards, your presence will be all that I desire."

"Then six o'clock it is and we shall work to right all affronts that have occurred in this first meeting."

* * *

THE STABLES
FREEDMEN'S BUREAU

Andrea watched the small cavalry detachment depart the Freedmen's Bureau headquarters.

She leaned against the side of the massive, oak desk that sat next to the window of her upstairs office. She fixed her gaze on Major Tyler's back as he trotted his mount at the head of the column. As a woman, she knew that a backward glance in the direction of her officer would signal his interest in her.

She waited and watched.

Just as the as the entourage was passing through the front lawn gate, She witnessed Robert turning in his saddle and fixing a departing look at the mansion.

Andrea's intuition told her that Tyler was in her spell and that if she could foil his carnal intent, she could glean anything she wanted from him.

"Angie Sue?" She picked up a white prochain bell and rang it once. She was aware of the young assistant entering the office from a side entrance. Her aide wore an apron over her full length dress. Points of perspiration sparkled on her forehead.

"Yesum, Missy Edwards?"

"Have you been helping wash the dishes from our garden conference?"

"Yessum."

"Don't do that. We have women who we pay to do that sort of thing."

"Yessum."

"Would you look up Big Joe and have him bring up Private Nichols from the stable. I'd like to talk with him. Have Joe tell him that I want to see him right away."

"Yessum. I tink that da Nichols fella is still walkin' toward de corral. Will dat be all?'

"Yes."

Andrealine busied herself looking over a ledger filled with descriptions of recent procurements and billings from providers of goods. In a few minutes, a knock sounded on her door jam. She looked up to see Homer Nichols standing in the doorway.

"You wished to see me, Ma'am?" The soldier was holding his battered kepi in front of him.

"Yes, I do. I'd like to discover the reason for the visit from the military just a few minutes ago? It's common knowledge, at least in government circles, that the bureau co-operates with the army but is not under its authority."

"I can't say as how I know much about all that."

"What was the nature of the lieutenant's questions?"

"He asked if the work was hard and if we'd been treated well. I told him that I had no complaints."

"Go on."

"I told him that me and Chance…er, uh."

"Wait, wait, you told me that you just vaguely knew Chance." Andrea's face displayed puzzlement.

Nichols swallowed and wiped his head with the back of his hand. He regained his composure and continued, "Well, Neunan come down to Brownville on the train with me. He and four others from the brigade stepped forward and answered the call for volunteers for a secret mission. I rode the cars with 'em to Fort Brown because I was replacing the farrier for the Sixteenth cavalry who'd got sick."

"Nichols are you telling me all, and I mean all, that you know about Chance?"

"Yes. Oh yes, Ma'am."

"Well, I'm going beyond you, Private."

'Oh, I wish that you wouldn't."

"Yes, I'm going to Major Tyler to learn about Chance."

Andrea saw the young man's body shiver.

"Please, I've told you what will happen to me if word of all this spying gets out."

"I'll be discrete, Nichols. Your name will not be revealed in my investigation."

Homer Nichols wrung his hands and shook his head. He moaned, "Oh, I wish that I'd never met Chance Neunan."

Andrea patted the distraught man's shoulder and said, "But I'm so glad that you befriended him. Don't you see what word of him that you've provided has given me hope? I know now that the man whom I've adored and loved has followed me to Texas."

* * *

UNION ARMY ENCAMPMENT
FORT BROWN

Major Tyler was simmering. He'd allowed the beautiful Andrea to best him in the seductive game that he'd devised. His actions were too rash and he had moved toward his goal too quickly.

At this particular juncture he'd have to throttle back and play the repentant gentleman.

As the contingent of riders halted before the command tent, the major waited as his aide, Private Fields, strode up and accepted his horse's reins.

Tyler did not dismount immediately but directed Lt. Wilson to dismiss the men. Major Tyler slid easily from his saddle as the aide steadied his mount.

"Wilson, I'd like your presence in my tent as soon as you're finished."

"Certainly Sir;" came the response.

Upon Wilson's return, he found his commander lounging on his folding cot enjoying one of his choice cheroots. The tent's interior sweltered from the mid-day heat.

"My private meeting with Miss Edwards did not go overly well, Lieutenant."

"How's that, Sir?"

"I'd rather not say. I have an opportunity to right myself in her eyes at a dinner to be held here in my tent tomorrow evening at six."

"A dinner party, Sir?"

"Yes. Get three, clean men with clean hands and nails. Make certain that they are newly bathed and send them to the medical tent for white over garments. These three shall serve as waiters for the soiree. Please make good choices, Wilson; none that chew or have filthy habits."

"How many shall be in attendance? How many shall I have the cook prepare for?"

"Just two, that's all. I should think that a brace of partridges taken from the surrounding bottom lands, some potatoes of the locally grown variety and vegetables. I will let you select the dessert for Andrea Edwards and myself. Oh, yes, let's have a nice, mild claret with the meal and coffee with the desert.

"Is that all understood? Wilson?"

"Yes Sir. Precisely, Sir."

"Good man, Wilson. I've always marveled at your ability to carry out orders. But before I send you on your way, Lieutenant, there is another matter that I'd like for you to attend to."

"Sir?"

"This infernal floor or lack of one. I'm sick to death of the dust and critters that are under foot. I have found grasshoppers in my bed and I want this stopped. You'll gather a crew of former carpenters from the regiment and put them to work immediately to rectify the problem.

"Yes, Major." As Wilson started to make his departure he stopped and turned back.

"You've given me a lot to do, Sir."

"You can handle it all, I'm sure. Oh, and one additional thing, Miss Edwards desires information on some soldier she's acquainted with in our command. I tried to beg off but she was persistent. You and I both know that we have no Negro men within the brigade."

"Perhaps the man of interest isn't black."

Tyler was indifferent to Wilson's suggestion.

"She's written the soldier's name on a slip of paper and entrusted it to me. Of course, if you can't turn up anything of importance, fabricate something."

Tyler took a draw on his cigar. "I think that I'll take a party of four troopers and swing down along the river and see if we can't flush some partridges for tomorrow night's festivities.

"In our hunt, I will reconnoiter the observation scaffold that's being erected, The 'High Tower,' I believe its being called."

"The slip of paper, if you please, Sir? I can put some desk people on the roster search once I've alerted the cook of the menu."

Tyler fished a finger into the vacant watch pocket on his vest and handed the little note to Wilson.

"Yes Wilson, what we need down here is one of Thaddeus Lowe's hot air balloons like we had on the Peninsula. Then we'd not have to rely on that rickety affair. How long do you think it would take going through military channels to get one of those balloons from the East here to Texas?"

When Tyler lifted his eyes to prompt a response from Wilson, the junior officer had left the tent. *It was just as well that Wilson was gone. Perhaps I can get a short nap before my jaunt to the tower and hunting foray for the game birds;* Tyler told himself.

* * *

"Excuse me Major. I'm sorry to disturb you but I have brought the carpenters with me. Have you fallen asleep?"

"By damn, I must have. Have the men wait outside so that I can change into more suitable clothes for the hunt. Will there be enough time for me to bag a few birds and get back with them to have them for dinner?"

"Sir, You told me the dinner is set for tomorrow. That is correct isn't it?"

"My word, yes. I'll go with my little group and shoot the birds this afternoon. The cook can dress them and put them on ice until they're needed. I'll be out of the way so that the construction can proceed."

Tyler was rummaging around in his foot locker but he stopped and said to no one in particular. "Candles. We must have candles, lots of them."

"They will be procured, Sir."

"Wonderful. Now all I have to do is to round up some wild fowl and everything will be falling into place."

"Sir."

"Yes."

"The soldier's name on the paper…"

"Speak up, man. Apparently he is well known if you have information on him all ready."

"This man, Chance Neunan, is one of the five spies we sent across the Rio Grande twelve days ago. We will be expecting him back within four days."

"How in thunder do you suppose she knows this man?"

"I wouldn't have any idea, Sir."

Tyler stopped tugging on his boot top. "I wonder what her motive is with this Neunan, fellow. How much should we tell her of Chance Neunan? Is she trying to tip our hand to the Imperialists?"

* * *

MAKING FOR THE RIO

Chance's bald faced horse was trotting along at a steady gait as the sun crested the distant horizon. The ascending orb cast a pinkish glow on the tops of the shadowy forms it touched. Chance had tried to avoid burdening his animal with too much extra equipment but even with what he considered the essentials, the slender equine groaned as it climbed the small inclines.

The country was not good for dogs and women as the old timers said. It was hard, dry and unforgiving. Lack of water and forage as well as sinister predators contributed to the land's insidious reputation. Only when the topography fell away at the edge of the Rio Grande's watershed could a settler have any hope of staking out a site that had any possibility of raising a crop.

Chance stopped twice in a futile search for landmarks resembling a bear in the rock formations. He was certain that he was heading north from his own reconnaissance but when he became addled, he consulted the compass Carter had given him. At each respite, Neunan slid out of the saddle and gingerly tested the sand for growing warmth. Withdrawing the tattered map from his shirt's breast pocket, he studied the faint ink drawing.

Somewhere ahead of him a prominence rose gradually from the midst of the mesquite and pine thickets to form a salient. Finding and following this formation while always keeping it on his right, he was to set a track which would eventually lead to the river's watercourse. The difficulty lay in locating one of the two gaps passing through the salient in order to gain access to the valley edging the Rio.

As the sun inched higher in the sky, its rays grew more intense and Chance avoided looking in that direction. The compass would come into play in the full light of day.

Poco limped through the low chaparral, the thorny twigs tearing at the horse's side and Chance's lower legs. The trooper was growing aware of just how much the sun was wearing him down. He dismounted again, wet his bandana with tepid water from his gourd jug and dabbed at the corners of his mouth. Taking his pocket knife from his sodden trousers, he cut away a small section of the saddle blanket. He sprinkled water on the shabby cloth and placed it on Poco's nose and mouth. Chance, in spite of his dehydration, knew that he was in a tight spot very similar to the one he'd been in previously. Hawbacker's and Carter's timely arrival had saved him but he could only rely on himself in the present situation. He had to forge on, in spite of the pounding, relentless heat, and find the opening in the towering ridge to his right. Chance remounted and clucked to his spindly mount.

"Come on, Boy. Don't give out on me now. We've got to find the nearest gap."

The jaded horse paid no heed to Neunan's digging his heels into its boney ribs. It was spent and no amount of urging could compel it to move any faster.

A tinkling sound, barely audible to the trooper's fevered sense of hearing alerted Chance that something unnatural was near by. His complacence was swept aside and his sense of survival was placed on high alert. Something or someone was moving parallel to him and he could hear the dry twigs snapping. Chance flicked the front brim of his sombrero away from his face causing the headgear to fall onto his back. Only the thong attached to the brim held it in place. He loosened the Spencer in the leather carbine socket buckled onto his saddle and waited.

Suddenly, an enormous billy goat leaped through an opening in the brushy barrier and stood eyeing the interloper who'd come into his domain. He lifted his head and shook it sideways causing the bell to tinkle slightly. Two smaller nannies followed close behind their leader and all three shifted around to face Neunan. They stood side by side, motionless except for the movement of their jaws as they chewed their cud. Chance was both happy and concerned with the animals' appearance. Their presence meant that human habitation was near but he was fearful because he had no way of knowing the allegiance of the animals' owner.

The repeating rifle was drawn slowly from its sheath until it rested, blue and sinister across the pommel of his saddle. Neunan waved his right hand in the air and startled the goats. He then guided Poco through the gap in the underbrush and past a slit in the jumbled rocks. Pressing closer to the scrambling animals, the goats commenced to bound sure footedly over and through centuries old rockslides.

Chance vacillated as to what course to follow. He chose to try to find his way out of the incumberment by selecting a game path leading in a northerly direction. The billy goat doubled back, climbed up through a declivity and stood looking down at the horse and rider. Neunan marveled at the curiosity displayed by the male goat. He continued away from the errant animals, guiding Poco down the narrow path through the under brush.

A waft of wood smoke jolted him from the distraction caused by the billy and his harem,

Moaning and pleading whimpering rose over the sound of satanic laughter. Neunan prodded his horse through the last swath of brambles to enter into a rock strewn clearing.

A carcass, seared black, lay sizzling in the remnants of a dying fire. Eight feet away two Mexican men held a teenaged girl to the ground. As she begged and pleaded their hands ravished her body from head to toe. The marauders were so absorbed with their groping that they took no notice of Neunan's appearance.

The hysterical Hispanic girl's face was smeared with blood and her dark hair tangled and filled with dried grass and pine needles. Clawing hands had torn away the top of her dress exposing her youthful breasts. Another pair of hands was digging between her kicking legs. The pair was taking turns slapping her face from side to side. When she seemed to be loosing consciousness, one turned his attention to her lower body and attempted to pry her thighs apart.

"Basta por hoy, amigos!" Chance shouted as he leveled the carbine on the aggressors.

One of the would- be rapists rolled to his side and attempted to draw his sidearm. With his trousers wadded over his gun belt, he stood no chance.

Christian Spencer's invention spit fire and opened the man's bare chest. He fell backwards, face to the sky.

"Compadre! Compadre!" Screamed the second ruffian as he reached for his pistol which was in a holstered belt hanging below his knees.

Neunan shot him in the mouth as he squared himself above the prostrated girl. The lead slug yanked his head backward in a splay of blood, brains and hair. His body never twitched once as it clumped down in the dirt like a gunny sack of rocks.

"Gracias, gracias, Senor. Mucho Gracias!" The gratitude, blubbered through weeping, drew Chance's attention back to the terrified girl and away from the two men he'd just disposed of.

"Como te llamas, Senior?" A man's voice emanated from a hog-tied form lying trussed in the shade of a wind sculpted stone formation.

"It's Chance Neuman. That's who I am. Who are you and how did these banditos come so close to killin' you and your daughter?"

"She ain't my daughter, Sir. You seem to be able to speak the Gringo language pretty good for a Mex. Why don't you light down offa that horse and cut me free." The bearded, dirty faced man with a red swelling under his left eye scooted sideways until he could wedge himself upright against the rock. He struggled using the heels of his boots until he wrenched himself into a sitting position.

"Now, Rosa, cover yourself and move away from them bastards. Ever thing is gonna be all right." The unidentified man spoke words of comfort.

The trooper dismounted and approached the bound man. Chance walked around the bedraggled, middle aged fellow before he asked; "You a Johnny reb? You're wearing a reb jacket."

"Yes sir, I am. I'm Richard Cross, formerly of John Bell Hood's Texas Infantry. Look here, Neunan, can't you cut me loose. I been eatin' dust for an hour at least. Ever since them two desperadoes got the drop on us."

Chance took his time in making his interrogation. He wasn't about to free a man who would spring at his throat once his bonds were severed.

"They aren't going to be getting the drop on anybody again except maybe in hell."

Neunan leaned against the rock and looked down at the ex-rebel named, Cross.

"What I want to know is why you and your woman are so far into Mexico. You're a Texan. You and your lady could have remained across the river and made a living."

"Not hardly. The blue bellies has got all the good jobs give to the freed niggers."

Chance didn't respond to the slur. He wouldn't have expected any other position from a man who had fought for the 'lost cause'.

"All right, I can see what you were up to. You skirted around the camp at Fort Brown, crossed the Rio Grande, and were making for Mexico City and the Maximilian forces. That's true isn't it?"

The bound ex-soldier let out a sigh as if he'd told the same story a number of times before.

"You're partly right, compadre, but I got off course and ran inta Rosa and her aged grandfather. I was expectin' to hook up with a group of Confederate soldiers and do exactly as you described. Only, I got stranded when my horse give out and Rosa and the old man saved my sorry ass. I stayed on with old Raul and Rosa for a couple of weeks 'til the old man up and died. He was sufferin' from consumption real bad and it was that which got him." Cross coughed when a breeze funneled a wisp of smoke in his face.

"Look here, Yank, Do you suppose that you could cut me loose now? I could tell my story a hell'uva a lot better."

"You're doing fine where you are. Continue."

"You're a son- of-a- bitch; you know that, Neunan or what ever you call yourself."

"Watch your mouth, Reb. Why don't you talk a little faster?"

Chance took a sideways glance at the young woman who was standing by the stack of firewood. She'd straightened herself and had tied the bodice of her dress so that she was no longer exposed. She was holding a hefty stick of wood in her right hand and glaring at the Illinois trooper.

"Ah, ah, Senorita Rosa. Drop the wood and come join Mr. Cross, here. Do it now!" Chance's hand went to the handle of his holstered Remington revolver.

"Do as he says, Rosa. I think he's a fair man. He'll let us go."

The disheveled young woman complied and stood away from Neunan, still glaring.

"Go ahead, Cross. Finish your story."

Cross grimaced and looked down at his hands which were turning red.

"Damn you, Yank." He spit into the gravel on his right side. Then he resumed his tale.

"The old feller waved me to the side of his deathbed and gave Rosa and his goat herd to me. Said he had no relatives and Rosa was too young to fend for herself." Cross spit again. "We put him in the ground and went to the routine of rasin' goats. We did that for maybe a month, all the time knowin' that a Union occupation army was on the way. I decided to get outta the country." Neunan placed his hand on the rebel and motioned to the girl who had now found a shady spot under a rock outcropping.

"Rosa, agua." Chance pointed to the gourd jug tied to Poco's saddle. He retrieved his clasp knife from his pants pocket and began to saw through the leather thongs that bound Cross.

"You should've stayed where you were, Cross. Rosa isn't a bad looking woman and with the live stock markets sure to go sky high, you two could'va made a go of it."

Richard Cross groaned as he got to his feet.

Chance closed his clasp knife and thrust it back into his pocket. He kicked the rawhide bindings with which the desperadoes had tied their captive into the smoldering embers of the fire.

Richard Cross dusted himself off and retrieved his kepi from the inner tangle of a thorn bush nearby. He spit into the dirt and took the pottery jug when Rosa offered it to him. His Adam's apple moved up and down as he swallowed a long draught. Finished, he wiped his mouth on the frayed sleeve of his coat.

"We would've stayed put but two fellas from Jo Shelby's command appeared at ol' Raul's place where Rosa was keepin' house with me. They claimed that Maximilian was givin' land for a colony bein' set up by rebels near Vera Cruz. That was an incitement to pull up stakes. We knowed that the emperor wasn't hirin' rebel soldiers but he was more than makin' up for this slight by givin' out land grants."

The girl was going through the pockets of the dead men, wiping her eyes and spitting in the distorted features of each man.

"Rosa, honey, go down to the spring and clean yourself up. Take the water jug along and fill that too" The senorita nodded agreement to his directive. She stood on the last thug's stomach rocking back and forth before she dropped to a squat over him and started to unbutton the dead man's shirt.

That was the last scene that Chance was conscious of as his head commenced to spin and his knees buckled beneath him.

* * *

"You all right, Pard? You keeled over like you'd been kicked in the head by a horse. What's the matter with you?"

Chance shook his head trying to clear his thinking.

"Weak I guess. I haven't had much to eat except for some tortillas and beans over the last three days."

"You had me and Rosa worried for certain. We're owin' you for savin' our bacon. I'd hate to think what would've become of us if you hadn't showed up."

Neunan sat up and looked around, still not certain of his faculties.

"Here, take some of this Neunan. It's the kid goat them bastards was roastin' when they got interested in Rosa. I scraped off most of the burn so the meat's edible and she's bringin' up fresh water, too."

"Thanks Cross." Chance took the greasy slab of meat and wolfed it down.

The former Confederate offered him another slice. "Rosa looks a lot better after takin' a bath. She is awful purty even with that split lip they gave her. I hope she ain't scarred from what she's gone through."

"It's hard to tell. Women are strange things" Neunan wiped his fingers on the thighs of his grimy peasant pants. "I will say that they are a hell'va lot tougher than we give them credit for. But, like I say, there's no two alike and that's why the men can never figure them out." Chance leaned his bare head on the coolness of the rock he was resting his back against.

"I never laid a hand on her...never! Although I wanted to." Cross pursed his mouth. "Them sons –a-bitches violated her like they did. Poor thing, she burned the dress she was a wearin' in the fire whilst you was passed out."

Neunan watched as Rosa, wrapped in the shirt that she'd stripped off the last bandito that the trooper had killed, stacked the booty she'd taken atop a level topped stone.

"What did you do with the bodies?"

"Me and Rosa dragged them off inta the brush. That's why we can't stay around here much longer. Their compadres will come searchin' for them. I don't know about you, but I don't intend to be here when their friends come lookin. Me and Rosa's got twenty head of goats to care for and they don't drive as easy as a cow do."

Cross handed Chance a U.S. issue canteen filled with water. "Took it off one of the greaser's horses. Hard tellin' how they come by the canteen but it's sure better than that gourd you're haulin' around."

Rosa brought Chance a hot tortilla she'd removed from a flat rock at the edge of the rekindled fire. Chance nodded his thanks but did not respond to the gift auditorily.

"I'm givin' you one of the banditos' six shooters. Its an old Colt Pocket model that'll make a good hide out weapon. It's loaded save for the chamber that the hammer's settin' on."

Neunan took the pistol and slid it in the sash which circled his waist.

"Me and Rosa is takin'off now but before we do, I'd like to know just what you're doin' in this part of the country. I mistook you for a 'pepper belly' and you ain't one. You ain't said but I ain't sure that you're not an ol' Rebel like myself."

"Right on both assumptions, Cross. But before we part company, can you give me some particulars on getting to the river across from Brownsville?"

"You mean at Pequeno Matamores? That's the little town layin' to the west of the big city. If that's where you're headed, I must tell you that the territory is damned dangerous. General Leonardo Marquez who's throwed in with the French is in full control there. There's Juarezesta's hangin' in trees every whip stitch on the road inta town."

Neunan mounted Poco without asking for more information.

"That's where you're headed ain't it? By God, you're up to somethin'. Why else would you be travelin' like a peon?"

"Let's leave well enough alone, Cross. You take Rosa and the goats and get out of here. I'll fend for myself."

* * *

Richard Cross, the ex-Confederate had told Chance nothing of importance regarding the Maximilian supporters and the methods that they were utilizing in patrolling the territory which he intended to move through.

Neunan sat astride Poco watching Cross and Rosa amble past mounted on the rebel's horse and a newly acquired animal that until recently had belonged to one of the dead men. The goats ran ahead of the mounted riders, stopping and starting as they chose vegetation which appealed to their taste.

Chance shook his head at the ignorant audacity of the two. They had yet to traverse hundreds of miles and all of it was through the most lawless vastness that any man could imagine. But for the grace of a merciful God the two pilgrims would wind up along the way with their throats slit.

Neunan loosened his grip on the reins and nudged Poco's ribs. He turned the animal's head to the northwest and kicked him a second time. He rode at the edge of the spiny vegetation in the shadow of the stony formation. Rested, with food in his stomach, Chance was prepared to set a track in the direction of the river and attempt to locate the spy camp. He was within three days of making the allotted crossing time but that no longer mattered to him. He'd urge any of the four men with whom he rendezvoused to leave in the darkness of the night of assembly. Neunan wasn't certain that Carter and Hawbacker would arrive at all. That fact placed everything in a quandary and he would argue for as much time as could be spared for the two.

* * *

FREEDMEN'S BUREAU
BROWNSVILLE, TEXAS

Andrea crammed in as much of the paperwork that she could in the afternoon of the humid day. She knew that on the following day a great deal of her time would be spent in preparation for the dinner with the major. She poured over vouchers and letters of complaint from venders and freed men who felt that their former masters weren't being forth right with them. At three thirty, Angie Sue stopped in and provided her employer with a glass of cool water. The liquid only partially sated Andrea's thirst because it was without ice. Ice was a precious and expensive commodity in the region and it was a luxury beyond the means of the bureau's budget. A few more perusals and Andrea decided that she'd had enough. The ink stained ledger cover was closed and she slid back in her high backed chair.

Before she took supper and retired to her room, Andrea notified Angie and informed her that she was going for a walk. She made her way to the Bureau's dispensary and caught William Downs as he was preparing to close. Mr. Downs, in addition to his overseeing work contracts entered into by the former slaves and the plantation owners, was the possessor of a pharmaceutical license. Downs spent two to three hours per day distributing elixirs and pills for every conceivable affliction known to man.

Andrea had one potent to secure before she made an entrance into Major Robert Tyler's tent.

"Potassium Nitrate, you say?" Downs stood with his back to Andrea as his eyes followed his boney finger pointing at the multi-colored bottles on the high shelving. "Now I believe I should know if you have a young buck runnin' amok with the colored girls."

The employee turned back to face Andrea, his watery gray eyes peering over his nez pence glasses.

"Don't be so inquisitive, William. I have a use for the material that won't disturb anyone on these premises." Andrea felt that her subordinate was being much too inquisitive.

William Downs dropped his chin to his chest to enable him to give his employer an even sterner look.

"This stuff is not to be trifled with, Miss Edwards. If it's improperly administered, it can cause male impotency for a lengthy time."

"All right, I know what the nitrate is supposed to do. Just measure out a dosage for two applications. I totally assure you that it won't be given to anyone in this compound."

"Then you do plan on doing some mischief with the nitrate."

"Just a little, William. Now provide me with the dosage, please, and don't make any notation of its issuance in your monthly ledger."

* * *

"By Jove, Wilson, this is a spanking smart looking floor." Major Tyler smacked his gauntlets into the palm of his uncovered right hand. "The men have done a fine job, Lieutenant."

"Yes Sir, I thought so."

"But what of the mud from my boots? Won't that stain the flooring?"

"Sir, I've made arrangements for you to stay with Lt. Becker two tents down after tomorrow evening's dinner. My men will come set your furnishings outside, clean the flooring, and paint the boards. I believe that I can get a requisition for the materials."

"Yes, I'll make an order out at once. Wilson, I'm constantly amazed to see what work you do. Have I told you that, previously?"

The lieutenant did not respond to his superior's compliment.

"How was your hunt and inspection?" the young office placed a piece of paper on the major's desk and scooted a pen and ink next to it.

"We bagged a half dozen partridge which we left off at the cook house upon our return. I was accompanied by four men and we cantered out and back. It was a bracing, little ride."

"What did you think of the tower?"

"An architectural masterpiece. But I chose not to climb it. I don't care for heights, particularly when the wind was blowing as it was."

"I've heard that there's to be a second such erection begun shortly."

"Is that so, Wilson? I should think the one tower will suffice once we have telegraph lines strung from it."

Tyler scribbled on the paper on his desk with the pen and handed the order to his junior officer.

"Have you ever heard of a medicinal compound known as 'Spanish fly'?"

"Er..I..yes, I have. Isn't that what is given to mares to increase their desire at the onset of coming into heat?"

The junior officer coughed into his hand and continued.

"Why do you ask about this drug? You have me puzzled."

"I was wondering if you would go to the farrier and obtain a dosage for me."

Wilson looked mystified for a second before his features calmed and then became contorted.

"Major are you considering using this potency on Miss Edwards tomorrow evening?"

"I, well, I"…the officer stammered.

"My God, Sir. How could you think of such a damnable act? Don't you know that "Fly' lowers a female's will to resist? Its power could turn her into a raving nymphomaniac."

"I am aware of the drug's affect on the female body."

Wilson stamped his foot in disgust on the newly laid planking. He was so disturbed by his superior's intent that he was shaking.

"No, sir! I will not be a party to your depraved plan. Your conduct is revolting and extremely ungentlemanly."

Wilson's face was flushed with anger and his body continued to shake.

A hand reached through the untied tent flap and knocked on the near support pole.

Art Fields, the major's aide, entered and looked around. "Is there something wrong in here? I heard quite a racket coming from inside and I decided to investigate."

"No, Fields we were discussing a topic that neither of us could agree on."

"I say, sir, this is a first rate floor you have here." The private was passing the toe of his boot over the smooth surface.

"You're dismissed, Fields. Thank you for your observation."

Lieutenant Wilson's temper was still up.

"Wilson, you know that I was merely testing your level of morality when I suggested procuring the aphrodisiac."

The junior officer remained stoic waiting for additional retractions from Tyler.

Robert Tyler broke the icy silence which was a mere number of seconds but seemed like an hour. "Miss Edwards is a damn fine woman. Wouldn't you agree?'

"Yes, Major."

"Quite possibly a white mix somewhere in her lineage"

"It's possible especially if we're to believe a third of the stories told about plantation life before the war."

"Lieutenant Wilson, my sole intent was to woo her in the most respectable way."

The junior officer bit his tongue, thinking better of speaking for the sake of his career. Wilson sought to change the subject in order to gain a respite from the major's amorous monologue.

"Major you are aware that in three days, actually three nights, beginning at two a.m., we will commence to gather in our spies who have been observing the emperor's movements?"

"Yes, I'm aware of that."

"Will you wish to be disturbed when the men come into our lines?"

Tyler's face flushed red. "Are you suggesting that I may be indisposed in some activity?"

"Who can say; especially if you carry out your diabolical intentions?"

"Stand down, Damn you, Wilson! I don't like your impudence!" The major's brow was furrowed in a frown and his hands holding onto the back of his wooden chair were shaking. The man's posture remained rigid but his features slowly softened, returning to an assemblance of normalcy.

"I shall overlook and dismiss your remark, Lieutenant. Have Captain Adkins assist you as our espionage agents come into the lines. I will be in attendance, say at seven, upon their return for their reports and assessments. There will be no need to contact me during the night. Do I make myself clear, Wilson?"

"Yes, Sir."

* * *

DEFENSIVE ARRANGEMENTS
FREEDMEN'S BUREAU

The bath water was the perfect temperature in the high backed galvanized tub that Angie Sue filled in the master bedroom. Andrea was on needles and pins throughout the morning. She practically sleep walked in executing her duties and was completely absorbed with how she was going to handle Major Tyler in the approaching evening encounter. She had laid the ground work in their initial meeting of the method she was going to utilize in order to gain access to factual material which would tell her of Chance Neunan's whereabouts. What had occurred on the previous morning led her to wonder if Tyler had followed through on having an underling review the regimental rosters as he had promised he would.

Andrea squeezed a sponge over her throat and shoulders as her nostrils took in the fragrance of jasmine. She recalled that Angie had discovered a cylindrical cardboard container on the upper shelf of the bedroom closet. The powdered bath salts were left with several other personal items when

Mrs. Baxter had vacated the plantation. Now, the essence dissolved in the warm water soothed her angst and tension.

* * *

UNION ARMY ENCAMPMENT

Bryce Wilson's early afternoon duty of providing the morning reports to Major Tyler had been most distasteful to him. He'd wished that his commanding officer was absent from his tent but he knew that this was unlikely with the dinner set for the evening. Seeing Major Tyler engrossed in writing some order, the lieutenant had placed the reports on the man's cot and spun on his heels to make his departure. In doing so; he nearly collided with Art Fields who stepped through the partially closed tent flap.

The soldier, short in stature and unobtrusive in appearance, stood holding a covered platter of cookies and a silver, half liter, pitcher of claret. The NCO avoided the collision and waited to be recognized by his commander.

"Excuse, Major, but the biggest black man I've ever seen wished these items delivered to you. He said that he came from the Freedmen's Bureau at the direction of the chief executive there, a Miss Edwards."

"My, how thoughtful of Miss Edwards." Tyler relaxed and stepped forward to accept the gifts.

Fields continued; "Got called to the main gate by the corporal of the guard. He said that the man was becoming belligerent over not being admitted to deliver this little repast to you personally. Big Joe; Yes, that's what he called himself, said that these morsels were made especially for your enjoyment before his employer arrives later to sup with you. Of course I followed orders and refused him entrance into the cantonment."

The major stopped in mid-stride and waved his aide to set the items on his camp desk.

"You may have a cookie, Fields, there seems to be plenty, but Lt. Wilson and I will have to share the wine. You are on duty are you not?"

"Yes, Sir. Thank you for the cookie."

Fields took a baked delicacy from the top of the tray and paused to look down at the planking underfoot.

"Yes, sir, this is a first rate tent floor. Say it appears to have been painted. No wonder it's so white."

"That will be all, Fields. You are dismissed." Tyler puzzled over the man's infatuation with the new floor.

Tyler went to his camp chest and removed two collapsible cups and filled them with the elixir from the silver pitcher. Neither spoke as they bit into the still warm bakery goods.

"My cookie is a bit tangy. I expected a buttery taste but I have a peculiar sensation in the roof of my mouth. Perhaps the ingredients were not mixed well before they entered the oven." The major removed a crumb from the corner of his mustache.

"Yes, there is a slight aftertaste in mine as well." Wilson brought the item closer to his eyes and looked at it intently. "There is something in the mix which I can't identify, a curry or sage like remnant."

The cups were filled and refilled twice but little conversation passed between the two.

"I must excuse myself in order for you to prepare yourself, Sir." Wilson nodded as he started to leave.

"Yes, I must see to my appearance." Tyler took the junior officer's cup and placed it with his on the empty tray.

"Just a moment, Wilson. I will not apologize for my part of what's been said. We have both overstepped a level of military decorum that has raised the ire of both of us. I shall question you tomorrow to determine if you wish to continue on my staff."

* * *

Andrea lounged in the foamy water and massaged her ankles and calves.

Perhaps Angie Sue was right in suggesting that she choose a different type of footwear. The heavy army shoes were taking a toll on her lower body and back.

Angie opened the pocket doors which separated the boudoir from the dressing room. She carried an oversized towel with her.

"Lordy, Missy Edwards, you been in dat water so long, you gonna look like a shriveled up ol' persimmon. Stand up and I'll dry you off."

The young girl went about her chore humming a religious song, patting and toweling Andrea's supple body. "Missy, I swear you gots da golden skin just like the finest shammy ever made. You's jest about the perfect woman, you are. Jest like dem Greek wimmen in de water fountains 'cept you is coffee colored 'stead of white gravy."

"Leave the towel, Angie so that I can dry my hair."

"No, Ma'am. I gots an extra for dat. Here's da robe that musta been da Baxter woman's. It'll fit you jest fine."

The beautiful administrator went to the ornately carved dressing table with its age spotted mirror and seated herself. Angie Parker followed her as a puppy would its master.

"Can I do your hair for you, Missy?"

"Would you, Angie. I haven't had it put up in a bun in such a long time. Perhaps that won't be practical. It's grown so long."

"Oh, I tink dat I can do dat for you."

"Do your magic then, girl."

* * *

The Baxter phaeton passed majestically down the company street, its enamel painted exterior gleaming in the dying rays of the autumn afternoon. Big Joe and his helper, Filmore, had applied a liberal amount of wax to the conveyance's curvaceous lines and now the large man sat in the driver's seat guiding it past the gawking troopers.

Homer Nichols, coming from the evening mess, saw that the animals pulling Andrea's carriage were curried and perfectly matched. He additionally had seen that the harness leather was polished and the brass haime knobs burnished to a high luster.

Lieutenant Wilson waved Big Joe to a halt, nodded to Fields to take the team's reins and stepped to the phaeton's door.

Andrea rose from her seat, took the lieutenant's hand and placed her feet lightly on the steps before stepping onto the gravel before the officer's tent.

Wilson was stunned by her beauty. He gulped as her gloved hand rested gently in his. It was as though a charge of electricity coursed up to his shoulder and back down.

She'd made up her eyes, added a touch of rouge high on the outsides of her cheeks and a hint of the same color to her lips.

Wilson tried to avert his eyes to avoid staring at the being who reminded him of something of another world. A glow seemed to radiate from her face as the lieutenant parted the tent flap to the candle lit tent's interior.

The celestial virgin has arrived for the sacrifice. He thought as he stepped aside for Tyler to receive her hand.

He must warn her of the danger she was entering into; but how? Wilson had lost trust in his superior and he could not be certain that Tyler had not continued with his acquiring of the seductive potion.

"My dear, I'm so happy to see you." The major purred. "My staff has prepared a wonderful meal and once we've dined we shall clear the air of the concerns that we have."

It was too late for Wilson to alert the beautiful creature of the peril that she had put herself in once she had accepted the lecherous hand of his commanding officer. The Freedmen's Bureau executive would have to use her skills to hold the major at bay.

Tyler's tent was lighted by far more candles than were necessary. Andrea stood before the white linen tablecloth spread over a collapsible table and waited for the major to draw out one of the two chairs and seat her. In the process of initiating the mannerly protocol, Tyler leaned close. His nostrils drew in the aroma of the jasmine fragrance that Andrea was wearing which heightened his senses to a new level.

The major's passage around the table to a seat opposite her allowed the bureau executive a few moments to study the monogram on the silver tableware. She concluded that the pieces' initials did not match the cavalry officers and very likely they had been pilfered from some plantation during the recently concluded hostilities.

Different servers filed in and out of the canvas enclosure setting down arrangements of covered containers and removing others as needed. Her brace of partridge were served with saffron covered rice with garden beans and new potatoes.

Ample time was allotted for the enjoyment of the course and the monologue which Major Tyler delivered. Andrea was blessed with a complete military biography and she faked interest in his every word. She learned that Tyler had graduated near the top of his class at 'the Point' and taken an evaluative tour of the European armies with General McClellan before the commencement of the Civil War. He described his fracture from the military of the United States to serve with the British in the Crimean War and then to throw his services to the forces of Garibaldi in the Italian War of unification.

Hardly catching his breath, the man ploughed on with his bombastic narrative to the point that Andrea was becoming ill.

Unaware that he was dominating the conversation, he paused and asked; "Did I mention my roll as an advisor with Robert Walker in Nicaragua? You do know of that shameful affair, don't you?"

" No, Robert, I don't believe that you have mentioned your involvement in that occurrence."

"Oh, that was a real mess. I signed on as a mercenary officer in Walker's invading army comprised of all the misfits in the world. We went through the Nicaraguan army like a hot knife through butter. Ol' Walker threw out the royalty, gave land grants to the peons and rewrote the country's constitution. He named himself supreme ruler for life and renamed the country Walkeraugua. The man went too far too quickly and scared have of Central and South America out of their pants with his liberal ways. About five adjoining counties, forgive me but I can't recall just who they were, formed a military coalition and defeated the mad man. I barely got out of that affair by the skin of my teeth."

Tyler waited, expecting questions from Andrea. She offered none so he fashioned an addendum.

"Shot him, they did, and rightfully so. He was as crazy as a loon."

Andrea sighed but said nothing. She was reluctant to interject in any manner, least it ignite another diatribe from the major. But she knew that Tyler would be upset if she failed to respond in some manner.

'My, Major, you have had such an adventuresome life, haven't you?"

Before the officer could launch into some phase of his life that he'd neglected to mention, Andrea hailed one of the waiters and asked for more water. Nearly all that Major Tyler related to her, she all ready knew. She had informants within the command headquarters who kept her apprised of the postings and resignations among the senior staff. Andrea had passively endured the monotone delivery of the exploits of a great man, or so he thought. In his assessment of himself, none stood as tall as he.

Major Tyler made small talk as pecan-rum cake was served with coffee. Once the desserts were positioned in front of the diners, the major summoned one of the waiters to have Lt. Wilson come into the tent.

"Sir?" the junior officer appeared in the tent's doorway.

"You may have the quartet sing a few airs at this time."

"Yes, Sir."

Wilson stepped outside and snapped his fingers as a directive to the assembled songsters. A group of male voices swung into a melancholy rendition of 'Tenting Tonight' followed by 'Old Folks at Home' and concluded with 'Lorena'.

Robert Tyler watched Andrea's face as the music began. She sat stoically with her hands folded in her lap listening to the blended voices but she failed to applaud when the music ceased. Tyler noticed a tear coursing down her cheeks from her glistening eyes.

"I'm sorry Andrea I fear that the selection of songs were too morose."

"No, just the second song; 'Old Folks at Home'. It brought back disagreeable memories; ones that I'd like to forget."

"Again, I'm sorry."

Andrea Edwards looked away and remained silent as she visibly struggled to choose the words which would best describe her hurt.

"Nothing will ever be the same again. What went on before this miserable war came upon us is now changed forever."

Major Tyler placed his hand on Andrea's shoulder but said nothing.

Struggling to force the distasteful memories from her mind, Andrea allowed Tyler to gently lift her to her feet. His large, strong arms pulled her to him in an embrace. She'd cried bitter tears into the fabric of his dress coat.

"I'm sorry, Robert. I've gotten your uniform wet."

"It's nothing, my Dear. I'm such a buffoon for having selected songs filled with such lament."

Andrea sniffed and spoke barely above a whisper as she responded to the large man's attempt at comforting her.

"Thank you for your concern. I so appreciate what your doing but I fear that our diverse backgrounds will prevent us from ever knowing each other fully."

"Let's let this evening's dinner be as you suggested; the sweeping away of the clouds between us and the creation of a new relationship." Tyler was being tactful playing on Andrea's every word.

The beautiful woman tried to push away from the man's grasp and as she did, she leaned back and peered into the officer's eyes.

"Very well, Robert, what can you tell me of my acquaintance, Chance Neunan?"

"One moment, my Dear."

The officer disengaged himself from the slender woman and took two steps away from her. "Your shoulders are cold. The autumn weather is hardly balmy as the nights grow longer. Lieutenant Wilson, please enter and fetch Miss Edwards a shawl from my trunk, would you?"

Bowing slightly, the young officer acquired the requested garment from the storage locker and handed it to Tyler.

"Dismiss our quartet, our waiters, and Private Fields for the evening. You have done a wonderful job planning and executing the activities tonight, Wilson. You are dismissed as well. Good night, Lieutenant."

Major Tyler turned and looked at Andrea as the junior officer made his departure.

Let me see, where we were in our conversation before the interruption." He took a stride toward the young woman.

Andrea recoiled away from Tyler's open arms.

"Let's hear about Mr. Neunan before you go further." Tyler was surprised by Miss Edwards' rebuff.

"I really have not met the soldier personally, Madam. I only know of him. You see Lieutenant Wilson handled the planning under my orders, of course."

"Where is Chance? Is he here in the cantonment?"

"Technically, he is assigned to this command, but bodily he is not available."

"He is alive and well, then?"

"This I can not verify and; well, no one knows of his well being." The officer shrugged his shoulders which angered Andrea.

"What do you know, Robert?" The high ranking Freedmen's Bureau executive's eyes flashed.

"I can tell you no more." Tyler went to Andrea and placed his forearms on either side of her neck. He was taller and more massive than she, and his size seemed formidable.

"Friends should have no secrets, Andrea." Tyler's breath was hot and close. "How did you learn that this Chance Neunan had been put on extended duty?"

The officer's fingers dropped to the top button on the back of the young woman's dress. His large digits fumbled with the second button before it came undone. Andrea flinched at the officer's touch but regained her composure.

"Robert, I'll allow you to continue if you tell me more of Chance's whereabouts."

The major was perspiring in spite of the coolness within the tent. He smirked a nasty smile and replied huskily, "I intend to continue whether you give me permission or not, my dear. My God, you are beautiful. What is that heavenly perfume you're wearing?"

He breathed out as the third button was released.

Andrea could feel the looseness at her throat as the dress's bodice began to slip down.

She stiffened. "I don't like your game, Robert." Her voice was steely and cold.

"I'm rather enjoying myself, Andrea. You are remarkably composed for a lady who is about to be violated."

"I think not, Robert."

"What are you going to do, my pretty, scream? One stroke from my hand would knock you senseless. You would not get out a syllable."

"I will not have to shout out for aid, Robert. Do you feel firmness at the third button of your vest?"

"Uh, yes."

"Don't look down!" Her voice was strong, forceful, as though she were in complete control of the situation.

"You see, I hold the upper hand or should I clarify my statement, the upper blade."

Tyler saw no terror now in the woman's eyes, only venom. He could feel growing pressure at the base of his breast bone.

"What you feel is a dirk, slender and sharp, placed in a position to enter your diaphragm. Our dinner is concluded as soon as you remove your hands from me. Step back and button your uniform coat."

"You Bitch. You beautiful, black bitch." Cautiously, he drew his massive hands away. "Damn you woman! I've deduced your source of information and like you, I'm going to make that son-of-a- bitch pay. You'll see."

She kept her eyes on the officer as he moved back from her.

"Private Fields!" She called.

The aide appeared at the door flap of the tent.

"I was just about to go off duty, Ma'am. What can I do for you?"

"Have Big Joe bring up my carriage, please."

"Yes Ma'am, right away, Ma'am."

* * *

IMPERIALISTS MEXICAN ARMY CAMP
MENDEZ, MEXICO

The Imperialists' camp at Mendez was spread over thirty acres of arid land devoid of vegetation except for a few agave cacti. The royalist bastion was without earthworks of any kind due to the coarseness of the rocky soil. The cantonment was laid out with four entrances and exits capped by post and lintel fabrications. Flying on both sides of the construction were the tri-colored flags of France and Mexico. The 'drapeau' of Napoleon III's regime hung on the left and the eagle and the snake fluttered on the opposite pole on the right.

Dust billowed up from the company streets laid out between a myriad of shelter styles. Animals whinnied, bawled or bleated in the clay colored atmosphere and were blended with the harsh, shouted commands topped by incessant bugle calls. From sunrise until ten o'clock, firing squads plied their trade at a nearby ravine massacring Juarezestas.

General Leonardo Marquez and his staff were ensconced in a multi storied hacienda in the midst of the madness. The manor had been commandeered by the forces loyal to Maximilian once its value had been ascertained and the owner had been conveniently killed in a peasant ambush. Marquez saw that the grieving family was packed off to the safety of Matamoras before ordering the camp's construction.

Now the stout, adobe structure was his to do with what he wished. The general chose a side bedroom for his main office. The room had high ceilings and an east window equipped with slat shuttered blinds. From the twelve foot tall corridors crisscrossing the habitation, cool breezes seemed to be ever present. Marquez told himself that he had made a wise selection many times over.

"Pardon, General;" a young lieutenant stood in the doorway to Marquez's office.

"Yes, Ricardo, what is it?"

"The 'gringo' captain has arrived as you requested."

"Good. Send in Captain Thome immediately." The Imperialist general straightened a few items on his desk, and then looked up at the junior aide. "Wait one moment, Ricardo. We must remember that we are not to address our American allies by the derogatory name, 'gringo'."

"I'm sorry, Sir. I must have forgotten."

"Do not fail to make this correction, Lieutenant. Thanks to the Americanos our artillery park has at least four batteries bearing the initials U.S. or C.S. on their barrel trunnions. We must take care not to ruffle feathers."

"Yes, my General."

"Send in the Captain. No, wait, Ricardo. He has not heard our conversation has he?"

"I think not, Sir. He is waiting in the ante room."

"Excellent. Have him come right in."

A few minutes elapsed before a burly man with shoulder length hair and an untrimmed beard entered the room and stood erect at the general's desk.

"Buenos dais, Captain Thome."

The captain responded with a tired salute.

"My, you look terrible, Captain. You have been in the field as ordered?"

"Yes, General."

The Mexican officer studied the man in front of him for a few seconds choosing the words he wished to say. "Before we go any further, may I suggest that the next time you report to me that you dress appropriately. I have a requisition here for you to see my tailor in order to have him measure you for a new uniform. He will make you such a suit, as mine, of the Imperialist cut of green material piped in red with gold braid accents. Not too much braid and certainly not as much as I have. We must be mindful of our rank."

"Yes, Sir. Certainly. Sir. I will take care of the matter as soon as I leave the office. But, Sir, if I may, I prefer to wear my old Confederate jacket in the field. It prevents me from being an easily seen target."

"I understand but from this time forward, I will expect you to be dressed in the prescribed uniform while in this building." Marquez shuffled some papers on his desk allowing Thome to digest his directive. "You may give me your report now. I will have it orally but you must repeat it in dictation to Ricardo so that he may translate it. Now proceed."

Captain Thome adjusted his weight from one foot to the other. "General, you are on to something. I have conferred with my head of Yaqui scouts named, el Halcon. The Indian believes that he and his men have killed two of the Americans spies late last night. The dead men could conceivably be the men who mauled the French lancer detachment on the previous day. El Halcon felt that there were three or more men involved in that skirmish and one of them escaped the Yaqui's pre- dawn attack or had parted company with the group sometime earlier. This man could still be on the loose. El Halcon added that when they examined the corpses that one of them was suffering from a nasty wound under his arm. On top of this, the two were riding captured French mounts with French saddlery."

The general, who sported a thin mustache and goatee in the style of Napoleon III, pursed his lips and rubbed his chin with his right fist. "So you believe that the reports of Americanos attempting to pass themselves off as Mexicans in Nuevo Leon province are connected to the two slain hombres?"

"Yes. In addition, one of the Yaqui scouts killed the bigger of the two men after he had emptied his revolver. The Yaqui attacked him with a machete and the two went mano a mano. El Halcon's man cut the fellow across the thigh before he finished him. In the effects taken from the bodies, el Halcon saw a wad of paper protruding from the gash in the man's holster. Here it is, General, exactly as el Halcon gave it to me; blood and all."

Thome laid the wrinkled, miniscule note on the desk between Marquez's manicured hands.

"What do you think of this, Thome? Are these figures some sort of encoded tabulation?"

"Yes, sir, I believe that they are. Look at the top of the note and you'll see the letter, C. I think the letter stands for Coahuila Provence. Then below that, are the letters, A, C, and I. which stands for artillery with the number across from the letter, the number 35. You can take it from there, Sir."

"Anything else?"

"Yes, a map of some sort. There are the abbreviations for the directions written in several places and notations such as Bear Rock and Black Mesa. What's really got me are the letters, PM inside of a square shape."

Marquez squinted at the map and turned it in different directions in an attempt to decipher the letters' meaning. Without directing his question to anyone in particular, he said aloud; "Do you think that these three men were responsible for the mayhem raised at Los Rios three nights ago?"

"Our reports indicate that only one man was responsible for the damage at that location. This man could have joined the two we caught sometime during the next day."

"Then this person is yet outside our net?"

"Yes. I believe that he is and so do the Yaqui scouts."

"Just a moment, Captain." Marquez opened a top desk drawer and removed a magnifying glass from the contents. He moved the glass back and forth over the spattered paper as though he believed that the device would translate the meaning of the letters; P.M.

The general set the glass aside and still holding the map up to a ray of light filtering through the window shade, he began moving his lips as though he was reading silently. Then he smiled at the epiphany that had come to him.

"Captain, I believe that the letters are, of course, an abbreviation which stands for Pequeno Matamoras."

* * *

FREEDMEN'S BUREAU
BAXTER PLANTATION

Angie Sue met her employer at the front door of the former Baxter plantation and read the distress on Andrea's face. Miss Edwards brushed past her without a word of greeting or the passage of any pleasantries. Before closing the huge pair of doors, the assistant walked onto the portico and looked at Big Joe and Fillmore sitting on the seat of the phaeton. Both had donned heavy cloaks to ward off the chill that appeared to be rising from the bottomland to the south. Steam wafted around the nostrils of the team which stood waiting for commands. Angie was baffled by the administrator's demeanor.

"What went on over to de camp, Joe?"

"Don't know, Angie. Somethin' must've gone bad wrong 'tween Missy and the major. We just was aware of how she was actin' and knew better than ax her about her dealin' with the big brass."

"Lands sakes, what coulda happened over der?"

Andrea's aide made her way up stairs to the master bedroom and knocked lightly on the pocket doors.

"Yes."

"It's me, Angie. Ain't nobody else awake in dis house."

"Come in, please."

Angie could see the wetness on Andrea's cheeks in the flicker light of a pair of candles on the dresser. Andrea was patting at her eyes with a handkerchief.

"Would you kindly go down to the kitchen and see if Effie left any hot water in the stove's reservoir? I'd like a bath."

"Lands sake, Missy, you just took one three hours ago."

"I know, but right now, I don't feel clean."

"Yessum, I'll see that you gets your bathwater." The aide paused at the doorway. "I'm surprised at dat officer. He seemed so nice and polite, not like most of da Yankees."

"I've warned you about first impressions of men, especially those that wear uniforms." Miss Edward's voice was etched with bitterness.

* * *

UNION ARMY ENCAMPMENT

It was nearly eleven o'clock by Major Tyler's pocket watch as he snapped the cover over the face of his time piece. He eased back his chair at his field desk and tapped the finger tips of his right hand on the ink stained, wood surface. Captain Adam's arresting party had yet to return with the farrier, Homer Nichols, but he expected them momentarily. In the interval he composed the meat of the report that Lt. Wilson would give to Colonel Archer. Tyler had read Wilson's preliminary account and he would insert it into his material indicating that the spy assignment had failed due to a leak in security. The seemingly innocuous horse shoer, Nichols, was privy to the operation and had unknowingly talked to counter Imperialist spies. Tyler was vacillating whether or not to implicate Andrea Edwards in the subterfuge. A besmirching of her reputation would end her career in the Freedmen's Bureau and if found guilty would send her to prison or worse.

No, he thought, she was far too beautiful to grow old in an eight by eight cell in Fort Jefferson on the Dry Tortugas. Her body, if not her spirit, could still be his. All that he had to do was to confront her with his evidence in a second meeting and reveal to her his expectations if he chose not to include her name in the report.

Tyler stopped drumming as he brought his gaze to his finger tips. Both digits on each of his hands had touched Andrea. He had used them as he traced the neck line of her dress bodice. They had sensed the softness of her graceful, Grecian like throat and they now thirsted for more titillation.

* * *

CLOSING IN ON THE UNION SPY CAMP

Chance marveled at the strength and composure of the Mexican horse he'd named Poco. The animal was nothing but skin and bones, yet if found the stamina from somewhere to carry him on. Poco had not bolted or shied when the two Mexican banditos were shot. He'd only thrown his head to the side as the two reports from Chance's carbine had sent the pair to a place in hell. Neunan's mount's behavior and steadiness was beyond that of the cavalry trained horses in such situations. Perhaps, in the course of his life as a gelding, he'd found that sudden exertions tired him. Neunan reached down and patted the animal on the front shoulder.

In the shade of the ridge, Chance's eyes discerned a glimmer from the valley below. He reined Poco to a halt and stared intently into the blue haze which drifted up from the brown- green verdant growth. The shimmering object repeated itself from between a swatch of timber.

If only he'd taken Lew Carter's binoculars instead of the compass.

Chance dismounted in the shade of a giant agave, pulled his sombrero to the back of his head and rested his firearms on the seat of the saddle. By cupping both hands above his eye brows, making a shield from the sun.

Yes! Yes! The glimmer, the sparkle, was light being reflected off water and that water would be in the bed of the Rio Grande!

Neunan dropped his forehead to within inches of the stained leather of his saddle and before he could stop himself, his shoulders commenced to shake and tears burst from his eyes. They streaked over the dirty contours of his cheeks and seeped through the hairs of his beard.

Poco, ever faithful or possibly oblivious to what his rider was doing, stood stoically, permitting Chance to vent both his joy and sadness at having reached the last natural obstacle before safety. Somewhere, miles behind him, were dead Mexicans a few French lancers who would never see their homes again, and two goat herding pilgrims. In the miles he'd cover Chance had left Carter and Hawbacker. Although he hoped that the two were on the trail behind him, he had little faith in their ever crossing the river to safety.

Ahead lay the border signifying river and on its northern bank, the United States. On that far shore was an oasis of relief for the newly freed slaves and within their ranks, he surmised, was the woman he had sought for months.'

* * *

Poco ambled along the base of the ridge that was Bear Mountain, shielding himself and his rider from the early afternoon sun which had passed its zenith three hours earlier.

Neunan was taking more care now, paying attention to smoke spiraling upward or dust devils skimming across the valley beneath the trail he was following. From his vantage point he began to distinguish fields of maze yet unharvested, shocks of wheat waiting to be carted from the acreage and grazing herds of livestock. The fields were patches of golden yellow and dull sections of brown. The animals, at the distance Chance was watching from. appeared miniscule and ill defined. Rock formations which shielded him previously were commencing to dwindle in height. Chance knew that within a few more miles the escarpments would disappear all together.

In the valley of the Rio Grande, the seasonal rains, he was told, followed the watercourse and nourished the tilled earth to make the area the bread basket of Mexico and Texas.

Small adobe dwellings materialized as the rider passed in and out of sun and shadow. Cumulus clouds drifted lazily above the weary trooper. As he had estimated, the stony formations had shrunken into low hillocks covered with timber and underbrush.

The trail had widened and he took notice of the number of hoof prints that scarred the dust. Neunan dismounted in a cleft in the few remaining boulders and fished the tiny map from his shirt pocket. As he studied the drawing, a tinkling sound alerted him that a herd of something was approaching. Quickly he replaced the map and placed his hand over Poco's muzzle to prevent him from whinnying. As during the day before, a billy goat and his harem walked stately up the path and then stopped. They all stood staring at Chance's place of concealment.

"Arriba, Arriba!" the young herder picking at the laggers with a long stick, begin to curse viciously but Neunan's Spanish was so lacking that he could not translate what the lad was saying. A few tense moments and several rocks cast into the smelly animal's ribs got the balky herd started again. Once the entourage moved further down the trail, the trooper took out his map and looked at it again. The crumpled paper was dirty and tattered but Chance came to recognize that approximately four miles further on he was to locate an abandoned pueblo and wait. This was the assembly point that all the spies were eager to reach in order to swim their horses to the other side of the Rio. The time allotted was twenty minutes on either side of the two o'clock a. m. deadline. Any attempt to gain the United States side of the river before or after that time would mean that they would be fired on.

Chance took a draw from his U.S. marked canteen and then dribbled a small amount of water on Poco's lips. Tired to the bone, the trooper swung himself up into the saddle once more. Placing himself in an ever higher alert mode, he guided his animal at a walk down the pathway. Poco maneuvered through multiple piles of goat droppings with no apparent concern. As the day wore on Chance's mind wandered in and out of consciousness into complacent oblivion. He lost control of his ability to judge time and without a watch, he could not decipher a quarter hour from an hour. When a smaller trail veered to the right from the main one, Neunan noted that dried grass grew in the tract's center and there was no evidence of goat shit. Poco slowed his rambling pace and lifted his eyes to look to the right. The animal seemed reluctant to go any faster and Chance was in key with his mount's wariness.

Ensconced in an opening in the pines, the trooper's gaze picked out an adobe wall and a shelter constructed of the same material. A closer examination brought Chance to the realization that the narrowing path led directly to an abandoned habitation's front door. To approach into an unobstructed field of fire did not sit well with the Illinois trooper. Instead he directed his mount in a circuitous route through the thorny brush that brought him to a side window. Quietly, Chance eased himself from the saddle and tied Poco to a weathered corral post which long ago had lost its rails. The Spencer repeater and the pocket Colt were left on the saddle rig as he crept to a glassless window. He untangled the Remington revolver from his sash and cocked the weapon making sure that the revolution of the cylinder revealed a percussion cap on the loaded chamber.

The late autumn sun had disappeared behind the low ridge at his back. He was aware of the chill in the air as the sunlight waned and the shadows lengthened in the ram shackled cabin's interior. Neunan's visual search of the two rooms revealed that no one had chosen to live there for sometime. A broken, wooden chair and a stained corn husk mattress were all the furnishing in the nearest room. The adjoining room, the kitchen, was littered with broken crockery and rusting tin cans laying helter-skelter next to a soot smeared fireplace.

Neunan was about to give up, deciding that the map was wrong or that the surviving scouts had by passed the place and gone on toward the river, when he noticed a sloping depression under the stone foundation. The opening beneath the house's floor sill was a partially filled cellar door.

Placing his sandals carefully so as to make as little noise as possible, he eased himself to the darkened excavation and listened. Poised, with his revolver at the ready, he leaned down and moved aside a cedar board partially obstructing the passageway. The cold, metallic, click, click, of a pistol being cocked brought the short hairs up on the back of Chance's neck.

"Como te llamas?" a hoarse voice demanded from the pitch darkness.

Neunan considered answering in Spanish but decided to use his English with as forceful a tone as he could.

"I'm Chance Neunan, By God! Who the hell are you?"

"You ain't one of Marquez's boys?"

"No, I'm an American."

"Ain't no Johnny Reb, either?"

"No."

"I hear the Johnnys are comin' over the river to join Maximilian."

Neunan took a quick step sideways at the hole's entrance removing the silhouette of his body in the weak light of the dying sun.

"You move again like that, Newman, and I'll damned kill you."

"It's Neunan. Who are you?" The dug confinement was heavy with humidity.

"Bill Blain."

There was silence as Chance tossed the unseen man's name around in his mind trying to make recognition.

Chance drew in a breath and exhaled. "I know you Blain. You and I were together with four other men over across the river two weeks ago. Could I come in?"

"Yeah. That'll be alright. You've come to the roost just like me."

The Illinois cavalryman bent over and squeezed through the opening. He was barely able to stand upright in the storage area but in the weakening light he was able to make out a figure sitting with his back against the earthen wall.

"Where's your pard?"

"Lem Jent?"

"Was that his name?"

"Yes." A hacking cough erupted for a few seconds before Blain could continue. "The Mex's got him. He's dead."

"Uhh, that's too bad."

"Where be yourn?"

"It's a long story, Blain. Are you able to get up and go outside?" There was a sickening stench in the cellar as though someone had excreted in a pile of rotten flesh. "Place down here smells like a gut pile."

"No, no, I'd expect that I better stay here."

"You, all right?"

"No, no, not really."

Chance heard the gravel comprising the floor grate as the man named Blain shifted himself to a new position.

"If you're expecting more fellows than me, I don't believe they're coming." Neunan uncocked his pistol and returned it to his waist sash. "I left two of 'em two nights ago and one of the men was bad wounded. His partner stayed back to take care of him. He felt that they'd make a try for the border regardless of the deadline for our return."

Blain groaned softly.

"What's the matter with you, Blain, and what is that God awful smell?"

"It's me, Dammit. I'm gut shot and been bleedin' inside for the past couple of days. I'm rottin' inside." Blain was straining to force his voice loud enough to make himself heard.

"It's bad isn't it?"

"Yeah, it's bad."

Chance heard the man crying in the darkness.

"Want me to take a look at your wound? I got matches in my pocket."

"Won't do no good. I'm a goner."

"'Don't say that."

"It's the truth. A man knows when he's on the road to meetin' his maker."

Neunan felt his way around the sloping edges of the earthen storage space until his sandal nudged Blain's thigh.

"Sorry, Pard."

"You had to do that"; the wounded man wheezed. "Can you find a candle and somethin' to cover me with? I been down here in the dark for hours. I'm kinda gettin' cold."

Chance fumbled about until he touched the wounded spy's hair. His finger tips traced the hairline briefly until they lingered on the feverous forehead.

"Just a minute, Blain, I've got a couple of candles in a bedroll tied behind my saddle. I'll go fetch them."

"No hurry, Neunan. I'm stayin' right here. 'Nother thing, you'd best not be goin' hand over hand in the dark on the walls to get to the doorway. I heard things scratchin' and tumblin' around when I got here last night and you know there's some critters here that'll bite ya."

The Illinois cavalryman returned within minutes in the glow of the last of the sun. He lighted a candle stub and searched about until he found a rusty can to set it in. Poco's saddle blanket soon shrouded the body of the dying man.

"What's become of your horse, Blain?"

"Don't know. Don't really know how many hours I been in this cellar, either. Two days, I think. I got a watch some place in my goods but I suppose that my horse wandered away with it."

"It's best that you stop talking, Partner. I won't ask any more questions."

"Go ahead, ask. You're talkin' to a dead man."

Chance ignored Blain and raised the candle nub. "Let's have a look at you." He knelt by Blain's side and opened his shirt front. The fabric stuck to an ooze of black corruption above the navel on the spy's right side.

"Uhh!" Neunan couldn't stifle his reaction.

"I told ya I was rottin'. Just like an old pumpkin that's been froze and thawed a dozen times. I believe that the doctors calls this stuff, gangrene."

Chance eased back on his haunches and turned sideways in order to find a more comfortable position.

"While you was outside pickin' up the goods I wanted, I got to thinkin' about the Mexican and Frenchie troops Lem and me had seen. We was assigned to reconnoiter Tamaulipas and Coahuila provinces. I got the figures in my goods if I can just recall where I stored it. Put them together with your stuff when you go across the Rio. Jest remember that two good men got themselves killed takin' all this information down."

Chance spit into the gravel. "We're to make our crossing early in the morning two days from now."

"I know." Blain drew in a sucking breath and whispered; "You'll leave me. That's the only way."

Chance cursed and took up a handful of loose stone and hurled it against the far wall. "Dammit, Blain, I can't do that."

"You'll do it. I'll be dead before the sun rises tomorrow. You'll do your duty, so shut up about it."

* * *

William Blain's face glistened with perspiration in the flickering light cast by the candle. His eyes were closed and his mouth agape working to draw in each labored breath from the fetid, cellar air.

Chance sat beside the horribly wounded spy watching his chest rise and shutter before repeating the process again. Whenever Blain started to thrash his arms, Chance calmed him by wetting his lips with water and bringing his wrists back to his sides.

Through the low entry way, Chance could see that the sun was sliding toward the horizon and that the out of doors was tinted a rose color. As the minutes dragged on, Neunan sought to exit himself from the dismal situation that he found himself in.

His last correspondence from Andrea Edwards bore a return address of the Freedmen's Bureau, Jefferson Barracks, St. Louis, Missouri. She, with her flourishing penmanship, informed him that she was completing her instruction which would place her in a high position with the organization. At the conclusion of her schooling, she would be interviewing for assignment and posting. If all went well, she could be sent to the far reaches of the defeated Confederacy; Texas. That was the closing sentence of the missive. No further appeal to him to follow and find her, nor encouragement indicating that they might have a future together. There was no evidence that Andrea had feelings for him or if she was ambivalent toward him.

Chance had read and reread the letter, looking for clues; looking for meaning. He had noticed that the closing before she'd signed her first name was marginally smeared. Had she been careless with her hand or had a tear dropped from her eye and fallen on the paper?

Neunan could only hope. The cherished letter reread repeatedly was tied in a packet of his personal things and entrusted to a Lieutenant Wilson at the cavalry camp. He recalled vividly the letter's arrival at the assembly point at Arlington across the Potomac from Washington City.

How his spirits had soared when he held the letter in his hands but his elation was short lived once it was opened and read. He tried to read between the lines, to formulate any hidden message but nothing was apparent in the missive. It was just a letter, not of tenderness but of accomplishments and expectations.

Yet, Andrea had dangled a shred of hope to Chance by telling him that she was to be posted soon in the occupied rebel state of Texas.

Blain groaned shaking Neunan from his reverie.

"Would you like a drink of water, Pard?" The young spy leaned close to the wounded man's face.

"Yes, I'm so dry." William Blain whispered. "Go outside to the left of the dugout's door and see if you can find my goods. Lord, I was in such pain that I cant....., I can't remember if I took my stuff off the horse."

"You left them outside? I'll go look in a minute. Here take a swig. Can you hold the canteen by yourself?"

Quivering hands reached up and clasped the wool covered receptacle.

"You go look now, Neunan, afore it gets too dark to see."

"I'll be right back so don't move."

A halting reply came from Blain. "Yes, doctor."

The departing sun was a slit of orange atop the darkening landscape. Chance emerged from the cellar and squinted as his eyes were repelled by the orb's dying intensity. He looked away and when he did, he spied a ragged bed roll leaning against a pier of the side porch of the pueblo. Recovering the items, he stepped back into the inner sanctum beneath the dwelling.

"I found your stuff, Bill."

"The pocket watch." Blain rose to one elbow, grimacing in pain. "Hand me the watch, Neunan." The mortally wounded trooper sank back to his reposed position. "Is the key still connected to the fob?"

"Yes, Bill. I see that your watch is inscribed too." The younger man handed it to Blain.

"From my father on the day I left for the service."

Blain tried to open the time piece's back with his shaking hands but he couldn't accomplish the simple task.

"Here, Bill, let me do that for you."

"Wait, Neunan, before we open it up, you've got to promise to take the watch back to the folks in Illinois. I know that that would mean a lot to them."

"Where in Illinois, would that be?"

"Leroy Center in Boone County."

"I promise that I will do that for you if I survive this mission."

"You will. You got grit." Blain smiled a drawn smile. "Open her up but be sure to take that little disc of paper out. Don't let it get away from you."

"Does it have figures on it?"

"Yes. We scouted the two provinces I told you about."

"Don't talk anymore, Bill. I know how important this material is. It seems I've been collecting numbers from fellows I've left stretched along the way over these past two weeks."

Blain coughed.

"Is the watch runnin', Neunan?"

"Yes, it appears to be."

"What time is it?"

"Says its nine minutes 'til nine."

"Then you've got to leave. Take the watch and go." The dying man coughed two; short dry coughs. Chance looked out of the depression's opening into the blackness that had fallen like a curtain within the last few minutes.

"I told you that I wouldn't leave you and I won't. I keep my word." Blain's left hand, claw like and withered, grasp Chance's arm and squeezed. Neunan was surprised the strength that the stricken man displayed.

"You've got to get across the river tomorrow night. The figures we've collected could mean war with Mexico and France. You've got them in a safe place don't you?"

"Yes. They're in an oil skin packet that I have tied around my throat."

Chance loosened Blain's grip on his bicep and returned the hand to the trooper's side. "I'm not rushing into a big turkey shoot. If the military doesn't get these numbers at the appointed time, it won't make any difference. The U.S. army can wait until daylight when they can see me coming. I'm not getting myself shot by some seventeen year old, green recruit blazing away at two o'clock in the morning."

Blain didn't reply. He appeared to have lost consciousness.

Chance unraveled short pieces of the yarn from Poco's saddle blanket, rolled then into balls and placed them in his nostrils. The reeking odor emanating from William Blain's body was becoming more than he could bear.

Blain was quiet for a time. The only sounds were the occasional spit from the candle flame that burned on the gravel floor and unseen crawling things in the darkness outside the radius of the light.

The wounded man's breathing was growing weaker as the time between oxygen intakes widened.

"Mother?" Blain whispered. "Mother," his voice was a bit louder. "Martin locked ol' Whitey in the corn crib." The trooper's fevered mind was in the throes of hallucination. "No, Mother, I didn't hurt Marty for what he did. Just cuffed him good. I'm sorry Mother."

Chance was growing uncomfortable with the one sided conversation that Blain was involved in.

"Mother, I'm so glad you're here with me. Will you hold my hand, please?"

Chance slipped his hand in the dying trooper's hand as gently as he could.

"I'm so tired, Mother. My legs are tired and I've come a long way."

Neunan felt a lump rise in his throat as Blain's failing eyesight focused on the flickering candle.

"I'm coming with you now, Mother."

Trooper William Blain from Leroy Center, Illinois, coughed one more time very weakly before his hand went limp in Neunan's grasp.

* * *

Poco watched Neunan as he approached in the pink, pre-dawn light. During the interlude when they'd arrived at the adobe dwelling and the present, the horse had browsed on thorny bushes at the furthest extent of his reins. The animal observed his rider as the man tossed metallic things into the partially washed out well.

"Poco, ol' boy, let's get you a drink of water and be on our way. I must say that you revived yourself over night."

Neunan led the bald faced horse to a rusty caldron tipped on its side next to the well's collapsed outer foundation. Chance found a discarded boot stuck upside down on a corral post next to the broken down gate, tied his lariat in one of the finger loops in its top edge and lowered it into the depths below. The rust color of the liquid did not matter to the animal and it drank it down in long, loud, swallows.

"Just a bit longer, ol' fellow, and you'll carry me across the river."

* * *

IMPERIALISTS MEXICAN ARMY CAMP
MENDEZ, MEXICO

General Leonardo Marquez stood looking out his office window at a drill sergeant attempted to teach a group of Mexican recruits how to march in formation. The majority of the soldiers were young dandies from the society hierarchy and desirous of a more lofty position within the Mexican military than that of a worm tramper. But, alas, not every man supporting the return of an emperor as the head of government could be an officer. Finding enthusiastic volunteers for Maximilian's armies was difficult at best and certainly very sparse among the peons who idolized Juarez for his land reform programs. Benito Juarez had pledged in the democratic election that he would expedite agrarian redistribution and put the peasants on their own farms. His proposition had made him a favored leader of the lower and middle classes. The numbers of his ill equipped army far exceeded those of the imperialists and their 'for hire' foreign supporters.

"Excuse me, my General." Lieutenant Ricardos stood at the door with Captain Thome at his side.

"Ah, Captain Thome, come in and have a seat. Have you reports for me regarding your counter intelligence mission?" General Marquez returned to his desk and placed a leather bound ledger on top of a stack of orders of execution.

"Yes, General." The mercenary officer advanced to the huge mahogany desk but side stepped the offered chair and remained standing. "We have news received within the hour. I have two American scouts in the field with the Yaqui contingent. My men are able trackers and were formerly with Nathan Forrest's Confederate cavalry."

"It's not necessary that you provide me with the men's pedigrees, Captain. I trust your judgment with the selection of the troops we employ. Please, get to the point."

"Your assumption as to the general location of the river crossing appears to be correct and the only piece missing from the plot of the spies is: how many men were sent into Mexico?"

"You haven't yet made your point, Thome." Marquez answered coolly.

"Here's the latest from our tracking party." Thome handed the commander a yellow sheet of paper.

General Marquez accepted the telegram, removed a pair of glasses from the inner pocket of his tunic and began to silently read.

DISCOVERED ABANDONED PUEBELO NEAR RATTLE SNAKE MESA stop BROKE DOWN HORSE IN THE BRUSH stop DEAD MAN IN THE CELLAR stop NO IDENTIFICATION stop BELIEVE MAN IS ONE OF THE YANKEE SPIES stop HORSE TRACKS LEADING TO THE NORTH EAST. SIGNED; SGT.YOUNGBLOOD.

Captain Thome, who was still wearing his ragged, short Confederate cavalry jacket, placed his hands on the top of the officer's ornately carved desk and said; "Tracks heading north-east, that could mean and probably does, Pequeno Matamoras, General."

Thome paused allowing the information to sink into his commanding officer's brain.

"What type of forces do you have stationed there?" Thome questioned.

"I am the General in this situation. Did you forget that, Captain?" The general snapped in reply.

"Sorry, Sir. I meant no affront to your authority."

Marquez did not offer a response to the apology but returned his gaze to the telegram.

He spoke as if he was putting together a dictated message in a report. "An inept force commanded by Colonel Carlos Calderon, a man who bought his commission in Mexico City. He has a tiny contingent made up of Yaquis, inexperienced militia, and a few regulars, mere cannon fodder for the Yankees if they choose to attack."

"A few hundred men?" Thome questioned.

"And a battery consisting of guns from your defeated country and the Yankee's best pieces which we have liberated from the Juaristas."

"Sounds like enough men to catch a couple of spies."

Marquez removed his glasses and gave the American captain a stern look. "Captain, they are mainly militia. We have but a handful of regulars stationed in that flea bitten town."

Captain Thome straightened and positioned his arms across his chest. "Can we get some dependable men up to that location?"

"Ricardos, how many miles from here to Pequeno Matamoras?"

"Forty-five miles, my General. That is by rail."

"And the Juaristas?"

"Sir, they have cut the rail line twice in the last six weeks."

Marquez threw up his hands, one holding his glasses and the other the telegram.

The gesture was not lost on Captain Thome.

"Look General, we've got to get some specialized help to this Colonel Calderon. I'd like to contact Sgt. Youngblood who very likely is hanging around the telegraph office in Reynosa waiting on orders from me as to what the next move will be. Of course, I am acting at your discretion."

"A plausible idea, Thome. I'll write out an order immediately and have Lt. Ricardos take it to out telegrapher."

"I want el Halcon and his Yaqui trackers to be on that train as well. Sergeant Youngblood is an excellent shot with the Whitworth sniper rifle and he may be of value to us especially if we have to take down the spies as they attempt their escape over the Rio."

"Very well, Captain Thome. Let us hope that the Reynosa rail line is in good repair."

* * *

UNITED STATE'S ARMY CANTONEMENT, FORT BROWN BROWNSVILLE, TEXAS

Reveille had sounded at five a.m. and Lieutenant Wilson rose and ate a scanty breakfast of fried bacon, hard tack and black coffee prepared by the officers' mess cook.

Following his morning repast, the officer returned to his tent, brushed his uniform and straightened the button alignment on his coat's front. Then he picked up a leather ledger before pausing near the tent's front flap to sharpen his pencil with a pen knife.

Before he could grasp the canvas with his left hand to make his exit, Major Tyler loomed in the opening.

Wilson stepped back in astonishment at seeing his superior in his tent. "Good morning, Sir. I didn't expect to see you for at least another half hour and in your tent, not mine."

"Yes, but I couldn't sleep and I decided to come see you in order to clear up a few things. My insomnia may have been caused by a combination of rich food and the company of a beautiful woman."

Wilson made no comment and backed deeper into his shelter. He set the recording book on his camp desk. He nodded to a chair next to the desk but Tyler waved his hand in refusal to the offered seat.

The lieutenant cleared his throat and said, "I'm afraid that I have some bad news in regard to our spying operation." He waited in silence for the reaction of his superior.

"I'm not surprised, Lt. Wilson."

"Major, not a single man has been heard from since they ascended into Mexican territory to begin their information gathering. We have no word from any of our agents."

Tyler whacked his gauntlets which he'd removed on his thigh.

"Damn! This entire operation is a failure!"

"I'm afraid that it's looking that way, Sir. But we yet have the day after tomorrow. And then…."

"Could our enemies have had forewarning of our intelligence work?"

"I think not, Major. We have had no desertions in the two weeks during the time that the plan has been in effect."

"Don't be too sure of that, Wilson. I gleaned something from Andrea Edwards which could have compromised what we'd set out to do."

"But Sir, the freed slaves are our most loyal allies here in Texas."

"Not the slaves, Lieutenant, or the personnel at the Freedmen's Bureau. The leak to our enemies could have come from one of our own."

"Preposterous, Sir!"

"Do you recall that the volunteers for the clandestine operation were from three cavalry regiments; the Twelfth Illinois, the Third Iowa, and the Fourth Wisconsin."

"Yes. There were six men in attendance at our initial meeting."

"But one of these six was a farrier who'd come by mistake with the compliment. This soldier attended the details' gathering, found out about the danger, and went to his sergeant the next day. He complained that he'd been called to Fort Brown as a replacement for a horse shoer who'd been discharged due to illness. He protested that he'd never agreed to go on a secret mission and had accepted the transfer in order to do his duty in a safe location. He was not paired with a partner and stayed on our side of the Rio Grande when our spies made their penetration."

"I see what you're saying but I have met with this Homer Nichols and other than having a serious case of homesickness, he seems loyal and patriotic."

"Who knows the reasons that a man does things? Money, women, or freedom from this hell hole we're serving in. These things are what tempt a man to commit vile acts."

"You're wrong, sir. You're barking up the wrong tree."

"You don't understand, do you, Wilson? This spying fiasco will do damage to my career, my reputation. I'm not going to take the blame for this project's failure when I can shift it to Private Nichols."

The lieutenant's gray eyes smoldered. "You're assuming that just because Nichols served with Chance Neunan in the Twelfth regiment and was acquainted with the four others at one time, that for some reason, he committed a military indiscretion."

"Or something beyond being discrete."

"I'll not be a part of this, Sir."

"You don't need to be, Wilson."

"Private Fields?" Tyler called his aide. "Take this order to Captain Adams and tell him to carry it out immediately."

Wilson stood dumbfounded as the interior of his tent commenced to spin.

Major Tyler was acting too rashly and proceeding on a course the he had not anticipated.

"There, Lieutenant, I have removed you from the responsibility that you consider detestable. You are not a party to any of this until you are required to testify at the court marshal. Nichols will be arrested at the Freedmen's Bureau and brought before me to be formally charged. He will be placed in shackles by Captain Adams and escorted to the stockade where he will be imprisoned."

* * *

FREEDMEN'S BUREAU
BAXTER PLANTATION

Andrea awakened to a pilliated woodpecker hammering on a dead elm on the perimeter of the fog shrouded lawn. The sun was struggling to make its entrance but the cool mists mingled with the increasing warmth dropped a gray veil over everything. Andrea rolled to her side and snuggled into the down filled pillow and clinched her eyes tightly. Her dreams had been a mélange of disturbing vignettes of Robert Tyler pawing at her in the amber glow of his tent and Chance Neunan ripping aside the flap and sending her antagonist sprawling. His appearance and his action to save her brought back images of the dark haired, handsome man. She missed him so and the separation that depressed her was nearly more than she could bear. Andrea worried about him and where he might be. Was he cold and wounded as he was when he had first came into her life? Her lover was performing perilous duty and she prayed to God that he would safely return to her.

There was a soft knock on the double doors.

"Missy, may I come in? You been sleepin' for an awful long time. I brung you a scaldin', hot cup of coffee and some soap and a washrag with water so's you can cleanup."

"Yes, come in, Angie. I'd like someone to talk to."

The young aide entered and nodded a greeting. Andrea sat up and yawned. "I did not have a pleasant evening with Major Tyler last night." The tousseled haired administrator threw her legs over the edge of the bed, stood erect and walked behind a privacy screen.

"Dat man, he touched you, didn't he?"

"Only on the back of the neck but it was more than I cared for. I still have a cold sensation where he pressed his fingers."

"As I've toad you, Missy, jest say da word and we'll get Big Joe to pay dat brass hat a visit. He oughta be taught some Southern manners like the white folks down here has.

"That won't be necessary, Angie."

"I put out some fresh bathin' stuff, Ma'am and I found another bar of dat jasmine soap.

"Thank you. You are dismissed."

The girlish assistant didn't openly answer to the directive but continued to grumble as she closed the pocket doors behind her.

The warmth of the water on the coarse wash cloth felt heavenly to Andrea. She held the heated cloth to the nape of her neck and proceeded to rub it back and forth over the spot where Tyler had touched her skin. The boorish major's digit tips were in no way as tender and caressing as Chance's were. Instead they were rough and fumbling.

Why must I, a beautiful woman, always be on the alert to the lechery of men whose sole game in life is to seduce me? Beauty, intelligence, and poise are a curse to a woman in a male dominated world. Men both adore you and resent you at the same time. They want you one step beneath them at every turn and it is rare to fine a man who is sensitive and attuned to a woman working on a higher level than he. Chance Neunan was such a man and she missed him terribly for his understanding and tolerance. Damn the major. He had been evasive and had offered very little in the way of information for her to hang her hopes on but she knew that if her lover was alive and physically could; he would return to her. Once the two of them had been united, she vowed that she would never permit a separation again.

The rising steam from the bathwater made Andrea drowsy and she eased her head back against the tub's elevated headrest.

She was unaware of how long she'd dozed but her absence from her duties was long enough to alarm Angie Sue who came looking for her.

"Wake up, Little Missy. You been sleepin' a long time. It's a wonder that you ain't slid under the water and drowned. Now stand up and 'low me to towel you off, then we'll get you dressed. Dey's somethin' goin' on down to da stables."

* * *

SECOND CHANCE

MAJOR ROBERT TYLER'S TENT
FORT BROWN, TEXAS

After issuing the order to apprehend Private Nichols, Tyler returned to his command tent along with Wilson's report which had been intended for Colonel Archer. The junior officer was in a huff about rewriting his report but he knew better than to argue the point with Tyler.

Robert Tyler expected unwavering support and loyalty from his subordinates and he was growing tired of the young lieutenant's obstinance. Perhaps after all this was cleared up and he was exonerated of the mission's failure, he would ask Lieutenant Wilson to accept a transfer to another regiment and another staff position. Life was too short to have to stumble over obstacles created by unhappy personnel.

Once this Nichols fellow was caught and charged with treason all would be copasetic. He would intercede on Nichols' behalf and ask the judge advocate for leniency for the farrier. The private was guilty of a mere slip of the tongue that put the Imperialists Mexican forces on the trail of the American spies almost from the outset. Nichols was a youthful young man totally unaccustomed to the secrecy demanded in such an intelligence endeavor.

The rusty bearded officer noticed a shadow on his tent flap.

"Yes. Who is it?" Tyler called.

"Private Fields, Sir."

"You may enter, Fields. What is the purpose of your duty, here, Private?"

"The party that you requested of Captain Adams to arrest the farrier at the Bureau location has returned and is waiting outside."

"Send them in immediately, Fields. You've been waiting outside with the enlisted men of his squad?"

"Yes Sir." The private parted the tent flap and motioned for the officer of the squad to enter.

"Lieutenant Thomas Bowen of the Fourth Wisconsin Cavalry, at your service, Sir." The young man snapped a perfect salute to Tyler. The major received it with a lazy motion of acceptance.

"Do you have our man, Nichols, with you or have you deposited him at the stockade?"

"No, sir, I regret to inform you that the man was not at the stables at the Freedmen's Bureau. He did not show up for his morning duty today and he has not been seen about the camp since last night at company mess. I fear that he has deserted."

"Dammit!" Tyler paced about for a few seconds before composing himself.

"Lieutenant, send an order with a reliable man to the 'High Tower' and have the telegrapher get a message off to Hempstead. We'll have a reception committee for the rascal at the depot if he's traveling by train. Then get a couple of Texican trackers in your employ and see if they can't pick up his trail. I want this man in custody before sunset. Is that clear to you, Lt. Bowen?"

"Yes, Sir. Fully, Sir."

* * *

ON THE TRAIL TO THE RIO GRAND NEAR PEQUENO MATAMORES

Neunan walked Poco whenever scrub trees overhung the trail so low that there was a danger of him being unhorsed. They were traveling on a tract that appeared to be growing wider and more heavily used by animals and the local inhabitants. The bald faced horse had recovered his strength at the abandoned pueblo and responded to Chance's urging whenever the man's heels were applied to his ribs. The equine was able to trot when called on, a gate he'd not been able to do two days previously.

The pathway wound around the cusp of a hillock that overlooked an even lower set of harvested fields. Back home in Moultrie County, Illinois, the locals would have referred to the sprawling expanse as a 'second bottom'. The trooper noted that the landowners had sited their rancheros on higher ground and permitted their peasant workers to construct their hovels in the marginal flood plain. Until Chance and Poco chose to leave the passageway and ride into the more populated areas, there seemed to be little danger. It would be when he approached the river across from the military compound at Fort Brown that his presence would be challenged by the curious Mexicans.

Neunan knew that he'd have a difficult time convincing the denizens that he was a Mexican national but he also was aware that the Texicans of mixed lineage often favored the garb of the region. He would have to impress upon those who challenged him that he was a mean hombre and not to be trifled with.

Maybe I'll put on a bold front. Trot into town and shoot the first dog that barks at me. Maybe yell a few sexual slurs at the senoritas standing in the shade of their casas.

The trooper's neck and shoulders ached from the fatigue created by his cautiousness as he ascended into the outer edges of the small town. Little farms surrounded by brush fences gave way to decrepit looking businesses and boarded up buildings. His boney mount plodded down the dusty street of the suffering burg which Chance was able to identify as Pequeno Matamores from the signage on the store fronts. Chance had been told in the briefing two weeks earlier that it was more sensible to attempt a river crossing outside the environs of this city than to try at the larger city of Matamoras. The trading center was too populated, too well guarded, and the waterfront was too choked with shipping and had more than one French naval vessel moored there.

No, he would settle into this dusty, little 'dog town' and wait for the best opportunity to make his escape regardless of when that time came. He knew that he would choose nightfall as the safest time but was wary of the number of curs he'd seen. Chance knew that the animals would sound the alarm as he passed through the sleeping town and made for the river in the early morning hours.

Neunan skirted the main street of the town, choosing instead side streets with their tumbled down appearance. Hovels of adobe brick, herds of goats, flocks of chickens and turkeys all jumped and flopped out of Poco's way as the young spy studied the lodgings for a sign reading; cantina. Late afternoon cooking fires lifted the aroma of tortillas and enchiladas on the heavy September air. The horse and rider ambled past two wheeled carts filled with hay, pumpkins and squash. Chance continued to scope the hovels and dingy places of business crammed against a narrow boardwalk with their doorways opening onto the street.

At last, a cantina appeared with a sign advertising tequila and sleeping rooms. Poco was reined in and Neunan dismounted tossing the lines of his mount over a gnawed hitching rail that did not appear to be very sturdy.

Chance looked up and down the narrow street searching for signs of danger. Seeing only an old, fat man hobbling across the roadway, Chance entered the establishment. He stood for a moment allowing his eyes to accustom themselves to the darkness of the interior of the room.

"Oala, Senorita."

"Si, Senor. How many nights do you wish to stay?" The proprietress answers in English. The raven haired young woman stood behind a bar consisting of a plank lying on top of two barrels, drying shot glasses.

"Don't know, Miss. It depends on a number of things."

"I won't ask what that means. In these times it isn't healthy to ask too many questions."

"How could you tell that I wasn't Mexican?"

"Just a guess. You dress like a Texican. We have two languages here being so close to the border. You can spit across the Rio from our side of the river on a windy day. But another thing that told me that you were a gringo was the way you walk. You see, a Mexican man your age has a certain strut, a certain bravado. This you do not have."

"I'm tired. I've come from Fort Worth. I need a bath and a one night stay will be all I'll need."

"Oh, senor, you have come a long way."

"It is and I'm thinking that these rags I have on need a good burning. Would you have something on hand that you'd sell me?"

"I could look into my grandfather's chest. He passed away last month."

Chance paid no heed to what the girl had said and offered no condolences.

"What about my horse?"

"Miguel, my little brother, will bring him grain and watch him every night that you stay. He charges but twenty-five centavos for the service."

"And the room?"

"Just seventy-five centavos. It is clean and located on a back alley. No noise."

"I'll take the room for one night. Then I'll decide if I have to have a second night or not."

"Oh Senor, if I was your girl, I'd want you at home with me every night." The young clerk rolled her eyes at Chance.

"I'm tired. I'll go out and bring in my gear."

"I'll be in the cantina late tonight, Senor."

"We'll see, eh,… is it Maria?"

"Yes."

"That's the name on the sign behind your desk registry?"

"And how are you called, Senor?"

"Chance Neunan."

* * *

FREEDMENS' BUREAU
BAXTER PLANTATION

Andrea Edwards paused in the lower kitchen of the plantation house and helped herself to a freshly baked biscuit. Betsy, one of the girls employed to prepare food for the administrative staff, set out a small crock of butter, a knife, and a bowl of honey. With the hot coffee that Angie had brought her, Andrea sat down at a long table next to the open fireplace and ate her morning meal.

"Betsy, May I bother you for a moment?"

The middle aged woman looked up from a dough trencher where she was kneading dough and wiped her hands on her apron.

"Sure, Missy Edwards. What is it that you want?"

"Well when Angie Sue woke me this morning she said that there was some kind of activity going on at the stables. Would you know anything about that situation?"

The door leading out to the side yard opened abruptly and Big Joe, wearing a well worn jacket, walked into the warm kitchen.

"'Spect I can tell you a little bit of the goings on at de barn. Five army boys who I'd never seed afore came to the corral leadin' an extra horse. Said that they was lookin' for Homer Nichols and that they was gonna arrest him. I told 'em that he hadn't showed up at the bureau with the rest of the volunteers this mornin' and that the last time I seed him was on the previous evenin' when the army wagon took the boys back to their camp."

Big Joe went to the coffee pot sitting on an iron spider by the fire and poured himself a cup of morning coffee. "Then they got kinda tough with me and said I would be in big trouble if I was hidin' him. I told them I wasn't and that I was gonna come up to see you about the way they was actin'."

"They're gone, then?"

"Yessum, but I don't think we've seed the last of them. I sure hope that Nichols feller dresses warm on his get away 'cause the nights are gettin' danged cold."

* * *

REINFORCEMENTS FOR THE IMPERIALIST'S FORT AT PEQUENO MATAMORES

Charles Thome was not happy with the assignment which he'd been given. The ex-Confederate officer sat disgruntled, leaning against the half lowered window in the railroad carriage as it rocked and jostled at a terrapin's pace.

His orderly, Sergeant Ben Louder, selected the first car behind the engine's tender for their journey to Pequeno Matamores. Louder had ridden a few trains during his military duty in the recently concluded hostilities and his experiences told him of the importance of car selection. Seats in cars nearer to the lumbering locomotive while noisier, offered shelter from the billowing smoke and hot embers cast off by the engine's stack.

Captain Thome sat pensively smoking one of General Marquez's cigars. His gray eyes were fixed on a hand drawn map of his command's destination at the river crossing.

" 'Spect that the boys in the tail end cars are getting' pretty well smoked." Sgt. Lauder rose from his seat opposite the captain and adjusted the height of the window.

"Just as long as we keep 'em all in one piece, Louder, that's all that counts."

Thome tapped the loose ash from the tip of his smoke on the thread bare arm of his seat.

"You ain't particularly pleased with the orders that you received, are you Captain?"

"I'll reserve my feelings regarding the general's decision but I will say that he has no confidence regarding the garrison's ability to thwart the Yankee spies crossing the Rio to Fort Brown."

The officer returned to his perusal of the map drawn on lined paper torn from a ledger.

"That's his reason for sending us. We're to rendezvous with Youngblood and his Yaqui trackers at Gila Junction. It looks like this place is about eight miles from our assigned deployment.

"We'll get off this backbreaker for a while then?"

"Yes. We'll make our hookup and proceed overland from the Gila depot."

"How come we ain't riding the rails right on into the town?"

Captain Thome did not allow the sergeant's inquiry to break his concentration and kept his eyes glued to the map.

"Juaristas ripped up the tracks in several places between the two points. Of course we'll go as far as we can by train once we've gathered up Youngblood and his group. General Marquez knows that these raiders, who he regards as insurgents, have destroyed communications and isolated the garrison there at the crossing."

Thome folded the map and placed it in an inside pocket of his jacket.

" At this miserable pace we're two hours behind schedule. It will hurry us to reach Pequeno Matamores before night fall."

"What about that lil' ol' jackass gun we're haulin' on the flat car at the end of the train?"

"The Woodruff cannon?"

"What ever it's called. I hope you don't intend to take on the 'Blue Bellies' with that pop gun?"

" Of course not. We're to augment what ever artillery pieces that the Imperialists have on hand. The general was unsure of the armament that was located in the arsenal there."

The sergeant sprang to his feet and began to brush a glowing ember from the thigh of his trouser leg. Louder cursed before raising the car window even higher. He settled down and returned to his the frayed seat. Louder never spoke but slid his hands over both his thighs to see if he'd missed any other incendiary particles.

"So if Youngblood can't pick off the spies with the special rifle of his, then you're gonna pull down on 'em with that little cannon?"

"Not very sporting, is it, Sergeant? My orders direct me to kill all the agents if they cannot be captured. Under no circumstances are they to be allowed to enter the Union lines. I'm certain that Marquez would be delighted to have me bring one or two of these fellows in alive. They'd be put on trial in the capitol which would set off a furor in the European courts. Such a happening could swing aid and support over to Maximilian's side."

Louder smiled a wane smile as he imagined the fate of any agents who wound fall into the hands of the Imperialists.

Neither man offered a topic which would commence a new conversation. The outside temperature of the late afternoon had risen and coupled with the lack of ventilation was forcing the carriage's interiors to grow stuffy and uncomfortable.

The sergeant stopped talking all together and within the passage of a few minutes, his head lolled against the semi closed window.

Captain Thome, too, was succumbing to the heat and he found himself dozing off only to be awakened by every sharp jolt that occurred in the train's undercarriage. He was, however; becoming more oblivious to the bumpy ride as the length of his consciousness waned.

"Captain?" Sergeant Louder called to his superior before correcting himself. "Oh, I'm sorry Sir but I thought you should know that there's a lot of smoke sweeping over the tracks and that the engine has slowed considerably."

"It's just the smoke from the locomotive's stack isn't it?" Thome asked sleepily.

"No Sir. There's lots more outside than this old steamer could generate."

Both men leaned forward and attempted to locate the source of the thick gray haze. They were so absorbed with their search that they were surprised when the car's rear connecting door was jerked open and a sooty faced lieutenant stepped into the isle.

"Sir, Lieutenant Abrams reporting. My squad assigned as lookouts on top of the cars are seeing vast amounts of smoke and fire at the station at Gila Junction."

As the officer submitted his observation, the engine sounded three short whistles. Immediately following the alarm, the men were aware of the large drive wheels on the conveyance grinding to a halt before reversing themselves.

* * *

The decrepit iron horse transporting the rebels now in the employ of the Mexican Imperialists forces sat hissing among the ruins of the depot and rail switches at Gila Junction. Orange flames licked at a vast stack of ties topped by glowing, twisted rails. The track had been taken up leaving a barren trail in the ballast. A single strand of telegraph wire hung forlornly on a lone pole which had been left standing by the attackers.

"Well, shit, Sir. Where have you seen rail track handled in this way before?"

The three men; Thome, Louder, and the well smoked Lieutenant Abrams, stood up wind of the smoke and marveled at the extent of the devastation.

"Looks just like the work of Sherman and his bummers down in Georgia. You can't tell me that the Juaristas aren't getting help from the Yankees across the river."

The stench of overcooked meat seared the nostrils of the three causing them to cast their gazes in three different directions in an attempt to locate the source of the odor.

"Over there, Louder. There's a half-burned body inside the depot's doorway. Check it out, will you?"

Sergeant Louder walked to the corpse and turned it over with his booted foot.

"'Peers to be a Yaqui, I'd say. Whose side he was on you can't say. Those sons-a- bitches switch sides at the drop of a hat."

Lt. Abrams unsnapped the catch on his revolver holster and focused on a brush covered swale beyond the station's water tower.

"I believe that there are some men emerging from that area beneath the tower, Sir."

"Louder, get the cannon crew riding on the flatcar up here at once. We'll take cover underneath the cars. Get those men up here damned quick!" Captain Thome was at his best in a command situation.

Louder ducked low and scampered up the three steps in the connection of the cars and down on the other side. He hunched over keeping the carriages between himself and the unidentified men observing them from a distance. Before he reached the artillerymen, a shot rang out and a lead projectile smashed into an outside lamp of the car that Thome and Abrahams were standing in front of. Both men fell flat on their stomach as the sound of the gunshot died away.

"Jesus Christ! What the hell is the range those birds fired from?" Lt. Abrams shouted, the tenor of his voice etched with excitement.

"I don't know what the distance is but there's only one man that I know of who would take a shot like that."

"And who is this William Tell?"

"Casper Youngblood of my command. He's got a Whitworth Rifle and that shot is intended to let us know that he's with the group at the tower."

* * *

The bulk of Thome's miniscule command pitched in to help unload the Woodruff gun while the remainder spread out on either side of the tracks to form skirmish lines.

Three by twelve Live Oak planks were located in a pile of lumber that the raiders hadn't burned. These the troopers used to make ramps in order to pass the small caliber gun from the high surface of the open car to the ground. The gunners fashioned tow ropes onto the trail of the piece and then brought up the draft horses from the stock car to assist them.

All went well until the weapon was turned to make its exit from the car. For some reason, possibly a wisp of smoke, the team of animal panicked and bolted sideway jerking the cannon out of the artillerymen's control and onto the rocky ballast of the rail line. The gun's unsupported fall broke its axle like a matchstick.

Captain Thome walked through the half dozen men gawking at the calamity and cursed silently to himself. One of the reasons for his being sent north by General Marquez was now an irreparable pile of iron lying before him. He paced back and forth formulating a plan in the shade of the cars as the men watched him.

All the switching mechanisms were destroyed by the Juarestas which left the train in the predictment of being capable of traveling only forward or backward. Forward was no longer an option so the locomotive would have to be driven in reverse pushing the cars behind it. To abandon the train was certainly out of the question and a serious military offense in any country's army. It would be imperative for the locomotive to start immediately on its return trip to avoid being surrounded and destroyed by the enemy. He could only hope that the anti- Imperialists would not sabotage the rails ahead of the train at some point in its return trip.

Lieutenant Abrams hitched up his waist belt and unbuttoned the top two buttons of his cavalry jacket before approaching Thome.

"Captain Thome, what are your orders, Sir?"

Thome said nothing but waved to the assembled men to join him out of the sun. He wiped his forehead with a handkerchief which he'd drawn from the inside pocket of his jacket.

"Gather round men. Here's what I propose to do. You may assume my remarks to be a direct order. The cannon will be jettisoned once we clear it from the tracks. Its ammunition will be destroyed by dumping it in the depot's well once we've taken ample water for our animals and us from it. I'll take ten men including Youngblood and his rifle and make for Pequeno Matamores, our original destination. We'll try to make that point by dark. That portion of General Marquez's order will at least be accomplished. Those whom I have not selected shall return with the train to the Mexican cantonment under the direction of Lieutenant Abrams."

"What about our Yaqui scouts?" Lauder asked.

We'll take El Halcon and two of his men. Have the others join your group. Are there any questions?" The captain's looked into the face of every man." Hearing none, we will begin as soon as the mounts needed are off loaded from the cattle cars. Gentlemen, this is a perilous situation we are in. The Juaristas have watched our passage to this point. They may be preparing ambushes on both our groups so certainly be on your guard at all times."

* * *

Even though the cavalry horses had been transported in a slat-sided cattle car, when they were released they seemed lethargic and listless.

Thome took the heat and jostling of the rail cars as contributing factors in the behavior of the equines. All the mounts were saddled within fifteen minutes and ready to start their passage to the river town some eight miles away. This distance was but an estimate for the last depot prior to reaching the destroyed rail juncture at Gila and was the only gauge that Thome and the Sergeant had to go on. A major concern arose when the cavalrymen searched the area for a well or spring so that their animals could slake their thirst.

In the very well that Thome was directing the canoneers to sink their useless ammunition, the men found the scalped body of the station agent. The man had been killed in the early morning hours before the train's arrival but not a trooper would step forward and fill his canteen with water after the body had been removed. Even the horses were hesitant about the water as if they could smell the blood contaminating the liquid.

El Halcon, the Yaqui leader, walked as only an Indian could through the milling troopers and in broken English assured Thome that he could locate a natural spring halfway between Gila Junction and Pequeno Matamores.

Taking the man at his word, Captain Thome mounted his detachment and led them onto the ballast where the tracks had been removed. In a matter of minutes they reached the undamaged portion of the rail line. Two outriders working cautiously ahead of the party peeled their eyes for the enemy as the remaining men watched their progress.

Thome angrily bit his lip and cursed as he heard the engine's whistle toot twice as a farewell to the returning detachment. *Nothing like alerting the enemy to our location and our departure, you damned fool*, he thought.

Thome waved to the departing men commanded by Lieutenant Abrams as they closed and latched the locks on the stock cars. The artillery crew had been allowed to remove the wheels from the Woodruff gun and stow the parts on the flat car. Then they were broken up, some joining Abrams and some going with Thome's detachment. The men joining the cavalry hurried to overtake the departing contingent mounted on horses that they'd never ridden before.

In two hours, Charles Thome knew that his men were in trouble. The canteens were nearly empty and the shifty eyed el Halcon either had lied to him about the water sources existing or was inept at locating them. The plight of the ten riders grew more dire as they plodded on in a north easterly direction. Lathered and sporting swollen, protruding tongues the cavalry mounts were noticeably distressed. As the sun commenced its descent its passage created long shadows in the thorny chaparral clinging to life alongside the rails.

"Louder, call a halt. We can't go much farther without a rest." Thome ordered. He knew that none of the animals could carry two riders if any one of the mounts became incapacitated.

"Dismount and stand at ease." Louder squawked through cracked lips. All the troupers wearily swung their right legs over the saddle tree and stood beside their jaded steeds.

"Have them hobble their horses, although I don't think the animals have enough energy to run. Send El Halcon to me as soon as he can be found."

"Yes Sir."

"Damn!" Thome was not a habitual blasphemer but he could control his temper no longer. In fifteen minutes the sun would be gone and the landscape would be as black as the inside of a stovepipe. His attempt to reach Pequeno Matamores to augment the force there had failed. The soldiers in the river town would have to proceed on their own.

"Damn!" The captain cursed this time under his breath. *First the loss of the Woodruff gun and now their tardiness would take Private Youngblood and his sniper rifle out of the equation. The rifleman would not be able to use his scope-sighted weapon in pitch blackness.*

Captain Thome removed his shabby cavalry jacket and used a leather strap from his saddlebag to lash his horse's front legs together. Then he stood with one hand resting on his saddle, head down with his eyes closed. He did not look up when he heard footsteps approaching. The Captain picked up the smell of the Indian even before the man stopped adjacent to him.

"El Halcon?"

"Yes."

"We are in a very serious spot. We must have water. Is there any to be had?"

"Yes."

"Find it for us. I'm giving up on trying to each the river crossing. We will retrace our march and follow the tracks to Gila Junction. Once we return to the break in the telegraph line, I'll get a man up a pole who can tap into the line. General Marquez can have water and fresh horses transported to us. Right now, however, we must have water or we will surely die."

"I will find you water, Thome. I now know that I have ridden past the markers for the water."

"How far away is this water?"

"Maybe an hour, maybe less."

"Good. Sergeant Louder?"

"Yes Sir."

"Gather up eight canteens from the men and give them to El Halcon. He and one of his Yaquis will be riding to the water hole. We won't try to reach it with him. I can't see how we could make that distance."

"Yes Sir." The Sergeant turned to begin his collection but Thome stopped him.

"We're going back to the junction and we'll try to tap into the telegraph line."

"Luck is with us Captain. We have Walt Cline in our group and he's worked as a telegrapher before he joined the cavalry. I've seen him tap and use a pair of pinchers and a screw driver to send messages outside of Perryville. He can do the job for us."

The troopers all had removed their jackets and tied them to the back of their saddles. Nearly every man sat, knees apart, with his head down. One man lit a pipe; the sound of the lucifer being struck was the only interruption to the silence which had settled around them. Far off, enveloped by the night's blackness, a coyote wailed for a short time. When it failed to arouse a response it stopped its howling. Someone in the group of splayed out bodies coughed, but no sounds of sleep were emitted. Every man jack in the group was too tired even to slumber, move, or blink. The minutes ticked off accumulating into hours as the sandy soil on which the men lay began to cool. Another trooper coughed and a horse in the tiny herd shook its head causing its halter to jingle.

"Hey look there! There on the horizon! There's a glow. It must be fire and a sizable one at that." The men rose to their feet, pointing and gesturing. Captain Thome awoke at the sound of the excitement and joined his detachment.

"What is it Sergeant?"

"Don't know, Sir. It must be Pequeno Matamores because that seems to be where these tracks are headed."

"Do you have any estimation of the distance?"

"No, but it might as well be on the other side of the world. We haven't got the strength to ride that far in the condition we're in."

"Riders comin'in!" Two troopers at the outer edge of the complement announced the approach of horsemen. El Halcon and a fellow tribesman, their perspiring bodies shimmering in the orange glow of the distant fire, halted their horses inside the circle of men and held aloft eight dripping canteens.

* * *

El Halcon had been absent since he and his cohort had departed with the canteens to re-locate the water hole.

His return from the spring with his tribesman carrying the life reviving water had saved the detachment. The troopers and artillerists gulped down their fill of water and stood watching as Thome sent the pair of Indians back with all the canteens they had. The men, replenished, set to digging two large holes in the ground with their hands and mess plates. Sergeant Lauder supervised the work and when the cavities were completed he asked for any of the men who had any of the new Goodyear rubber ponchos in their possession to bring them to him. With judicious arrangement, the rain covers were quickly in place lining the make shift watering troughs.

El Halcon appeared again and the troopers took the vessels from him and emptied the contents into the poncho lined holes. It was all that the horse handlers could do to hold back their thirst maddened mounts so that they would not rush forward and trample down the ingenious watering devices. Even with their hobbles in place, the animals were far from stationary. They smelled the water and hopped around like so many giant jack rabbits while awaiting their turn.

The Indian returned to the hole for a third and last time before Thome felt that the steeds could travel to the valuable spring. The breech clothed chieftain slipped away for another absence as the troopers walked the mile to the spring. When the man next appeared, he was in the midst of the tired riders before they knew it. It was as if the scout was a mist that had drifted in on the morning dew. Captain Thome was bent over pouring liquid from his full canteen onto an oversized neckerchief. He was using the cloth to mop at the grit on his face when his scout strode up.

"Thome, me go to the rim of the hill lookin' down into Pequeno Matamores. Whole town about half burned up. Much shootin' in the dark. Don't know why Mexicans and Gringos so mad at each other."

"I can only guess, el Halcon". The captain answered. "I'd like for you to scout back toward the junction at Gila and report to me if there is anything going on there. It's possible that the engine that we left last evening has reached the depot further back and reequipped.

"I do this. My horse very strong. He hold up for me to go see what goes on there."

"Good. Here's a mirror for you to signal to us. The sun will have risen by the time you and your scouts get back to the junction. If you flash once with the looking glass that will mean that we should join you on the tracks at Gila. If you find that there is no train then leave the mirror in your pocket."

"Thome expects the fire wagon will come with water and supplies from Mendez."

"Yes. We should be on hand as soon as it arrives to board the cars and get away from here."

* * *

Sgt. Louder climbed to the top of a rocky prominence jutting out of the thorn trees and spiny bushes in the vicinity of the junction. Thome had moved the complement away from the water hole to a point within two hundred yards of the ruined station. Hydrated and refreshed the troops and horses had covered the distance on their return trip easily and awaited the signal from el Halcon before they proceeded.

The site of the ambush continued to smolder. It flamed anew whenever a layer of oxygen- infused material was uncovered by the collapse of a burned section of a wall or floor.

The foliage was so dense that it hid the riders from anyone watching from the tracks. Horses shifted their feet and threw up their heads indicating a desire to move away from the brush and the biting insects preying on their rumps and hind legs.

El Halcon appeared beside Captain Thome as if by magic. He had a way about revealing himself briefly and then disappearing without saying a word. This time he spoke in a broken delivery.

"Me no like look of train, but can not get close enough to see why."

"The engine has steam up. I can see the smoke coming from the stack. It surely has just arrived."

"Something not right."

Charles Thome vacillated for a few moments before responding. He set his gray eyes on the locomotive and studied it. "Let's go down and see what's going on. I can make out Imperialists in their green uniforms in the cars looking out the windows." The captain waved at a formation of sweat bees that buzzed around his chin. "I'd give anything to have a pair of field glasses."

The Yaqui chief didn't say anything. He sat immobile and stared. "Men not move in cars. Me watch 'em."

"Probably they're asleep. They've been roused out of the barracks at an early hour in order to have arrived as quickly as they have. This is most fortuitous for us." Thome was interrupted by two sharp toots from the hissing engine.

"Sergeant Louder, bring up two men and we'll go to see if the relief has brought provisions and aid to us."

"Me stay here, Thome."

"Do as you like."

The Captain waited until the Sergeant and his two selections passed through the brush to fall in behind him. Louder and Thome walked their horses from the chaparral into the morning sun and chose a course in alignment with the tracks. Louder, who wore a battered Yankee, wide-brimmed hat, passed his commander, mounted his stead and rode at a walk along side Captain Thome.

"Hallooo, we're Thome's command and we need water and provisions." Louder called.

Two shots, fired in quick succession, replied to Lauder's inquiry which unhorsed a private at the back of the group. The second shot struck the Sergeant's head gear, knocking it askew.

"Don't shoot! Don't shoot! We are friends!"

In the brush behind them the three troopers could hear additional shots being fired. Thome raised his hands as a signal that the party was surrendering. Louder and the remaining uninjured private followed their commanding officer's lead.

The Mexican Army uniformed men sitting in the carriage seats stared out at the three riders with dead eyes. In seconds the bodies were pulled from the seats at the windows and replaced by live Juaristas who thrust weapons through the broken glass.

Thome chanced a look behind at the group they'd left and saw that they had been rounded up by sombrero wearing men clothed in civilian garb.

El Halcon still mounted, broke from the captives, reached down and grasped a slight man by his shirt collar as he bore through the would be captors. In a flash he knocked a soldier's gun away and pulled the struggling Juarista up behind him. Using the man as a shield the Indian rode his horse at top speed into the spiky foliage and disappearing.

Charles Thome had been hornswaggled and he knew it.

* * *

The prisoners sat in a circle, their hands bound tightly behind their backs with their headgear removed. Overhead, the sun blazed down relentlessly forcing rivulets of perspiration to soak through their linsey-woolsey shirts that the majority of them wore. There mounts had been taken from them and moved to the opposite side of the train where a group of their captors were going through their saddle bags while laughing at their good fortune.

"Well, well, what a bunch of gringos we have captured." A plump man shaded by a giant hat stood with his hands on his hips looking down at the ex-Confederates.

"You will notice that we have spared only the gringos. We don't bother with the Yaquis and we don't waste bullets on them."

The heavy man laughed.

"It is too bad that when we took your train yesterday evening that we had to convince some of your friends of the justness of our cause. It only took a few bullets to prove out point." The corpulent leader motioned to his aide to hand him a gourd full of water.

"You see, all this talking makes one thirsty." He tortured his captives by taking a long draught from the vessel, sloshing the water around in his mouth and then spitting it in the sand at his feet. He handed the gourd back to his assistant.

"Excuse me, Senors. I have not introduced myself to you. I am Don Carlos Rojas of President Juarez's national army. I control this district within this province."

Don Carlos looked down at the sweating men before him before continuing, "With these niceties out of the way we will get down to the matter of our recruiting." He cleared his throat while removing a massive Pettingill revolver from his waist sash.

"You men are all rebel gringos who have fought against the 'Blue Bellies' as you call them on the other side of the river. You fought your war for what you claim was a just cause. You lost and then you came here and what did you choose to fight for, money?"

Rojas fanned a blue bottle fly away from his face.

"If you will fight for money in Maximilian's army why not change sides and fight for Juarez? You will be paid less but there is one important benefit which you will receive that is a very important one to you."

The perspiring, big man brought the gun up from his side and pointed it at the nearest private sitting at his feet.

The youngster cowed, turning his face away from the muzzle of the revolver.

He aimed down the barrel at the trembling youth keeping one eye closed.

"This pistol, she ain't real accurate at a distance but up close, she never misses."

Rojas lowered the revolver.

"I did mention the main benefit for switching sides didn't I?"

Not one of the men stirred.

"We'll, I'll tell you. It's your life, compadres. It's your life."

"If you cannot understand my recruiting conditions and you say no to my proposal, then I will have to waste a bullet. Now, if you refuse to join us my bullet will not be wasted."

Rojas laughed a wicked laugh.

"Calderon come with the roster ledger and let us begin."

Charles Thome thought that surely no man of his command would hesitate at the Juarista's offer. He would enlist without a second thought. He had no compunctions about either side in this dirty war. There were rumors that there were land grants distributed by both factions. He would play along and when the circumstance permitted, he'd escape and look into the opportunities of starting a ranch.

* * *

THE CANTINA, PEQUENO MATAMORAS, MEXICO

The spy re-entered the cantina and found Maria talking to two Mexicans in low tones. He waited at a distance from the conversation, his bedroll at his feet. When the men left, Chance picked up the huge key from the bar that he assumed unlocked his door.

"Yes, that is your room key but my employer expects me to collect for the night's charges before you are allowed to move in. We will accept Yankee greenbacks, Mexican gold or silver coins but none of the Confederate worthless stuff."

"I haven't a cent or a centavo with me."

"You don't?" The raven haired girl was incredulous. "How did you expect to pay for your lodging? We are heavily taxed by the Marquez army." The clerk was commencing a rant. "My boss is not in the habit of providing free board to Texicans."

Chance held up his hand indicating that he had a solution to the dilemma. "I have a pistol which I'll trade for my room, my horse's care and two bottles of your tequila. One must be your best and the other bottle of a poor, less expensive quality."

"Are you a bandillaro, Senor?"

"No, just a man down on his luck. Now don't scream and faint. I'm going to show you what you've traded for. Your boss will be pleased at the good deal that you've made for him."

* * *

SECOND CHANCE

UNION CAVALRY CAMP
FORT BROWN, TEXAS

Private Art Field stood outside Major Tyler's tent in the sparkling sunlight of a crisp mid-September morning. A light frost had slipped in just prior to the emergence of the sun and left a veil of white on the dying grass.

He cleared his throat and waited to be acknowledged by his superior.

"You may enter, Fields." The major looked up from the rewritten report that Lt. Wilson had reluctatantly surrendered to him.

Fields saluted and blurted, "Captain Adam's men have returned to camp with the deserter, Nichols, Sir. They have escorted him to the stockade as you ordered."

"Good. That man will be punished for his big mouth."

"Sir?"

"Never mind, Fields. The matter doesn't concern you."

"Will that be all, Sir?"

"Yes, you may leave."

There was an exchange of words outside the partially opened tent flap. Tyler could make out his aide's voice but the other speaker's words were unrecognizable.

"Yes, Fields, what is it?"

"Sir, there are three men with a captain from Colonel Archer's headquarters delivering an order for you."

"Send the officer in, then."

Robert Tyler twirled the left end of his mustache as he waited to receive the order.

Finally, someone was acknowledging his establishment of a spy network and the pursuit of the leak that caused the effort's downfall. But how could the Colonel know about his good work? Didn't he, himself, have on his camp desk Lt. Wilson's revised report?

"Good morning, sir." A nattily dressed captain snapped a crisp salute. "Captain Charles Coulter of Colonel Archer's staff."

Tyler waved a weary salute from his seated position at the desk. "What is it that you have for me, Captain?"

The junior officer handed him a paper folded in triplicate, sealed with red wax.

"Thank you, Coulter." Tyler accepted the directive, slid a finger under one of the folds and opened the message.

"Shall I wait for a reply, Sir?"

Robert Tyler was dumfounded by the order's content: MAJOR TYLER, I AM ORDERING YOU TO ATTEND A CONFERENCE BETWEEN THE TWO OF US WITHIN THE HOUR. YOUR COMMANDING COLONEL, ABSOLUM ARCHER.

* * *

MAJOR ROBERT TYLER'S TENT; FORT BROWN, TEXAS
ONE HOUR LATER

Major Tyler returned from his meeting with Colonel Archer a thoroughly whipped and despondent man. His position had been that of a man standing on shifting sand during his commander's questioning. Archer was adamant about Tyler's initiation of his spy gathering network across the border into Mexico as verging on the commencement of hostilities with the Maximilian regime. The one eyed, white whiskered, veteran of the war with Mexico in 1846, had dressed him down and never let up. He derided Tyler for having hatched a hair brained scheme without official approval. Then, out of the blue, the old professional had attacked Major Tyler's attempt to cover up his failure by inventing flimsy and false accusations against a lowly private.

Archer's words still rang in Tyler's ears.

"I have learned from one source that this entire operation was of your making without any consultation within military channels. Another source has pleaded the case for the farrier that he had nothing to do with, or was ever in a position to signal to the Mexican Imperialist forces of the spy network's activities."

"I tell you, Sir," Colonel Archer was unable to, or did not care, to hide his fury. "It's due time that we got rid of you damned 'soldiers of fortune'."

Upon his return to his tent, Robert Tyler flopped into his camp chair and tossed the report into one of the shelter's corners. He removed his hat and put it on the folded blankets on his bed. He placed the finger tips of both hands on the sides of his heads and began to rub his temples.

Archer had explicitly ordered him to destroy the report that lay beyond his reach on the newly installed tent floor. Archer had said; " I cannot impress upon you the importance of the destruction of this document. We have fifty newspaper reporters in the area who would give anything to get their dirty hands on this information."

Archer had become even more agitated with each passing moment. He ranted and stamped his feet as he strutted around Tyler.

"You fool! Can't you see we are in a fish bowl here in Texas? We have these reporters clamoring for anything that they can sensationalize. True or not, they could get us into a shooting war with whatever coalition attempting to run Mexico within twenty four hours of the first publication of an exclusive in the newspapers."

Archer had paused to catch his breath. "And further more, Sir, you will release this Illinois private and return him to his regiment. There will be no charges filed except possibly his taking 'French leave'. You may punish him for that, but by God, nothing else. Let this whole affair die."

Colonel Archer's face was beet red and the tendons in his neck stood out. "And don't try to uncover the outside sources to which I've referred. The officer straightened his eye patch. "If I find that you have acted in retribution against those who exposed you, I'll recommend that you be cashiered from the army. You'll be working for the Sultan of the Maldives as your next means of employment."

* * *

THE CANTINA
PEQUENO MATAMORAS

Chance slept fitfully in the darkness of the sparse room he'd bartered for. The 1849 Colt was worth more than what he'd received but it was the one item he could comfortably part with. Bathing in the clear water had refreshed him and the clothing he'd obtained from Maria with his last few coins, while ill fitting, was clean. A search of his saddlebags had garnered the coins that the girl had accepted for her grandfather's apparel.

Chance checked the time on the gold watch that Pvt. Blaine had given him two days before. In the light of the room's single candle, the hands pointed to 9:30 p.m. In a half hour he'd wander into the kitchen area of the cantina and beg Maria for a tortilla or whatever she'd give him. He readjusted the oil skin pouch in which he carried the precious military figures so that its bulge was not apparent around his neck.

Neunan eased open his room's back door and looked up and down the boardwalk. Torches thrust into metal holders illuminated the street and the mercantile exchanges on both of the roadways sides. A sputtering pine knot torch wavered over Chance's head in the gloom.

He closed the portal and picked up the short jacket that had belonged to a dead man up until a few hours ago. His Remington .44 was shoved down under the folds of his red sash which he'd wound around his middle.

Chance paused before the cracked mirror on the back of the room's door entering into the corridor. Maria provided her deceased relative's straight razor, as well as the old man's clothing. The cavalryman honed the razors edge on the leather sole of his sandal before attacking his two week old beard. His appearance shocked him as he turned his face both left and then to the right. Chance was astonished at how white the lower portion of his visage was. The surface from his nose up was as dark as any Mexican's but from his nostrils down his skin was as white as lamb's wool. He mulled over a solution to the crack in his disguise before uncorking the cheap bottle of tequila and soaking a rag taken from the dry sink. This he wiped on the inside of his sandal until enough of the dye in the footwear leached into the cloth to be applied to his snow white lower face. If the cantina was dark, the correction would not give away his nationality.

Chance checked his revolver before exiting his room into the hallway. He passed the entry to the saloon and stepped onto the establishment's outdoor boardwalk.

"Are you Miguel?"

"Si, senor."

"Has my horse been fed and curried?"

"Si, senor."

"Beuno, Miguel. Put the saddle and bridle on him and keep them on him. Comprendes?"

"Si, senor. Do you plan to leave quickly?"

"Perhaps."

"Sometimes our customers leave plenty pronto."

"Just do your job, Miguel."

Upon entering the saloon which reeked of old, spilled liquor, cigars, and perspiration, Neunan perused the scantily furnished room. Four Mexican caballeros were playing cards at the corner table and two more hombres stood at the plank substitution for a bar.

Maria waited until Chance took a vacant chair opposite the card players. Then she motioned for her relief and walked over to greet him. Instead of taking his drink order, the young woman sat down quickly on Neunan's lap. She laughed a mischievous laugh and pulled the soldier's ear next to her lips,

"Senor Neunan, the two men at the bar are following you. They are Imperialists with Marquez's army," Maria nibbled at Chance's ear lobe.

"Now laugh and smile at me. Then get up, take my hand and lead me to your room."

"Uh, I'd rather not."

"Listen you fool, those men can signal for reinforcements and you can be charged on the weakest pretense. You'll be shot at sunrise."

Neunan shook his head slightly affirming that he understood his perilous situation. He laughed his best mock laugh and swung Maria from his lap and onto her feet.

The girl smiled and taking her right hand she fluffed up her tresses. She slid her arm under Chance's and directed him to the corridor.

* * *

When Maria stepped into Chance's room, she turned back quickly and looked to see if they were being followed.

They weren't.

Neunan went to the horse hide covered chair and pulled Maria to him. She slid into his lap and encircled his neck with her arms.

"All right, Maria, what's this you're telling me about being watched?"

"More than you know, Senor Neunan," Maria changed the subject and nuzzled his face.

"You're even more handsome without your whiskers," she purred. Her fingers caressed the nape of his neck before she pressed her lips to his.

"Do you like us dark skinned women, Senor Chance?"

"Of course, I have no preference either way."

"Then you should acquaint yourself with the director who operates the black people's bureau across the Rio. I have not seen her personally but my compadres, who have, say that she is a ravishing beautiful creature. So exquisite that she takes away the breath of men who first lay eyes on her."

"Wait, what are you telling me? Here you are sparkin' with me while you tell me about some earthly angel I don't know."

"The lady's first name is, uh, Andrea, I believe."

"What?" Neunan sprang to his feet launching Senorita Casteel from his lap.

Chance turned his back to the Mexican girl and walked about in a daze. His fingers trembled as he ran them through his tangled hair. He shook his head several times in an attempt to clear his thoughts.

Neunan groaned and smacked the fist of his right hand into the palm of his left.

"How? How could this be? She was right here with me not two miles away." Chance muttered oblivious to the woman who stood staring at his agonizing.

Maria's voice from the corner of the room next to the street side door brought Chance back to reality.

"I see that you have met this Andrea before. Apparently your acquaintance with her was more than casual."

Chance turned his attention to the female speaker.

"I have told you the truth about myself up to a point Senor Neunan. I have not lied to you once. Now I will take the oil cloth pouch."

Maria Casteel stood facing Chance, the small Colt pistol that he had bartered away earlier that afternoon aimed at his mid section.

"Senor, you do not take me seriously?"

"Oh yes, Maria, that pistol is a convincer."

"Senor Chance, you are too handsome of a man to die over such a trivial thing that you carry. This war is so much larger than you or I. Now give me the packet."

Chance's eyes focused on the brass mounted revolver the young woman pointed at his stomach barely six feet away. He always carried his pistols regardless of their make, with the hammer on an empty chamber. He could see that Maria hadn't yet cocked the gun's hammer to rotate the cylinder to a loaded bullet.

"How did you know I was one of the United States spies?"

"You are the last and only one who has gotten to the river. The Imperialists followed you and we Republicans follow them."

"But aren't we and the Juaristas allies? Aren't we both desirous of getting the French out of Mexico?"

"True. But your military and General Sheridan who gave our magnificent general arms and equipment, will never cross the border and fight at our side. We know that."

Maria Casteel took a step closer and extended her right hand, palm up demanding the surrender of the packet.

Chance swallowed once and asked, "How do I know that you won't shoot me and sell the information to Marquez?"

"You don't, do you?"

The Mexican bar maid reached closer as Neunan made a move with both hands as if he was untying the thong at the base of his neck.

Then, in a split second, his left hand grasped the small gun's cylinder preventing it from rotating and firing the gun. His right hand, doubled in a fist flashed from Maria's right and struck her squarely in the jaw.

She collapsed in a heap as the cavalryman wrestled the small revolver from her grasp. Maria was not a heavy woman and the sound of her fall was overshadowed by the throbbing notes of a mariachi band playing in the street.

Neunan swept her unconscious form from the floor and flopped her on the bed. Loosening the strings on the front of her bare shoulder blouse, Chance tier her hands behind her back and her ankles to the bed's footboard. He ripped apart the pitiful excuse for a towel hanging at the dry sink and gagged the Republican spy. Then he shredded the remainder into strips which he stuck in the uncorked bottles of tequila to form crude wicks.

The band continued to play outside as the last spy of Major Tyler's ring exited the front entrance of the cantina. He tossed two centavos taken from Maria's apron to Miguel. He took his time attaching his bed roll and blanket to Poco's saddle.

Hysterical female laughter emerging from down the dusty street mingled with the barking of dogs and Mexican troubadours' music.

"Muchas gracias, Miguel." Chance touched the brim of his sombrero as a parting gesture. Then he said in English, "Go find your sister."

Neunan walked his horse through two intersections to the east before turning north on a more dimly lighted route.

Earlier that afternoon before his lengthy nap, he'd reconnoitered the best passage way, not from the public ferry but at a ford further downstream on the on the Rio Grande. His intent had been to attempt a passage over the waterway in the early pre-dawn hours but Maria Casteel had disrupted his plan. Still he had formulated a diversion that would buy him time as he made his escape.

Passing himself off as a drunken Mexican street person, he'd staggered down the myriad of dusty and cobblestone roadways fronting on the river. He'd liberally sprinkled his clothes with cactus whiskey and no one had acknowledged or bothered him.

His charade had proven fruitful, for in his wanderings, he'd located one of General Marquez's command posts two doors adjacent to an Imperialist army check point.

Now, he was temporarily lost for a short period but by studying a derelict store front without any sign of illumination, Chance saw that the Marquez command post was two intersections to his right. Neunan stuck the wicked tequila bottle under his left arm and fished for his match safe in his pocket. The Lucifer flecked brightly under his fingernail and caught fire on the raveling dangling from the liquor bottle. His heels dug into

Poco's ribs and away they went, the crow bait horse's hooves thumping over the cobblestones.

An Imperialist militia man dozing at his post was roused to a frightening sight of a shadowy figure riding pell-mell toward him trailing sparks and sputtering shards of fire. The guard's eyes grew larger as they focused on a flaming bottle turning end over end nearing the post's thatched roof.

"Alarm, Alarm," the guardsman squealed just as the fire bomb smashed onto the straw material and spewed fire all over the front door of the adobe walled structure. The antique flintlock musket the man was holding clattered to the street as he cast it aside to make his retreat into a nearby alley.

Poco clattered past the growing inferno with his rider crouched low, his face buried in the animals flowing mane.

From within the confines of the Marquez camp bugles announced a signal that all was not well. Two silhouettes appeared at the entry gate and drew fire from Neunan's revolver. Poco was bouncing over the unlevel street surface so violently that Chance could not tell if his pistol shots had struck either of the soldiers.

Reaching the next cross street, he turned his mount's head left and kicked the animal once more.

No blasts of musketry sounded to his rear and no leaden missiles whizzed past Chance's ears. He had made the escape he'd wanted and was travelling the street which would end at the outskirts of town.

A finger of sparse timber receding down to the river's banks met the roads juncture which would afford Neunan a measure of cover. Chance knew, however, that the area would be swarming with armed searchers within minutes once the turmoil he'd created was sorted out. He needed time but obtaining it would be precious. Time would permit him and his horse to swim across the Rio in the mists and fog that always arose from the river as day break approached. But, his course was immersed in blackness as dark as the inside of a hat and his studying the area during the daylight had been cursory at best. Still he had to find safety for as long as possible while waiting the streaking of the eastern skyline.

* * *

UNION ARMY ENCAMPMENT
FORT BROWN, TEXAS

Lieutenant Wilson had purposely avoided Major Tyler during the afternoon of the headquarters' conference. He eluded his superior by sending small missives through Private Fields to Tyler. Additionally, Wilson made himself scarce with a ride away from the encampment at the head of a small group of cavalrymen but hurried back to the cantonment with an important message received at the 'High Tower'. He reined up before the major's tent and turned the command of the compliment over to a sergeant. Wilson was in awe of the observation post which was truly an engineering marvel that rose two hundred feet into the air and afforded an unobstructed view of the Rio Grande two miles in either direction. There had been talk of the second erection of a similar type but with the coming of the communication engineers and the telegraph system, the project had been scraped. Within the past week, shiny wires had been stretched between a myriad of smoke pole pines, trimmed and sunk into the ground.

Bryce Wilson, riding at the front of the detachment, noted an officer waving to him from the tall platform. The officer turned back to his duty, placing his hand on the shoulder of a signal corpsman that seemed to be peering at something to the south through a fixed telescope.

"You there! Yes, you. Identify yourself." The officer looked down and demanded.

"Lt. Wilson of the Fourth Wisconsin Cavalry."

"Can you take back a message to Colonel Archer? We are having some problem with our communication line."

"Yes, of course, Sir."

"Very well. This information is to be delivered to Archer and I'd suggest that it goes through the proper chain of command."

"Yes, Sir. I'll take it to Major Tyler."

"Tell him to expedite this material as quickly as possible."

"Yes, Sir."

"Pay attention, now."

"Yes, Sir."

A tin canister equipped with a string harness and an orange bandanna came floating down from the platform.

"Don't delay in getting this back to camp."

"Yes, Sir." Wilson saluted, foolishly realizing that the officer couldn't see him from his vantage point.

Lt. Wilson dismounted and strode up to Pvt. Fields who rose from his seat on a wooden hog's head and saluted. He took the lieutenant's horse's reins and stood at attention as the junior officer passed and entered through the open tent flap.

"Lieutenant Wilson reporting with information from the 'High Tower', Sir." The young officer was unsure of the reception he was about to receive from his commander.

Tyler gave Wilson a scowl before arising from his chair.

"What is it, Wilson?"

"The information is in this Signal Corps container. I have not opened it, Sir."

"Allow me to see what's so urgent."

The major worked at unfastening the canister's lid while stamping his left foot which had gone to sleep while he was seated. He removed the top and opened the folded note. Tyler looked down at the writing on the salmon colored paper.

"This Captain Woodward says that Marquez has his men digging rifle pits and erecting a strong command post well back from the river. The pits extend over two hundred yards on either side of the ferry crossing. He adds that he can only guess at the reason that this is being done." Tyler continued to look at the paper as he rubbed at the front of his left thigh.

"Dammit, where is this Juarez fellow? We seem to be doing more than our share of dealing with the Frenchies and the Imperialists."

Lt. Wilson was anxious to put distance between himself and the major. "Shall I carry this information to Colonel Archer, Sir?"

"Yes, immediately. You were at his headquarters earlier today were you not?"

"Yes, Sir." Wilson thought it best not to lie.

Tyler took up a pencil and scribbled a few lines on a separate sheet of paper before folding the two notations together and putting them back in the signal corps container.

"Take this to Archer and tell him that I await his orders."

* * *

FREEDMEN'S BUREAU
BAXTER PLANTATION

Andrea had spent the morning away from her duties trusting that William Downs and Whit Leonard would carry on in her absence. She was still shaken from the confrontation with Major Tyler at the dinner soiree two evenings ago. Although she felt fresh and clean outwardly, she could not erase from her mind, the lecherous action taken by the officer. It was unforgivable for a Christian gentleman to act in such a way toward any woman regardless of her race. The man was an insufferable brute and a danger to any female that he might take a fancy to. Her morning note carried to Colonel Archer by Big Joe described the type of man that she felt Tyler was and the underhanded chicanery that he was fermenting against Private Nichols. She sought to exclude any involvement or knowledge of the spy network so as not to be entangled in it herself. She merely gave a shining report regarding the farrier's work for the Bureau and asked for the Colonel's sympathy in reviewing the charges against the trooper.

Andrea experienced a twinge of joy at having sullied the major's reputation. Andrea had her own sources within the cantonment and her 'eyes' provided her with useful information. While her operatives were diligent, they were not especially fast and it was sometimes days before they could substantiate the rumors that they'd heard. It was from these informants that Andrea had word of Nichols' capture and incarceration within an hour of the arresting party's return to Fort Brown.

She arose from her writing desk in the corner of her bedroom and went to her closet. She removed riding apparel feeling that a canter on a horse in the coolness of the September morning might be bracing and help her clear her mind. She laid out the garments on her bed and knelt to peer deeper into the depths of her wardrobe for her riding boots. Her thoughts drifted back to the last time that she'd ridden. *Could it have been three years ago? Was the last time when she accompanied Nell Edwards as they rode through the cotton fields during the fall of 1860? They had watched the slaves as they toiled in the boiling sun, bent over, drenched with sweat, yet singing. That last ride was before the war came and the horses were not yet confiscated, and the cotton bales not yet burned and the slaves not yet run away. No, how could she have forgotten. She and Chance had spent time together on his farm before they had parted company. This, like the dreadful scenes of the slaves in the cotton fields at the plantation, was even more painful for her. It was the last time she had seen Chance Neunan.*

Andrea stood up, a boot in her hand, its leather dry and cracked. *What was she thinking? The garments might fit her; she had worn some of Mrs. Baxter's dresses in the early days of her posting when the transport had not yet arrived from the headquarters in St. Louis. Out of necessity she'd clothed herself with the borrowed clothes but she had felt odd doing it.* She studied the boot and surmised that the footwear was at least a size smaller than her foot. Andrea sank down on her brocaded bed spread and wept.

All she'd known, all that she'd endured, and all she'd loved were nothing but memories. Chance Neunan, wherever he was, it was as though he'd never existed. His image came to her in her dreams but her life had changed so much that she questioned if he were really real and if the love that they'd shared was real as well.

Her lips began to quiver as tears streaked down her cheeks. She could no longer contain her sadness and before she could control her emotions, she broke down and allowed herself to endure body shaking sobs.

* * *

ANDREA EDWARDS' BED CHAMBERS
FREEDMEN'S BUREAU AN HOUR LATER

The administrator had fallen into a deep sleep following her cry. She felt better when she awoke, not rested exactly but with a clear mind and a desire to confront the situation that was becoming more and more muddled by the hour. She sat up and touched the puffiness under her eyes. She would definitely have to give that condition a little attention but she could manage to restore herself to a presentable appearance in a short time. Andrea took all the clothing and boots and threw them in the bottom of the chifferobe and picked out a pillow sleeved dress, long gloves and a shawl. Then she rang for Angie Sue to come to her assistance.

"Yess'um," her aide stood just inside the pocket doors.

"Go find Big Joe and Alvie Fillmore and have them harness the team and bring the carriage around to the front doors. I plan to pay Private Nichols a visit in the stockade. Now go on and don't dally."

Angie left in a ruffle of skirts without a word perhaps sensing that there was a degree of urgency involved.

Andrea busied herself at the dry sink attempting to rid her face of the hard sleep than she'd fallen into. She'd originally thought that she would try to wangle a pass to see the imprisoned but she knew that if she followed this approach she'd have to confront Major Tyler. This she refused to do.

She'd settled on a more direct approach instead. Big Joe and Fillmore would convey her to the stockade and she would demand an audience with Nichols. She would make her strong request due to his being an employee of the Freedmen's Bureau on loan from the army. Nichols would be scared and depressed; liable to say anything without thinking. His honest innocence and the manner that he would be interrogated by Tyler could implicate him in any type of plot that the officer broached.

Her plan had a slim chance of success but Andrea knew that she had to see Homer Nichols first before Robert Tyler did.

There was a soft knock on the pocket doors of the bedroom and Angie Sue made her entrance without being formally received.

"Big Joe and Fillmore is getting' up da team and da carriage. Big Joe says he'll drive the closed one 'cause da wind is up and it's gettin' colder."

"I'll be along shortly, Angie, but while they wait for me, go down to the kitchen and have Betsy get up two dozen sugar cookies and a pitcher of sweet apple cider. I mean to cheer up Private Nichols.

"Yess'um, I'll get to them tasks right away, Ma'am."

* * *

UNION ARMY STOCKADE
FORT BROWN, BROWNSVILLE, TEXAS

Andrea chose her time wisely when she entered the outer admissions room of the prison.

The captain in charge of the stout penitentiary ensconced inside the earthen breastworks of Fort Brown had passed his responsibilities to a Lieutenant Sims. The officer had excused himself while he partook of his noon day meal.

The surrogate commander sprang to his feet when a sergeant opened the entry room door exposing the holding area. Andrea Edwards stood with a small smile on her face and held a covered basket in her gloved hands. She wore a grape colored shawl trimmed in cream.

"Good afternoon, Madam, I, er… it is afternoon isn't it Ma'am?" The officer shot a glance at a Seth Thomas clock ticking on an adjoining desk.

"It's afternoon, Lieutenant." Andrea gave him her most alluring smile. "I'm Andrea Edwards of the Freedmen's Bureau at the Baxter Plantation. I understand that you people have a Private Homer Nichols. He was arrested in the afternoon yesterday."

Lt. Sims did not offer his hand in introduction since it was customary for the female to initiate the gesture of greeting. Andrea's hand gripped the handle of the basket and remained there.

Sims flipped open a thick ledger and used his finger to trace the names of the prison entries. He took his time, drawing his ink stained index finger along each line.

"Yes, here's the man's name. Brought here under guard this very morning. But I'm not sure that you can see him."

"With what infraction has Private Nichols been charged?"

"Uh, says here, desertion."

"Nothing too serious, then? No pillaging, no mayhem?"

Lt. Sims gave Andrea a stern look. "Miss Edwards, desertion in the time of war committed by any rank within the military is a serious offence."

"He's just a lonely young man who's been in the army too long."

"Perhaps"

"I've brought him freshly baked sugar cookies to lift his spirits and I've added an extra half dozen for any nice officer who would allow me to have an audience with him."

Sims took a second look at the clock.

"All right. I'll have the prisoner brought to an ante room next door. We will place a guard outside the door for our peace of mind. I can see that you feel that you will be safe in his presence but I can tell you that we've seen the most docile inmates turn on us." The junior officer cleared his throat before continuing. "I'll give you fifteen minutes with Nichols and no more."

"Oh, thank you, Sir!" Andrea gushed. She offered her gloved hand to Sims and added, "Here are your cookies."

"Wait in the hall while I have the prisoner brought up. I'll not record that you've been here or have seen the prisoner. That's for my sake."

* * *

In the passage of a few minutes, Andrea heard the sounds of footsteps and the rattle of chains. Homer Nichols, dirty and wearing pieces of civilian clothing approached in front of a burly guard. Nichols nodded to Andrea as they waited for the hefty jailer to unlock the dimly lighted cell.

"Fifteen minutes Ma'am. Then I'm comin' to take him back. Now you mind that he don't start nothin' with you."

"He'll be a perfect gentleman." Andrea stated firmly.

The massive barred door thudded behind them and both heard the lock fall into place.

"Sit here, Homer. How have they treated you?" Nichols pulled out a chair at one end of a long table and sat down. He exhaled before answering.

"Oh, not too bad. They roughed me up a bit when they first caught me along the tracks. Told me that if I'd have switched my coat for a civilian one that they'd have shot me on the spot as being a spy."

The disheveled young man didn't raise his eyes from the worn boots he was wearing. Andrea stood beside him and reached down to take and open his dirty hands. She drew out several cookies from underneath the white cloth covering the plate and placed them on a napkin before the dejected soldier. She pulled the cork from the cider jug and watched his Adam's apple move up and down in short swallows.

When the container was empty he removed it from his lips, set the vessel in the middle of the table, and groaned.

"I'm afeared that I'm in deep trouble, Ma'am." Nichols wiped his mouth on the back of his hand.

"I'm working with Major Tyler to have the charges lessened or dropped that exist against you."

"Thank you, Miss Edwards, I'm much obliged."

Andrea touched his hand and leaned down to look into Homer's blood shot eyes. "I just couldn't allow any harm to come to you."

She removed a small bottle of water, uncorked it and wet her handkerchief. She dabbed at the dirt smudges on Nichols' face.

"Here, let me do that Ma'am. You're too young and too pretty to be my mom." The trooper took the dainty cloth and wiped under his eyes and around his mouth.

Andrea rewet the handkerchief and allowed Homer to become more thorough with his washing.

"I'd like more information in specifics regarding Chance Neunan. There are no reasons to hold back now. You have only insinuated that the man that I seek was on a mission in Mexico."

"Er, uh,..." Nichols stammered. "I've told you too much all ready."

"Andrea leaned even closer and clutched the farrier's shoulder as though she was correcting a school boy. "Don't clam up on me, now, Homer. That card you've played before. I must know; was Chance Neunan one of the five spies that was sent across the Rio Grande?"

Nichols sighed and hunched down in his chair. Then he reached for the cider jug, shook it, removed its cork and swallowed the last dregs of the liquid.

"Yes! Chance Neunan was one of the agents."

* * *

APPROACHING THE RIO GRANDE
PEQUENO MATAMORAS

Neunan gave Poco his head and permitted his stead to pick his way through the discarded debris of the small town. Weeds and thorny shrubs hid broken parts of wagons, stacks of adobe brick razed from buildings and several mounds of broken crockery, bottles and tin cans. The bald faced horse whose eyesight was keener that that of his rider managed to wind his way through the jumble of castoffs jettisoned in the ravine by the inhabitants.

Further on, down the defile, the detritus thinned and finally ended except for a few items which had been swept downhill by spring freshets.

Chance was coming down off the adrenaline high that the excitement of his escape had created. His clothing was drenched with perspiration and his body seemed incapable of sitting upright in the saddle. When he felt that he was loosing his ability to stay upright, Neunan dismounted and located a sapling which made a ready hitching post for Poco. The Illinois trooper looked around and with the aid of a growing conflagration at his back, found a patch of dry grass. He fell into the dry stems and allowed his muscles to relax.

Above him and behind him, Chance's ears discerned a cornucopia of bugle calls from a variety of points in the town. The Mexicans were fond of bugle calls and Chance thought to himself that if one were to list the national characteristics of the Hispanic race, one notation would be their love for the brass musical instruments. The muffled shouts arising in the streets he'd just passed through didn't concern Neunan. Apparently, the command post which he'd set afire with his tequila fire bomb had spread evidenced by a bright orange glow wavering through the dark trees lining either side of the defile.

Chance unbuttoned the short jacket and cotton shirt. He felt about his arm pit and brought out the waterproof pouch encasing the all-important troop figures. Taking precaution to shield the flame of his match by kneeling behind a tree trunk, he examined the five pieces of paper. He struck a second match and held it close to Blain's watch and determined what time it was. The time piece's hands read two o'clock.

Neunan sighed. If he could stay hidden for two more hours, the dawn would begin to break and the fog to rise from the surface of the water with the change in temperature. To be flushed from his place of concealment before then and have to take to the water would place him in great peril. Chance believed that the Rio Grande was not deeper than six feet on the

Mexican side but somewhere near the middle of the river, in the ship channel, the waterway deepened. Sea going transports from all over the world nudged into Bagdad, a Gulf seaport, located in Tamaulipas province, just a few miles below Brownsville. In high water, the crafts could navigate up within a mile of the United States encampment but now with the fall season, shallow draft lighters were employed to move freight and supplies. Chance couldn't be certain but he suspected that the depth of the water beyond the center of the Rio and nearer the American side was eight to ten feet.

The trooper's attention was drawn back to the activities taking place behind him. The volume of the voices and the kindled torches sharpened the level of his angst. A string of wavering blazes was advancing down both sides of the declivity and approaching more quickly than Chance would have liked. He could tell from the shouted commands that the militiamen were walking in alignment and commencing a descending sweep toward the river.

Neunan's nerves were raw and his strength flagging as he pulled himself to his feet. He quickly took stock of his riding gear and threw his extra clothes into the darkness. He paused for a few moments to rip shards of cloth from his blanket before jettisoning the unneeded bed roll. Before mounting, he fashioned a crude sling for his Spencer rifle and swung that over his right shoulder. The Blakeslee box went over the other shoulder and the revolver was shoved deeper into his waist sash. Chance took a long drink of the tepid water in his canteen before turning to watch his pursers advancing toward him. He spit into the murkiness, untied Poco, and led him downhill toward the river.

* * *

UNION ARMY STOCKADE
FORT BROWN, TEXAS

Andrea was devastated by Nichols' revelation but she managed to restrain her emotions, hiding her anxiety and dread from the prisoner private until he'd been marched back to his cell.

She walked straight back to the open entry door and through the post's office never acknowledging the lieutenant on duty. He remained stoic and watched her departure through the door leading to the outer yard.

Big Joe stood holding open the carriage door and made certain that the train of her dress cleared the opening's frame. Once inside, she could no longer restrain herself and she burst into tears. The dainty kerchief, wet with water earlier, was ill prepared to absorb the flood that coursed down her face. The tea towel from the basket helped to some extent but she quickly cried that damp as well.

At the Bureau, her feet barely touched the front steps as she blindly made her way into the manor and ascended the broad staircase to her room.

Angie Sue followed her through the pocket doors and watched as Andrea ripped at the buttons of her bodice and tore the material of the dress in a frenzied desire to escape its restraint. She stood naked, her slender shoulders shaking and the once crafted hair style in shambles. She stumbled two steps and flung her body onto the bed. Sobbing in the most unbearable tones, she muffled the torture she was enduring by burying her face in the bed clothes.

Angie removed a cotton coverlet from a brass blanket stand and covered her employer.

"Der, der, Missy. Want to tell me what grieves you so?"

Andrea seemed oblivious to her aide's presence.

The faithful black assistant eased down beside Andrea and began to massage the back of her neck and shoulders.

"Tell Angie Sue, Missy. Can I help in any way?"

"Oh Lord, he's dead! He's dead! I just know it!" Andrea screamed. "Why, oh why, did I ever leave that man?"

Angie Sue patted Andrea and wiped at her moist face with the corner of the coverlet.

"Who is dis man that's 'causin' you so much sadness?"

"Oh, Angie, you don't know him. He was the kindest, most loving man any woman could ever wish to meet."

"Dis man's got a name, don't he?"

Andrea stopped crying, sat up and wiped at her eyes with her index finger. "His name was Chance Neunan. He was a spy the army sent into Mexico with four other men. None of them returned from their mission."

The heart broken administrator rolled onto her back, turned, and buried her face into her pillow.

"Why, God, did you take him from me? You've carved the heart out of me;" she wailed.

"Der, der, Missy." Angie Sue comforted. "Let me get you some brandy from de cook house. It'll relax you, honey."

"Yes, yes, anything to put me in a delirium. God, oh merciful God, why did you have to take him?"

* * *

APPROACHING THE RIVER
PEQUENO MATAMORES, MEXICO

The man and his horse descended cautiously in the direction that both knew the river flowed. Chance stopped with every sound that rose from the gloom. He told himself that he could not rush head long to the water's edge in spite of the pursuers' speed in closing on him. Each time the trooper paused, he raised his eyes upward to the line of torches ever relentlessly moving closer. The fire from Pequeno Matamores continued to glow above the black tree line at the outer perimeter of the miserable little village. As Neunan drew ever closer to the watercourse, his measure of careful progress paid off. To his right, he smelled the smoke from a twig fire and heard the voices of two men speaking in low tones. Chance instantly calculated that he was passing a vidette post and that he needed to use the utmost care in navigating past it.

This he managed to do and his progress increased as he forced Poco through a willow growth into what appeared to be a dry flat edging the Rio. The weak light cast over the area by the illumination from Brownsville enabled him to see that the willows would be the last vegetation he would encounter before reaching the water.

Neunan mounted Poco and allowed him to carry him over the cracked, dry mud surface where last spring's water had flowed. At the distance from the river that they were, Chance knew that the footing would be sound. It was as they neared the darkened waterway that the soil would become moister and the horse's hooves would commence to sink in. Once in the river, the problem would be ameliorated but he worried about the quicksand like mud they'd have to hazard across to reach the water.

From behind him, at the end of the ravine, a musket popped and a ball zipped five feet over his head. More gunfire erupted as the ears of the militiamen picked up the cracking sound of Poco's hooves on the flats. All were sounding shots wildly placed in the hope that the leaden missiles would find their mark. Chance heard the balls striking the mud in his rear and to his right. He didn't dare halt Poco and turn to see if he was being followed by a mounted party. All he wanted to do was to reach the Rio in the mists of the morning and escape the eyes of his pursuers. He urged his mount on and was soon passing through dead vegetation, killed by the first frost a week ago.

In a few more moments, Neunan heard the crunch of gravel under his horse's feet and in the next instant, the animal plunged into the water. The cavalryman loosened the reins and gave Poco his head as he began to swim. Poco extended his neck and coughed when his nostrils temporarily dipped beneath the surface of the river. Chance was surprised that his mount was such a strong swimmer and that he was carrying him so high above the level of the water. The trooper set his eyes on the twinkling lights on the distant shore. He kicked his foot out of the right stirrup as the current caught them and drifted the horse in that direction.

A salvo of musketry erupted behind the desperate rider, followed by a second flight of lead balls.

Suddenly, Poco hunched his body rigidly and dropped his head beneath the water. He struggled to maintain his head above the surface for a few moments but then the animal gave up and dropped into the depths. Chance felt the mass of horseflesh slipping away from his sandaled feet. His horse had just vanished from beneath Neunan's thrashing legs and was gone.

Chance was fighting to keep his own head above the water as the weight of his rifle pulled him down. He flayed about attempting to right his body from the vertical to the horizontal in order to swim. He used all the strength he had to force his body upward, draw in a breath before being submerged once more. He was growing weaker as the current swept him downriver in the blackness of the night.

Then his legs bumped into a sunken log and a tangle of spiny branches. The relentless current pushed him harder into the entanglement and Neunan grasped for anything that would provide a handhold and stop his bumping passage. If he could not stop his movement, he feared that he would be swept under a log jam that he could not see in the murkiness.

He stopped his erratic passage and commenced to struggle up a sunken log that was suspended at the right angle to place him higher on the jumble of flotsam. Nothing underfoot seemed stable. Every object he touched or stood on seemed to be rocking and swaying in the fast flowing water. The Spencer got tangled more than once but Chance did not panic and retrieved his carbine each time. His snail paced progress eventually elevated him higher until his sandaled feet were stepping on and through small flotsam interwedged between the logs. Chance, in his eagerness to get out of the water, was oblivious to the musket fire and directed his efforts toward getting onto some piece of dry land no matter how small it was. He was coming to the realization that he was marooned on an island shorn of trees or vegetation but covered instead with a monstrous amount of dead trees and flood debris. He shivered in the darkness as the river current rocked his perch. In broad daylight he would have been visible to the militiamen and would not have lasted five minutes before he'd have been riddled by musketry. His spirits were ebbing; he was wet, cold, and exhausted and not yet in the safety of the United States' cantonment. Chance huddled, dejected and worn out listening to the gun fire glance from the giant logs he had sheltered himself behind.

After a time, he regained control of his faculties and began to formulate a direction for his escape. Chance, by careful placement of his feet, could inch higher to what he thought was the apex of the jam and work his way into a deeper, more secure lodgment in the debris. The black water beneath openings in the entanglement splashed and gurgled as it sped downstream. To make a misstep and fall would be fatal for him.

Like a blind man, he wound his way around obstacles until he reached the top of the jam. He commenced to swing under and through obstructions until his footing found solid ground and the sensation of sand wedging between his toes evidenced that he'd found dry ground beneath the towering mass. It was as though the trooper had discovered a tangled amphitheatre of safety within the tossed and twisted formation. The firing from the Mexican side of the river was incessant but Chance felt that he was now safe for a time.

* * *

UNION CAVALRY CAMP
FORT BROWN
BROWNSVILLE, TEXAS

"Major Tyler! Major Tyler! I beg your permission to enter, Sir!"

The excited voice of Lieutenant Wilson jarred the major from the depths of a restful sleep.

"What in tarnation is it, Wilson?"

"Sir, it's a big fire in Pequeno Matamores and there's a passel of firing going on down by the river!"

"Be specific, Lieutenant. Give me your report in prescise terms." Major Tyler was standing, attempting to stuff his night shirt into his double seated cavalry trousers.

"Sorry Sir, too excited I guess."

"Commence again, Wilson." Major Tyler adjusted the wick on a small, whale oil lamp which was sitting on his portable writing desk. He turned a half circle to locate his boots and then sat down and started to tug them onto his bare feet.

"Pequeno Matamores is aflame mostly in the area around the Imperialists' army camp. Our observers on the High Tower telegraphed that there seems to be firing up and down a ravine leading to the river. There appears to be musketry now aimed at an island adjacent to our position here at Fort Brown."

"Aha!" Major Tyler hooted. "It's about time that Juarez got off his duff and did some fighting on his own." The officer was smiling from ear to ear. "Help me with my uniform coat will you Wilson?"

Tyler paused before changing his mind. "No, call in Fields to do that. You gather a squad of twelve good men and assemble them fully armed outside my tent. When Fields is finished with me, I'll send him with an order to the First Illinois Light to get a four gun battery in position on the earth works right across from the island." Tyler was searching for his hat and putting together a defensive plan as he was occupied. "What is the number of that island, Wilson?"

"It's number thirteen, Sir."

"Good. Now be off with you and remember that time is of the essence."

* * *

ISLAND # 13 IN THE RIO GRANDE RIVER

Chance found a drier area by squeezing under a sawyer that must have been four feet in diameter. The sand was not totally dry but it was not covered with a slimy mud overlayment either. Every movement he'd made since sundown had been done in degrees of blackness. Now, he searched for dry twigs and sticks using only his sense of touch. When he'd acquired enough debris that would provide him with a small fire, he brought out his match safe from his sodden shirt pocket. The hinged, embellished container's lid was tightly sealed and when he opened the device, he was pleased to see that no moisture had leaked in and ruined them. The match sparked on the case's serrated edge and burst into flame. In seconds, Chance had the rudiments of a fire and he added more and larger twigs as it grew in brightness and warmth. Piling on even more wrist sized limbs, he had a cheery blaze going and his spirits were rising. His chilled muscles were locking in his arms and legs and the heat of the flames loosened them. He cast his eyes into the depths of the hidden chamber as he searched for objects that might be of use to him. His eyes came to rest on a frayed, gray piece of canvas cloth caught fast between two logs which had been shorn of their bark eons ago. Tugging and sawing at the fabric with his pocket knife, he secured a piece of cloth from the twisted mass. Chance reasoned that the tarpaulin was washed overboard from the deck of one of the river vessels that plied its goods from Bagdad to Brownsville.

The trooper shook the sand from his newest acquisition and spread it next to his fire. He retrieved his carbine and Blakeslee box from the darkness and returned to the canvas. He jacked the brass cartridges from his weapon and sat down to wipe dry each piece of ammunition on a section of sleeve from his shirt. He laid each load near the blaze but not so close that they could be ignited. He did the same with each cartridge he removed from the loading tubes in his ammunition box. Chance shook the droplets of water from the Spencer's mechanism and held the short cavalry arm up to the fire. He knew that the rimfire cartridges had been immersed in water only for a short time and he fully expected the weapon to function properly.

He withdrew the Remington revolver from his sash and examined the pistol, it being a cap and ball weapon, Chance was doubtful that the piece would ignite its loads as it should. Still, he toweled away the moisture from the steel surface as well as he could and stuck the weapon back into his waist binding.

A musket ball struck the interwoven mast overhead and dropped down into the sand at the edge of his fire light.

Chance looked up from his examination of Blain's pocket watch. Its hands had stopped and water droplets specked the piece's face beneath the crystal. The watch read; ten minutes passed three o'clock when he and Poco had entered the river. The shirt sleeve was used on the watch but he had little hope that the timepiece could be salvaged. Finally, he examined the minute notes sealed in his oil cloth pouch and saw that they still were whole and only slightly dampened.

A branch broke in the interlocked bower in the darkened depths further away. Chance tensed and listened. Only the rush of the river's water could be heard. Neunan kicked himself mentally for lowering his guard and becoming complacent sitting by the warmth of the fire. He had to battle his fatigue and stay alert or he would be caught or killed and all that he'd strived for would have gone for naught.

His mind went immediately to his pursuers. He had little to fear from the poorly trained militiamen but much to fear from the Yaqui Indian scouts. He detested these distant relatives of the Apaches. They had no morals in battle and no scruples regarding prisoners taken in conflict. The Yaquis allied with whoever was strongest and whoever promised the most booty. These were the people he had no use for and if it came to it, he would show them no quarter.

For all he knew, these evil men could be just now floating down the current on brush covered logs attempting to gain a foothold on the island on which he was hiding.

Neunan gather his belongings and took up his carbine. Removing a brand from the perimeter of the fire, he held it aloft and began walking deeper into his sheltered refuge. He had only gone a few feet when an idea came into his head. He put his goods and the weapon aside and returned to the dying fire. He found larger limbs and began to throw them on the fire kindling it back to life. Soon he had the flames leaping higher than his head and licking at the jumble of intertwined limbs and branches above. Chance was falling back to an old divergent that he'd used several times before... fire.

It was only when sweat formed on his brow and the front of his peasant shirt started to steam that he backed away from his task and recovered the items he'd set down. Driven by the rush of adrenaline and the thought of the Indian hirelings, Chance wiggled and crawled through openings that enabled him to progress even higher. He was aware of the advantage of height in his situation and an elevated position would permit him to see the Yaquis silhouetted against the orange glare of the fire.

The Illinois trooper forged on, ignoring his barked shins and bruised elbows until he stood before a massive form half buried in the sand. The torch which he held was sputtering and loosing it illuminating power as Neunan strained to identify what he'd bumped into. He reached forward to feel what the gigantic black form was just as his torch flicked its last. A wad of dry grass and a few twigs brought the flame back to life.

Square nails and ochered joints told him that the form was some sort of a river vessel that had become lodged in the log jam. The rotting craft was a lighter of the type used on the Rio for the transportation of goods during low water. Somehow the boat had broken free of its mooring or struck a submerged obstruction which sank it. It had drifted into the position where it now lay buried beneath layers of debris.

Neunan scrambled up the inclined deck, slipping and sliding on the dried mud covering the rotting boards. He pushed his way through and over heaps of dried corn stalks, weeds, stems, and tree branches until he emerged at the bow of the craft.

The flame he'd started in the mid section of the jam was now roaring skyward sending sparks and miniature fire brands spiraling in every direction. The orange glow illuminated a circumference of seventy yards or more and brought relief to Chance by not revealing any Yaquis creeping over the tangled mass toward him.

* * *

CAVALRY ENCAMPMENT OUTSIDE MAJOR TYLER'S TENT FORT BROWN, TEXAS

Lt. Wilson shivered in the chill of the pre-dawn darkness and the fog which had slipped like a gray cloak over the area. The mounts that the twelve troopers rode, stamped their feet and shook their heads. They'd been quickly saddled and released from the company corral and the urgency in which this had been done made them nervous and fidgety. The shouting and grousing by their riders as steel bits were shoved between their teeth had spooked the animals

Now, as they awaited further action, the equines grew impatient.

"Look there, Major." Lt. Wilson pointed a gloved finger at the flames glowing in the midst of the massive drift on Island # 13. "I can't tell if the fire is a signal to us or just what it is. It may well be what I've first suspected."

"Whoever is laying musket fire on the island hasn't let up one bit, have they? I can't fathom what's so damned important about that mud bank." Major Tyler placed his left foot into his mount's stirrup and swung easily into the saddle.

"You don't suppose?" Lieutenant Wilson's voice trailed away.

"That's enough, Lieutenant. Let us pass behind the men and out of their hearing if you have concerns regarding what may be happening."

Wilson turned his head to the right and called, "Sergeant Sawyer?"

"Yes Sir."

"Take charge of the squad. You are to remain mounted and await Major Tyler's orders."

"Yes Sir."

"Mind you that Private Fields will be returning shortly with a message for the major."

"Yes Sir."

"Very well, carry on."

* * *

FREEDMEN'S BUREAU
BAXTER PLANTATION, BROWNSVILLE, TEXAS

"Missy! Oh, Missy, open de door!"

Andrea heard Angie Sue pleading from outside in the parlor adjoining her bedroom.

Groggy from her sudden awakening, Andrea responded hoarsely; "Yes, what is it? Why are you rousting me at twenty minutes after four?"

The sleepy administrator sat up, rubbed her eyes and focused her eyes on the face of porcelain clock sitting on a bed stand near her pillow. "My God girl, it's not even day light yet."

"Missy, please open de door. Da whole river is afire and days shootin' goin' on down der. Maybe the Mexican and the Frenchies is comin' across."

Andrea found a dressing gown and covered her sleep wear with the garment. She walked quickly in her bare feet and turned the lock beneath the knob.

Her aide, dressed in a coarse gown fell into her employer's arms as the door opened. Her voice was uncontrollable, nothing more than unintelligible babble. She was trying to explain things that were beyond her comprehension.

"Stop it, Angie. Slow down! I can't understand a word you're saying." With that, Andrea grabbed Angie by the shoulders and shook her.

"Oh, Missy, Lord God, it must be da end of de world."

"No it's not. How did you learn of all this?"

Angie caught her breath momentarily, and then pointed to the wall opposite Andre's bed.

"Der! You can see the fire's 'flection on de wall." The aide let out a wail and kept looking at the orange glow wavering on the room's wallpaper. "Big Joe come poundin' on de front doors and said dat der was a big doin's at the camp. Bugles was blowin' like Jubilee an some cannons came bustin' out of de gate and headed for de river."

Andrea hugged Angie to her bosom in a joyful embrace and was laughing all at the same time.

"What's got into you, Missy? You's actin' plumb mystifin.'"

"I'll tell you later, Angie. Now get dressed and run find Big Joe. Have him saddle one of Mr. Baxter's best purebreds and bring him to the front gate."

"You want him to put Mrs. Baxter's side saddle on de horse, Missy?"

"No, a regular, good fox hunting saddle will do. Also see if he can get Fillmore or Lil' Alvie to join us. I don't know what we'll get ourselves into but we're going to the river."

"Oh, Ma'am, goin' to da river with all that shootin' goin' on could be awful dangerous."

"I'll take my chances. There could be a man on the Mexican shore and he could be Chance Neunan. I hope to God it's him."

* * *

ISLAND #13, IN THE MIDDLE OF THE RIO GRANDE

Neunan gained the front of the derelict boat and edged to a broken section where the gunwale had broken through which allowed him to observe the fire he'd ignited. The flames were breaking through the mélange of tree trunks and had become a raging inferno. A movement at the base of the hellish glow caught his attention and caused him to duck his head down. He cautiously eased the top of his head up in order to identify what he'd seen. Scrambling among the upturned roots of a centuries old behemoth were two men, both wearing rag head bands and small breech cloths. Chance recoiled backward and flopped down.

Could these approaching men be Carter and Hawbacker whom he'd left days ago, miles from their destination? No, this was impossible. Hawbacker was dying in the arroyo and there was no way that Carter could have made up the distance separating him from Chance short of having been carried there by some mythical Thunderbird. No, though Neunan wanted it to be otherwise, the men were Yaqui warriors, paid assassins, coming to kill him.

Neunan pointed the Spencer through the hole in the broken gunnel and sighted down its dark barrel. When he pressed the trigger on the carbine, the hammer fell but the mechanism only clicked. Frantically, he ejected the malfunctioning round and chambered in a new one.

BANG! The report sounded above the crackle and sizzle of the roaring fire. Framed by the intensity of the flames, one of the crouched figures dropped his bow and clawed at his chest.

Neunan chambered a third round and caught the second warrior just as he gathered himself to leap a gap in the entanglement. The Yaqui screamed and fell sideways. His lifeless body slid head first down the length of a limbless log and fell into the river leaving a black smear marking the path his body had taken.

Neunan worked the trigger guard for a forth time and moved away from his vantage point. He would have to be even more vigilant than he'd been now that his fears had come to fruition. He was growing more desperate now that he realized his circumstances. He'd have to work his way to the end of the jam, pass the vessel's stern and enter the river. The odds of reaching the American side of the Rio were slim but this was the only alternative left to him.

* * *

UNITED STATES' CAVALRY ENCAMPMENT, FORT BROWN, TEXAS, ON THE LEVEE

Sergeant Sawyer cantered up to his two superiors and saluted. "I mean no interruption, Sir, but I felt that you should know that there are reports of gunfire now taking place near the end of the island. The men picked up two shots that sounded as if they were fired from a cavalry carbine."

"Well, Wilson, Your guess as to who is on the island may be correct."

Half of Tyler's face was bathed by the orange glow of the inferno. "Still I can't understand why our intelligence people didn't come to the crossing at the appointed time. How late are they, Lieutenant?"

"One day and two hours, sir. You must consider that they've most likely been discovered and hounded all the way back to the Rio Grande."

"Have we any indication of the number of men trying to get into our lines?"

"Major, with this fog and the sun just beginning to rise plus the smoke from the log jam, we cannot reach any kind of estimation. The observers on the tower are just as blind as we are. On the good side, the sun should be up in the next ten minutes or so. Then we'll be able to see more clearly."

"I guess it doesn't really matter how many of the spies get back, does it? Archer has disavowed any involvement in the mission and severely reprimanded me for my part in its formulation." Major Tyler wiped at a drip of moisture which clung to the tip of his nose.

"But those men out there in the river are our soldiers, Sir."

"I know, I know. Perhaps rescuing them will restore me somewhat in the Colonel's eyes." Tyler shifted his weight in his McClellan saddle. "Are we taking any direct fire into our lines? Have we taken any casualties?"

"Nothing reported, Sir."

"Good. If we do begin to take their fire, we'll be obligated to return fire."

"Sir?"

"Yes, by God, we will get involved. The men need a bit of a moral boost, you know, a little smell of gunpowder."

Lt. Wilson sat dumbfounded at what he'd just heard. Then he implored; "We cannot commence something that will lead to a serious incident between us and the foreign powers across the Rio."

"To hell with niceties!" Tyler thundered. "I'm tired of cow towing to the damned Frenchies and the Beaners."

"It's not your decision to make, Sir. This issue is bigger than the both of us."

Tyler slapped the bow at the front of his saddle and stewed, attempting to make the correct decision.

"Get Fields up here and I will write out an order to deliver to the Illinois Light Artillery. It will tell them to load their guns with blank charges. If we have people attempting to cross to our side, the smoke from our battery will give them a chance."

"Yes, Sir." Lt. Wilson called to Fields to act as a courier.

* * *

ON A SIDEROAD LEADING TO THE RIVER OUTSIDE FORT BROWN

"Halt! Who goes there?"

The command was direct and forceful. There was a lack of timidity in the strong voice that indicated that the speaker meant business.

"Andrea Edwards, director of the regional Freemen's Bureau."

"Advance and be recognized."

Andrea shot a glance at Big Joe and he nodded for her to go forward. Both the hulking escort and Lil' Alvie stayed behind.

Andrea Edwards nudged her mount and walked it toward the sentry. Two other armed men stood in the glow of a camp fire next to a pup tent.

"What's your business for being out so early and on this road, Ma'am?"

"We've heard shooting from the direction of the river and Fort Brown. My assistants and I rode out to see the basis for the commotion?"

"You hear that racket, Ma'am?"

"Yes, we've been hearing it since perhaps forty-five minutes ago."

"Well, who the hell ever it is that's firing ain't shootin' spit wads. You and your boys is in imminent danger. No body is to pass this point."

"But…."

"I've told you my orders, Lady. If you don't want to get arrested, you'll go right back from whence you've come."

"Yes Sir, we'll do that. We don't want to make trouble for anyone."

Andrea tugged on he mount's right rein and turned the animal around. She took her time and walked him to where big Joe and Alvi were waiting. She burned at a remark that she'd overheard from one of the guards standing at the side of the tent; *Damned niggers, you give 'em a taste of freedom and they think that they can go anyplace they damned well please*.

Big Joe took hold of Andrea's horse's bridle and said, "Don't fret none, Missy. We can cut across to a bitty point of land that the Mexicans calls dedo de bruja."

"What does that mean?"

"Da witch's toe. Me and Lil' Alvie goes fishin' there all the time. Its got timber on the land right down to da water an nobody'll be able to see us."

The three retraced their steps for a quarter mile before the massive man servant found the necessary path. In the east, the sky at the horizon was streaked with yellow.

Shots could still be heard as the group picked their way through the sagging branches of the water oaks.

"What's this going to gain us, Big Joe?" Andrea asked as they rode single file in the emerging light.

"Water comes right up to de Ol' Witch's Toe before it gets swift and deep on t'other side. A sand bar pushes out into the river from the bank for several yards. We knows about it 'cause that's where me an Alvie catches mussels for catfish bait. We'll be able to see all up and down that ol' island cross from the fort. We'll have a better view than them soldier boys."

* * *

THE ISLAND IN THE RIO GRANDE

Neunan barged his way back through the tangle of debris to the stern of the buried boat. The fog rising from the water was tinted a straw color from the gathering dawn. A westerly breeze kicked up, changing the direction of the rolling smoke, pushing the acrid, lung searing odor into his face. It was time to make his exit, for with the growing daylight he was easily seen from both banks of the water course.

* * *

Private Fields, acting courier for Major Tyler, galloped up to the assembled cavalry squad, saluted the senior officer and handed him a folded sheet of paper.

"Report from Captain Howard of the artillery battery, Sir."

"Let me see what he has to say." Tyler opened the message.

"Ah, good. All's ready with the blanks loaded in the guns, Hmm, just a minute. This Captain Howard has received a report from the observation tower that the Imperialists have positioned two brass mountain howitzer's on the river banks at an angle to us. The guns are fully crewed and ready for action."

Bam! Bam! Almost as if in recognition of their position being discovered, the two pieces belched smoke and flame toward the island.

"Dammit!" Major Tyler's horse reared on its hind legs before the officer sawed its bit in its slobbering mouth and recovered control.

On island number thirteen, Chance heard the gun's report and instinctively ducked. The burning logs at the pinnacle of the jam were splintered asunder as the canister loads struck the mass. Neunan instantly saw that the guns would have to be repositioned in order for them to be effective in their quest to kill him. He leaped up and renewed his jumping, zigzagging run over the piled obstructions.

Four artillery guns from the American side replied to the Imperialist's blast with a deafening roar. The black powder cannon smoke mixed with the wood smoke shrouding the escaping man.

Neunan dropped from within a mass of intertwined roots to the lower surface that formed a narrow sand beach. His carbine had beaten him unmercifully around his neck and right shoulder. Gaining a more level footing, the trooper slung the Spencer off and was preparing to throw the firearm into the river. But he hesitated when his eyes spied a freshly cut cottonwood log pulled onto the washed gravel of the island's lower point.

Before he could cast his eyes in a different direction, a painted Yaqui leaped from the top of a gigantic sawyer and rolled Neunan onto his side. Chance spun away from the enemy as the savage dived on the spot the cavalryman had just vacated.

Chance regained his feet in time to turn his body away from the knife thrust executed by the tribesman. He brought his carbine's barrel flat against the attacker's jaw. A second swing dented the assailant's skull, broke the gun's stock and sent the man onto his back. He never moved and was unconscious.

Neunan threw the shattered firearm into the swift water on the American side of the Rio. He bent forward to push the log into the current which was now filled with smoking shards of charcoal and sticks.

A second salvo belched from the two Imperialist's mountain guns knocking wrist sized branches from the tangle of the jam.

Taking a breath of the pungent air, Chance loosened the fresh log, placed it under his arm and launched himself into the swift flowing water.

* * *

"Listen to those sons-a-bitches over there. They think that our four blank loads were misses." Major Tyler screwed up his face. "Those Illinois boys could blast those bean eatin' bastards all the way back to Mexico City if they were shooting live rounds."

"You've chosen the right course of action, Sir." Wilson congratulated his superior. The lieutenant noted the redness of the Major's face and knew that he was excited.

Private Fields broke from his position in the assembled squad and galloped up to Wilson and Tyler. He saluted and reported.

"We've got a man in the water just off the end of the island."

SECOND CHANCE

"Where?" Major Tyler stood up in his stirrups and strained to pick up the swimming figure.

"There! Just ahead of that smoldering pile of junk!" Fields rode alongside the senior officer and pointed.

"Oh yes, I see him. Is he one of ours, Private?"

"We thought at first he was Mexican but he ain't."

"Wilson, can you see our swimmer?"

"Yes, Sir."

"Can you identify him as being one of our agents? You hand picked them."

"Can't say for sure, Major. He's too far out in the middle of the river to see anything definitive about him."

Field's eyes followed the current and the flotsam being carried southeasterly.

"I think he's goin' to make shore on that spit of land stickin' out into the Rio 'bout a quarter mile from here."

Major Tyler vacillated for a moment then turned to his lieutenant.

"Wilson, hoist a flag of truce. I don't see a need for one since we have every right to inspect what this man is doing on the United State's side of the river. Perhaps, however, it'll save us from being fired on by those brigands on the Mexican side."

Wilson didn't wait for a direct order from the Major but took the initiate himself.

"Sgt. Sawyer, form the men in two columns and be ready to ride. We'll proceed along the top of the levee leading down to that finger of woods protruding out into the river. Major Tyler will give the order to move."

* * *

The fog covering the river close to the eastern fringe of the burning island had lifted enough that the Edward's entourage could witness the fight between Tyler's spy and the Yaqui warrior.

"He's in de water now, Missy, and he's comin' pretty fast. If he kicks hard, he can hang up de log he's on up on de sandbar. If he don't, he'll sweep in close to us but we'll only have one chance at catchin' him. He could drift on down to Bagdad and the Mexs will catch him for sure."

"We'll do our best then to gather him in, won't we, Joe?"

"Yes, Missy."

Joe looked back behind where the two were waiting. Little Alvie sat on his small pony with the reins of the mounts in hand. The big, man-servant who had dismounted, quickly searched around in the dead fall of saplings killed by the spring floods. He selected a sturdy shaft that still was green enough to snap back once it was bowed.

"Dis will do good." The massive black man stripped the slender trunk of small branches and wedged it's base between the trunks of two live trees.

"I can wade out into the current and hang on to dis to snag this fella who's comin'."

"I can help, Joe." Andrea said firmly.

"No, no. You just stay outta da way, Missy. I'll catch that man jist like I would a big old catfish."

* * *

Neunan was fighting to keep his head above water as he was carried rapidly down river by the swift current. The cottonwood log he'd commandeered from the comatose Yaqui at the base of the island did not have enough ballast to keep him afloat. Even with the bulk of his body hanging feet down from the flotation he'd chosen, Chance strained to breathe. He kicked with what little strength remained hoping that his progress would roll him onto a sandbar or against the overhanging limbs of trees on the opposite bank. Neunan felt submerged obstacles striking his feet as the unforgiving Rio Grande carried him in a south easterly direction. He felt his ability continue to wane as he frog-kicked to the surface for gulps of life giving oxygen.

* * *

Forward!" Major Tyler waited for the passage of a few seconds, then with a wave of his arm, "At a trot, yo!"

The squad spurred their mounts and fell in behind Tyler, Wilson and Fields who carried the flag of truce. Jingling reins and squeaking leather signaled their advance along with the thump of their horses' hooves. The entourage was covering ground rapidly as it traversed the smooth path along the top of the levee. Every man had his eyes on the lone figure moving parallel with them in the muddy water.

"Sir, we'll have to increase our speed if we are to pass our spy and get in position on the finger of land ahead. We'll have to catch him as he sweeps past. This will be our best chance of recovering him."

Major Tyler looked out at their quarry that was out distancing them to the point of interception and back at Lieutenant Wilson.

His mouth was open in the instant that the rifle's report sounded from the Mexican side of the water course. Another gunshot followed the first.

Robert Tyler, the officer and soldier of fortune, clutched at a ragged hole that suddenly appeared on the upper right side of his tunic. The impact of the bullet rocked him backward in his saddle and knocked his hat from his head. The following shot broke the staff of the truce flag carried by Private Fields and buried itself in the neck of Lt. Wilson's horse.

Before either of the two uninjured men in the column's forefront could act, Tyler was unhorsed and under Wilson's mount which was screaming and kicking in death spasms.

Lt. Wilson leaped clear of his stricken horse as it fell and watched in horror as the dying animal's hooves pulverized Major Tyler's lifeless body between its front and back legs. Private Fields had managed to rein his horse out of the way of the fallen equine's withering body.

From his position on the ground, Wilson shouted orders to the horrified squad.

"Dismount and prepare to return fire! Number four men take the reins of the horses and retire over the far side of the levee!"

* * *

Lil' Alvie swung his gaze from the preparations on the river bank and looked over at the stricken squadron three hundred yards away."

"Dey is shootin' goin' on over ta the levee. Looks like the soldier boys is in some kinda trouble."

"We'll let them take care of themselves. I gots my hand full here." Big Joe was crotch deep in the fast flowing water. He'd fastened the sapling in a steely grip and was watching the bobbing log as it made it approach.

Alvie kept shifting his eyes between the troopers and the man in the water, The cavalrymen were aligned in a prone position with their carbines pointing south from where the ambush had sprung. A dead horse lay on its side in the narrow roadway with an equally dead officer sprawled beside it.

"Here he comes, Joe! Get ready and don't miss him."

Big Joe's massive hand reached towards the head full of black hair and clutched the figure's shirt collar. Half drowned, the escaping agent turned his body away from Joe in a feeble attempt to twist free but he was caught fast. Chance lost his hold on his crude conveyance and it surged off into the deeper ship channel.

"I can't hold him, Missy! Help me!"

In one cat- like movement, Andrea was in the water and pulling in tandem with Big Joe. It took all the strength of the two to hoist the exhausted body through the tall bull rushes and onto the shore.

Andrea, Big Joe, and the rescued man lay on their backs, chests heaving as the morning sun touched the leaves above them.

Andrea wiped her hair from her eyes and rolled herself sideways to look at the spent man.

"Is that you, Chance?"

"Andrea?" The dark haired trooper gasped.

"Yes, Yes. It's me Chance! God has given you back to me and now you're safe."

"Ain't nobody gonna be safe if dem soldier boys come lookin' for us. Let's get up and outta here. You, Mister," the massive man clasped Chance by the shoulder. "Get up behind Lil' Alvie on his horse, I know a back way outta dis place so them troopers won't never know we was here."

Chance was so exhausted he could hardly maintain his grip on little Alvie's waist as the foursome wound their way out of the willow thicket alongside the thrashing waters of the Rio. He was unaware the group had evaded the squad of Union cavalrymen galloping their way to the Witches' Toe where Big Joe had pulled him from the river. He fought to regain his reasoning as the horses trotted through the underbrush. The passageway made it essential for the group to ride single file, thus Chance could only catch glimpses of the slight figure riding in the middle of the entourage. As the trio and their horses passed in and out of the bottomland, fog enveloped them on both sides. Big Joe rode ahead, ducking low beneath the overhanging limbs. Those following took their lead from the large man and initiated evasions whenever Joe ducked or held up his hand to shield his face. Delirium was overtaking Chance's ability to think and he could not be certain the form ahead of him was the woman he'd traveled a half continent to find.

The cannon firing and the small arms reports had ceased in the direction of the levee. Birds, oblivious to the unfamiliar noises of war, flitted in the low briars and autumn colored leaves of the trees. The rising sun peeked above the horizon and commenced to chase away the violet tinted fog of the new day. Big Joe chose a hidden wagon trace that paralleled the river for half a mile before it curved into a swale between two hills and coursed up to the fields of the former Baxter Plantation. The escape route the group's leader selected was masked from the sight of the embattled cavalry squad and the observers on the High Tower.

As the pathway widened, Andrea guided her mount to the tract's side and waited for Little Alvie to pass to her left. Alvie reined his mule to a halt which permitted Chance to raise his head from where it rested on the little man's back.

With half-closed eyes the surviving secret agent gazed into Andrea's beautiful face. She wiped away a wisp of hair from over her right eye and smiled a lip-quivering smile as tears streaked down her cheeks.

"Hello Darlin'. It's been a long time hasn't it?" Chance mumbled.

"It doesn't matter how many hours or days or years or, or.." Andrea stammered. "I will always love you and I'm so very happy that you've found me." Chance held out his quaking hand and the love of his life reached forward and grasped his fingers.

"I'll never ever leave you again, Chance Neunan. Not ever."

* * *

A pall of white wood smoke hung over the area north of the Rio for a day following Chance Neunan's escape. Andrea only opened her bedroom window on the morning of the second day of her lover's freedom. The closed boudoir smelled of her enchanting lavender and Squire Baxter's talc which Neunan had taken a liking to.

A cloth bag containing the Illinois soldier's Mexican disguise awaited laundering or burning whichever course Angie Sue chose to take.

Neither of the two had much need of anything to wear during the time that Chance had taken up his abode in the plantation house leased to the Freedmen's Bureau.

Angie Sue, ever mindful of their privacy, did not interrupt them in any way once the two galvanized tubs were filled.

The bathing basins sat side by side filled with used water that had grown cold and crumpled towels draped over their back rests. Plates of half eaten food sat desolate and forgotten on the stands on both sides of the canopied bed.

The lovers forgot the passage of time and only took note of the sun light or moon glow on the lacy curtains at the window. Both nestled into each other's arms and only awoke when one or the other lightly placed a tender kiss on the partner's lips. Gentle fingers meandered down the delicate skin on the inside of upper arms and inner thighs. Giggles of joyful glee flowed into moans of ecstasy as the lovers rediscovered each other's bodies. The shrouds of two years of separation were swept away in a few hours of unification.

In Andrea's elated delirium, she awoke in the early hours of dawn and looked at the slumbering man lying at her side. The bearded soldier was yet a boy in years but a man in experience.

Gently she trailed the back of her right hand over the sheet drawn tightly over the soldier's left hip until she roused him enough to cause him to sift his position next to her. He breathed deeply for three breaths before falling back into a rhythmic sleep. Andrea took up the corner of the cotton fabric and moved it aside.

There, on the lower left of his back was a two inch long scar which had turned pale as it contrasted with the brown-tan of his skin. The scar was emblematic of how they'd first met on a cold, misty morning alongside a burning blockhouse.

A soft knock at the pocket doors requested her attention.

"Yes." Andrea rolled on her side and faced Chance who'd been roused by the disturbance. She slowly drew the sheets over her nakedness watching her lover's face as her charms were covered from his adoring eyes. "What is it?"

"It's me, Angie Sue, Missy. Big Joe says that there's a giant goin's on at Fort Brown. He says da Mexican 'Perialists come over da river in a boat carryin' a white flag. Does dat mean dey's surrenderin'?"

"No, more than likely the Mexican forces want to talk. The white flag signals that."

"Oh."

There was a moment of silence.

"Would you want me to come into the bedroom and straighten up things?"

"That's not necessary, Angie. Just keep me apprised of what Big Joe learns. All right?"

"Yes, Missy."

Both Chance and Andrea listened for Angie's departing footsteps. Once they were certain that she had passed out into the hallway, Chance's finger tips took the bed sheet's hem and pulled it down. His gesture likened itself to a man removing a veil from a sleeping child's face.

"You are so exquisitely beautiful?" Neunan murmured as he lowered his lips to Andrea's shoulder.

* * *

The afternoon came and went all without removing Andrea's gown from where it had been draped over the face of the table clock next to the bed. In the interims between devouring each others bodies, both Chance and Andrea had brought their minds back to reality.

"While you were sleeping, Love, Angie Sue brought your revolver upstairs in our noon meal food basket. Joe took it apart, drew the charges, oiled and dried it. He reloaded it and told Angie to tell you it was as good as new."

"Good. I expect that I'll be needing that when I leave."

Andrea rose on her elbows and stared into Chance's dark eyes before asking, "Will you be traveling alone?"

Chance noted Andrea's concern and smiled his infatuating little smile.

"I'd hoped that I'd have a beautiful traveling companion."

"And where would this nomad take his beautiful lady?"

Chance sighed and trailed his index finger under Andrea's lower lip.

"Oh, way west. Clean across the Great Plains to California."

"Really?"

"Yes, really."

"Why don't you describe this beautiful travelling companion? Perhaps I could help you locate such a person."

Neunan sighed once again. It was obvious that he was enjoying the game.

"Let's see, I don't want to waste too much of my time grousing around looking for this person. Maybe a Mexican senorita would do. Most of them are pretty 'til they have ninos and then the bottom falls out."

Andrea gave Chance a jab in the ribs.

"All right, all right. I got sidetracked." Neunan feinted injury. "Let's see, where was I? Oh, yes, the description of my beautiful companion. She'd have to be tall, well proportioned with long, silky legs, shiny ebony hair, coffee colored skin, small, athletic breast which turn up and a face that only an angel in heaven could match. Smart, oh yes, she'd have to be smart and oh so spirited."

Andrea lowered her body from her elbows and snuggled close to Chance. She nibbled at his ear lobe which peeked from beneath a swatch of long hair.

"Would I do, Chance Neunan, or are you still searching for this perfect woman?"

Chance looked deeply into Andrea Edward's brown irises and murmured, "You'll do, my love. My search has ended and I thank God that I've found you."

* * *

A discrete knock sounded on the parlor side of the double pocket doors.

"Excuse me, Missy, are you awake?"

Andrea rubbed her eyes and sat up. The shadows on the drawn curtains told her that several hours had expired, and that the evening was upon them.

"Yes, Angie Sue."

"Dere's three soldiers in de lower parlor dat wants to talk to you. Da man dat seems to be in charge is dat feller, Wilson. I tink you knows him."

Andrea felt Chance's thigh lying next to hers, tense.

"Tell him that I'll be right down and Angie, you haven't said anything about Mr. Neunan being here, have you?"

"Oh no, Ma'am. I knows when to keep my mouff shut."

* * *

Andrea Edwards hadn't much time to fix her hair and dress. She wanted to present herself in the best possible manner namely because she was suspicious of Wilson's visit. At this hour in the early evenings, junior officers were busy with end of day parade reviews. The man's visit had to have a special purpose.

"Clean up, Chance, and select anything that fits from the chiffarobe. Mr. Baxter's clothing has been locked in the room off the bedroom since they let the lease. Break the lock if you have to."

"Break it?" Neunan looked at Andrea, questioning her.

"Yes. Do whatever you must to outfit yourself for a trip to California."

"Acting a bit abruptly don't you think?"

Andrea turned back from the double doors and said, "It's best to be prepared to make an exit. We don't know what the military people have up their sleeves."

She placed her finger tips in the sliding door's handle divots and paused once more.

"I kept your red sash and your oil skin packet out of the wash sack for Angie. The items are on the dresser. Fetch them for me, please."

"What do you want those things for?"

"I have a plan, trust me."

* * *

Lt. Wilson and his two escorts sat uneasily in their red velvet side chairs in the parlor. Angie Sue had seen to illuminating the room with four large wax candles. The thought of a fire in the tiled fire place crossed her mind but she felt the extra work of kindling a blaze was not worth the effort.

All the men had removed their head gear and rested them on their knees. The gold braid and polished buttons on the enlisted men's short cavalry jackets dazzled Angie's eyes. Wilson's sitting position, while erect and efficient; indicated that he was more relaxed than were the two troopers who were accompanying him.

Andrea made her entrance from the upper floor walking regally down the broad staircase. The troopers sprang to their feet and dipped their heads in a high bow as she walked toward them.

"Good afternoon, or should I say evening, Miss Edwards."

Andrea extended her hand to the lieutenant.

"I'm Lt. Wilson of Major Tyler's Fourth Wisconsin Cavalry."

"Yes, of course, Lt. Wilson. I remember you from my dinner with your commanding officer."

The officer looked down at the toes of his boots, and then raised his eyes to Andrea's face. She read the concern in his features.

"I'm afraid that I have sad news regarding Major Tyler."

"Oh, what is it?"

"Major Tyler is dead."

Shock registered on Andrea's countenance.

"Oh, my word!"

"He was killed two mornings ago at the river. We were ambushed by Mexican Imperialists."

"How tragic! Was this the reason for the group of Imperialists coming across the Rio with a flag of truce?" Andrea withdrew a handkerchief and dabbed the crocodile tears she forced herself to shed. While she strongly disliked Robert Tyler she was genuinely shocked to learn of his death.

"Yes. The Imperialists carried a letter of apology for what they called, 'the mishap'. General Marquez assured us that the offenders had been dealt with in the severest manner."

Andrea sighed and looked away. Her gesture was for effect.

"You surely did not come here to tell me of Major Tyler's death. I must say that I am saddened by the news."

"Miss Edwards I have been assigned by Colonel Archer to examine the circumstances of this action. We know that you have inquired about a trooper serving in our intelligence branch named Chance Neunan?"

"Yes."

"And that you queried both Major Tyler and a Twelfth Illinois farrier working here at the Bureau concerning this Neunan."

"Yes, I did. Mr. Neunan and I had met earlier in the war and we were romantically inclined toward one another."

Wilson looked down at his feet once more. He cleared his throat and looked back at Andrea's eyes.

"Madam, I fear that I have more bad news beyond what I've revealed. We believe that one of our agents was attempting to cross the river to our lines." The lieutenant swallowed.

"We suspect that he was drowned in the action two days ago. He was one of the five and although we cannot be sure, we strongly believe that he did not survive the attempt."

Andrea sank to her knees, crying and ringing her hands. She supplied sufficient tears to cover the faked anguish she was displaying.

Wilson motioned to the two troopers that had accompanied him. They leaned down and helped the Freedmen's Bureau administrator to a loveseat.

"I'm so sorry to have to convey this information to you, Miss Edwards." Lt. Wilson placed his left hand on the supposedly distraught woman's shoulder.

Andrea continued her display of grief for a few more moments. Then she shortened the frequency of her sobs before straightening and wiping her cheeks with the moistened kerchief.

"Its, its, just that we had been separated by my ambition and he by his duties in the war. He had been searching for me for the past two and a half years. Chance was so close to joining me and this horrible event prevented our juncture."

"Was your desire to locate your affectionate interest the cause for your attempt at going to the Rio two nights ago? We have a report from one of our sentry posts that you and two men were on the river road during the firing from the Mexican side of the river."

"Yes, Lieutenant. We were turned away by your videttes and obeyed their order to retrace our steps back here to the Bureau. I wish now that we had disregarded them and gone to the waterway."

Wilson kept his hand on Andrea's upper arm.

"It's good that you didn't, Ma'am."

"Lieutenant?" Andrea paused as thought she was in mid-thought.

"Yes, Ma'am. What is it?"

"Yesterday afternoon, one of our residents went fishing on the river below a point known as the Witch's Toe. He recovered these two items from a drift of sticks and logs wedged against the near bank. They may be of interest to you."

Andrea handed up the red waist sash worn by Chance which was wrapped around an oil skin packet.

"The waterproof folder has a side pocket containing some tiny papers with letters and numbers on them. Moisture has seeped into the protective packet and it doesn't appear that the figures are legible. They may or may not be a part of the intelligence being gathered by our military."

Wilson accepted the two river recoveries and studied the still damp surfaces.

"Even if these figures were compiled by our agents, there value is negligible. You see Major Tyler initiated the entire plot himself without upper echelon approval. He was censored for this and there was to be a review of his conduct for hatching the secret operation."

"I don't understand."

"The plain and simple of all this is that we have sacrificed the lives of five good men to carry out a plan proposed by an over zealous officer. He is now deceased as well."

"But…"

"I shall take the oil skin and its contents to file with my report for Colonel Archer. Since we had no inventory of what our agents were wearing, we cannot ascertain which of the five possessed this waist wrap."

"May I have it then, Lieutenant?"

"I see no reason why not, Miss Edwards."

Wilson handed Andrea the waist scarf and bowed slightly as he did so. He said nothing more as he turned his attention to placing his kepi on his head and adjusting it. The officer bowed for a second time as he touched the bill of his cap with the fingertips of his right hand. Lt. Wilson motioned for the pair who'd accompanied him to stand and follow his lead at replacing their headgear. She stood motionless and listened as Lt. Wilson and his compliment exited the front doors, mounted and rode away into the gathering glooming of the autumn evening.

Once the young lady was certain of their departure, she made her way up the staircase to her sleeping quarters. In the growing shadows of the upper story, Andrea made out a figure peeping through a gap in the pocket doors which led into the sitting room outside the master bedroom.

"Angie, is that you?" The beautiful executive called out.

Startled, the young girl threw up her hands to cover her face.

"Stop it Angie!" Andrea took her by the wrists and pulled her hands from their protective position. "Stop it! Do you hear? I'm not your mistress and I am not going to strike you! That was the old way but we live in a new age. We're equal to everyone, now. Stop your crying."

Angie was blubbering apologies as Angie took her in an embrace.

"There, there, child. It was a bad thing to eavesdrop but I forgive you."

Angie wept bitter tears on Andrea's shoulder.

"You'uns are gonna leave ain't you? I could see Mr. Neunan tryin' on the stuff that belonged to Mr. Baxter."

Andrea kissed the girl's forehead.

"Have I ever lied to you, Angie?"

"No you h'aint, never."

"Then I'll not start now. Yes, we'll leave during the night. What our destination is, I don't know. All I know is that we will find a new life in California."

"I don't even now where dat is, Missy Andrea."

"It's a long, long way from here. Who knows, you may travel to this place in your lifetime. Now listen carefully for I trust you like the sister I never had."

"Yes, Ma'am."

"There will be a letter in the top drawer of my desk in the office. This will be my letter of resignation. I've had it composed for several months when I believed that the man I loved would never be a part of my life again."

"Oh, Missy. I is so happy for you."

"Thank you, Angie. You've been such a good girl, honest and loyal. Now, a few more loose ends and I'll leave you alone."

"Yes, Missy."

"Go catch Big Joe before he goes to bed. Have him pick two dependable horses from the stable and saddle them. Tell him to put two sacks of grain on each animal and bring them to the back door where they're to be tied to the railing. Then stop in the cook house and put together a linen bag of food for Mr. Chance and me to eat. Can you do all that?"

"Oh, yes, Missy."

"Two other things, please. Remember, I'm counting on you."

"Yessum."

"Under my letter of resignation will be a second envelope filled with money. There will be enough inside to pay for the horses, tack and the food we're leaving with."

"Oh, Missy, I hates to see you go away."

"Don't fret, Angie. The Freedmen's Bureau will send another person that can fill my position. Remember to remind Big Joe and Lil' Alvie that they shouldn't talk of Mr. Chance for a few weeks or even after we've gone."

Angie was sobbing once more but was shaking her head that she understood and all the tasks which Andrea had set down would be attended to.

* * *

The newly rescued Illinois trooper awoke to discover Andrea gone and only the rumpled bedclothes were evidence that she had once laid beside him. Chance was disgusted with himself with having drifted back to sleep once his lover had exited the boudoir. He couldn't help himself he reasoned; the frantic flight and close brush with death were the culprits in the development of his fatigue.

Hastily, he dropped his feet over the edge of the bed and stood upright. A pair of silk under garments was laid out on a high backed chair next to the upstairs window. Before making a foray into the contents of Master Baxter's armoire, Chance opened a cabinet inside the closet and found a straight razor and talc which were, no doubt, the property of the manse's prior owner. He'd neglected to use the items on the night that Big Joe had yanked him from the Rio Grande because a more pressing need had arisen between Andrea and the half drowned soldier. Succumbing to their desire had left Andrea with roughened skin on her cheeks and throat.

Chance used a basin to dip cold water from one of the bath tubs and commence his attack on the week old growth sprouting from his face. Once the tonsorial task was completed he stood naked in front of the tall chest and picked one of every type of garment stored there and stacked them on the unmade bed. As he worked, Neunan came across a pair of pale, doe skin pantaloons and an exquisite pair of riding boots that fit him like a glove. Further digging turned up a cedar box containing a dozen or more, fine Cuban cigars.

The young man donned the attire save for a shirt and stepped to the mirror.

A bit wasted, I guess, but considering what I've been through not too bad. With this dark hair and smooth face, I'm rather handsome if I do say so. Chance complimented himself.

Turning, he spied a glass decanter partially filled with brandy. Chance wet his finger tips and applied a small amount of the liquor to the cheroot's outer wrapper. He lighted his smoke and wandered to the huge window overlooking the lawn and rose garden. Neunan, still feeling the effects of his adventures in the log drift, eased himself onto a cushioned seat on the window sill and took in the beauty of the setting sun. The evening was approaching and with the sun's demise, the temperature was dropping as well. The growing twilight signaled to the birds that they should utter the last notes of their songs for the day.

Andrea entered the master bedroom and set two carpet bags next to the bed. She was so absorbed with the tasks to be finished that she paid little attention to Neunan.

"Are you smoking, Chance, or is that smell coming off the burning log jam in the river?" The beautiful executive raised her head and sniffed the air.

"Yes, I'm smoking and all at the expense of the former Reb who owns this place. Say what was that commotion outside in the outer room? It sounded pretty intense."

"It was nothing, really; just Angie Sue spying on you. I scolded her for it and she confessed that she had figured out that we were leaving. She broke down and beseeched me not to go away with you. She learned of my earnestness when I gave her a list of things to do in order for us to begin our journey."

Chance said nothing but instead walked in front of the mirror and struck a pose.

"I picked out several garments from the armoire. What do you think of this outfit?"

Andrea turned her attention to the young man standing next to the window.

"Well, well and my, my. I believe that Beau Brummell has crept into my bedroom in my absence."

Andrea swallowed as her eyes swept over Chance and his attire. Chance's chiseled upper body, naked to the waist and his well formed legs filling the snug fitting trousers intrigued her.

Chance gave her his most seductive smile before removing the smoke from his lips and placing it in a silver hair pin dish he was employing as an ash tray.

"Yes, ol' Beau has stolen into the sanctity of you room with salacious thoughts on his mind."

"Well, Master Brummell, I can see that you have things other than packing on your mind at this particular moment."

Chance smiled and patted the bed's mattress.

"Why don't you come and join me and we'll see if you can take care of what's bothering me. We still have a few hours left."

* * *

Sometime after midnight, Big Joe, Angie Sue and Lil' Alvie, stood on the back steps of the Freedmen's Bureau's plantation house. The crushed stone drive leading through the manor's garden was dark with a skittering moon peeking on occasion, from behind high clouds.

Andrea Edwards had kissed them all and reined her mount next to Neunan's. She fought back tears steadying her voice as she spoke.

"I, along with Mr. Neunan, wish to thank you all for your assistance and kindness. We both feel that we have been blessed to have been in your presence during our short time here. We thank you for everything you've done for us and we fervently hope that you will find joy and happiness in the new society. We may never pass this way again so may God keep and guide you."

The former slaves were crying in unison with their employer, moaning and whimpering as they did so.

Andrea loosened her horse's reins and nudged her mount with the heels of her riding boots.

Both she and Chance never looked back and were soon swallowed by the ebony darkness.

THE END